PENGUIN BOOKS

# A BOY'S OWN STORY

EDMUND WHITE'S novels include *Fanny: A Fiction*, *The Farewell Symphony*, and *A Married Man*. He has received a Guggenheim Fellowship and the Award for Literature from the American Academy of Arts and Letters. He was awarded the National Book Critics Circle Award and the Lambda Literary Award for *Genet: A Biography*.

# EDMUND WHITE

# A Boy's Own Story

PENGUIN BOOKS

PENGUIN BOOKS

Published by the Penguin Group
Penguin Group (USA) Inc., 375 Hudson Street, New York, New York 10014, U.S.A.
Penguin Group (Canada), 90 Eglinton Avenue East, Suite 700, Toronto, Ontario, Canada M4P 2Y3
(a division of Pearson Penguin Canada Inc.)
Penguin Books Ltd, 80 Strand, London WC2R oRL, England
Penguin Ireland, 25 St Stephen's Green, Dublin 2, Ireland (a division of Penguin Books Ltd)
Penguin Group (Australia), 250 Camberwell Road, Camberwell, Victoria 3124, Australia
(a division of Pearson Australia Group Pty Ltd)
Penguin Books India Pvt Ltd, 11 Community Centre, Panchsheel Park, New Delhi – 110 017, India
Penguin Group (NZ), 67 Apollo Drive, Rosedale, North Shore 0632, New Zealand
(a division of Pearson New Zealand Ltd)
Penguin Books (South Africa) (Pty) Ltd, 24 Sturdee Avenue, Rosebank, Johannesburg 2196, South Africa

Penguin Books Ltd, Registered Offices:
80 Strand, London WC2R oRL, England

First published in the United States of America by E. P. Dutton 1982
Published by Plume, an imprint of The New American Library, Inc. 1983
Published in Penguin Books 2009

1  3  5  7  9  10  8  6  4  2

PUBLISHER'S NOTE
This is a work of fiction. Names, characters, places, and incidents are either the product of the author's
imagination or are used fictitiously, and any resemblance to actual persons, living or dead,
business establishments, events, or locales is entirely coincidental.

THE LIBRARY OF CONGRESS HAS CATALOGED THE HARDCOVER EDITION AS FOLLOWS:
White, Edmund, 1940–
A boy's own story / Edmund White.
p. cm.
ISBN 0-525-24128-0 (hc.)
ISBN 978-0-14-311484-0 (pbk.)
1. Teenage boys—Fiction.   2. Gay youth—United States—Fiction.   I. Title.
PS3573.H463B6   1982
813'.54   82-9536

Printed in the United States of America

*To Christopher Cox*

# ONE

We're going for a midnight boat ride. It's a cold, clear summer night and four of us—the two boys, my dad and I—are descending the stairs that zigzag down the hill from the house to the dock. Old Boy, my dad's dog, knows where we're headed; he rushes down the slope beside us, looks back, snorts and tears up a bit of grass as he twirls in a circle. "What is it, Old Boy, what is it?" my father says, smiling faintly, delighted to be providing excitement for the dog, whom he always called his best friend.

I was bundled up, a sweater and a Windbreaker over today's sunburn. My father stopped to examine the bottom two steps just above the footpath that traveled from cottage to cottage on our side of the lake. This afternoon he had put in the new steps: fresh boards placed vertically to retain the sand and dirt, each braced by four wooden stakes pounded into the ground. Soon the steps would sag and sprawl and need to be redone. Whenever I came back from a swim or a trip in the outboard down to the village grocery store, I passed him crouched over his eternal steps or saw him up on a ladder painting the house, or heard his power saw arguing with itself in the garage, still higher up the hill on the road.

My father regarded guests as nuisances who had to be entertained over and over again. Tonight's expedition was just such a duty. But the boys, our guests' sons, didn't register the cheerlessness of the occasion and thought it was exciting still to be up at such an hour. They had run on down to the water as I lingered obediently beside my father, who caressed the steps with the flashlight. The boys were racing to the end of the dock, feet pounding the boards. Old Boy started out after them, but then came back to round us up. Now Kevin was threatening to push his little brother in. Squeals, breathing, a tussle, then release, followed by the sound of two boys just being.

As Dad and I went on down, his flashlight veered off into the water, scaring a school of minnows and illuminating bands of sand. The Chris-Craft, moored to the short end of the L formed by the dock, was big, heavy, imposing. Two tarpaulins covered it: one was a square, corners rounded, that fitted over the two seats in front; the other was a smaller, perfect rectangle that protected the bucket seat aft of the engine, which itself lay concealed, redolent of gasoline, under the double wood doors trimmed in chrome. The canvas, as I undid the grommets and gathered in its folds, had the familiar smell of a sour washcloth. Neither my father nor I moved very gracefully over that boat. We were both afraid of the water, he because he couldn't swim, I because I was afraid of everything.

Dad's most constant attribute was the cigar clenched between his small, stained teeth. Since he could usually be found in an air-conditioned house or office or car, the system under his control, he saw to it that the smoke and smell filtered evenly and thickly into every corner of his world, subduing those around him; perhaps, like a skunk parent, he was steeping us in his protective stink.

Although it was chilly and I had on a sweater and jacket, I was wearing Bermuda shorts; the wind raised goose bumps on my legs as I installed the wooden flagpole at the stern, an accoutrement patriotism forbade at night but which we needed for the white light that glowed from its top. How the electricity could run through this pole as soon as it was plugged into its socket mystified me; I dared not ask Dad for an explanation lest he give me one. The leather seats were cold, but they warmed under flesh soon enough, skin to skin.

Pulling away from the dock generated high anxiety (pulling in was worse). My father, who'd been a Texas cowboy as a young man, could laugh at twisters and rattlers, but everything about this alien medium—cold, bottomless, sliding—alarmed him. He was wearing his absurd "captain's" hat (all his leisure clothes were absurd—jokes, really—as though leisure itself had to be ridiculed). He was half standing behind the wheel. The motors were churning, the spotlight on the bow was gyrating, the red tip of his cigar was pulsing. I'd ventured out on the deck, untied the ropes, tossed them in, jumped in the boat myself; now I was crouched just behind my father. I was wielding a long pole with a hook on one end, the sort used to open upper windows in stuffy grade schools. My job was to push us safely out of the berth before my father threw the toiling motors into gear. It was all an embarrassment. Other men moored their powerboats with a single line, backed away from docks in a simple, graceful arc, talking all the while, and other men's sons scrambled like agile monkeys across lacquered decks, joking and smiling.

We were under way. The speedboat lunged forward with so much force that we were pressed back against our seats. Peter, Kevin's seven-year-old brother, was in the rumble seat, his hair streaming under the rippling flag, his mouth open to scream with delighted fear, though the sound was lost behind gales of wind. He waved a skinny arm and with his other hand clutched a chromium grip beside him; even so, he was posting high as we spanked over someone else's wake. Our own was thrown back from the prow. The night, intent seamstress, fed the fabric of water under the needle of our hull, steadily, firmly, except the boat wasn't stitching the water together but ripping it apart into long white shreds. Along the shore a few house lights here and there peered through the pines, as fleeting as stars glimpsed through the moving clouds above. We shot past an anchored boat of fishermen and their single kerosene lamp; one of them shook his fist at us.

The lake narrowed. Over to the right lay the nine-hole golf course (I knew it was there, though I couldn't see it) with its ramshackle clubhouse and wicker armchairs painted green, its porch swing on creaking chains. Once a month we showed up there late for Sunday supper, our clothes not right, our talk too distant and forthright, the cigar a foul smudge pot set out to ward off the incoming social frost.

Now Dad's cigar had gone out and he stopped the boat to relight it. From our high windy perch we drifted down, engine cut to a mild churning. When the exhaust pipe dipped above water level, it blatted rudely. "Boy, I'm soaked!" Peter was screaming in his soprano. "I'm freezing. Gee, you sure let me have it!"

"Too much for you, young fellow?" my father asked, chuckling. He winked at me. The children of visitors (and sometimes their fathers) were usually called "young fellow," since Dad could never remember their names. Old Boy, who had been squinting into the wind, his head stuck out beyond and around the windshield, was now prancing happily across the cushions to receive a pat from his master. Kevin, sitting just behind my father, said, "Those fishermen were mad as hell. I'd've been, too, if some guy in a big fat-ass powerboat scared off my fish."

My father winced, then grumbled something about how they had no business . . .

He was hurt.

I was appalled by Kevin's frankness. At such moments, tears would come to my eyes in impotent compassion for Daddy: this invalid despot, this man who bullied everyone but suffered the consequences with such a tender, uneducated heart! Tears would also well up when I had to correct my father on a matter of fact. Usually I'd avoid the bother and smugly watch him compound his mistakes. But if he asked my opinion point-blank, a euphoria of sadness would overtake me, panicky wings would beat at the corners of the shrinking room and, as quietly and as levelly as possible, I'd supply the correct name or date. For I was a lot more knowledgeable than he about the things that could come up in conversation even in those days, the 1950s.

But knowledge wasn't power. He was the one with the power, the money, the right to read the paper through dinner as my stepmother and I watched him in silence; he was the one with the thirty tailor-made suits, the twenty gleaming pairs of shoes and the starched white dress shirts, the ties from Countess Mara and the two Cadillacs that waited for him in the garage, dripping oil on the concrete in the shape of a black Saturn and its gray blur of moons. It was his power that stupefied me and made me regard my knowledge as nothing more than hired cleverness he might choose to show off at a dinner party ("Ask this young fellow, he reads, he'll know"). Then why did his occasional faltering bring tears to my eyes? Was I grieving because he didn't possess everything, absolutely everything, or because I owned nothing? Perhaps, despite my timidity, I was in a struggle against him. Did I want to hurt him because he didn't love me?

Within a moment Kevin had made things right by asking Daddy how he thought the hometown baseball team would do next season. My father was soon expatiating on names and averages and strategies that meant nothing to me, the good spring training and the bad trade-off. When Kevin challenged him on one point, Dad laughed good-naturedly at the boy's spunk (and error) and set him straight. I rested my arm on the rubber tread of the gunwale beside me and my chin on my arm and stared into the shiny water, which was busy analyzing a distant yellow porch light, shattering the simple glow into a hundred shifting possibilities.

The baseball talk went on for some time as we rocked in our own wake, which had overtaken us. We were drifting toward an island and its abandoned summer hotel, moth-white behind slender, silver-white birches. The motor wallowed, the sound of an old car with a bad muffler. My father usually felt uncomfortable with other men, but he and Kevin had now found a way to talk to each other and I half listened to the low murmurs of their voices—or rather of Daddy's monologue and Kevin's sounds of assent or disagreement. This was Dad's late-night voice: ruminative, confiding, unending. Old Boy recognized it from their dawn walks together and circumspectly placed his nose between his paws on the cushion beside Dad. Little Peter crawled up over the hatch and listened to the sports talk; even he knew names and averages and had an opinion or two. After he'd been silent for a while I looked around and saw he'd fallen asleep, his head thrown back over the edge of the cushion and his mouth open, his right hand twitching.

By now we'd entered the narrows that led into a smaller, colder branch of the lake. The lights of a car, after excavating a tunnel out of the pines halfway up the shore, dipped from view and then suddenly shot out across the water, which looked all the blacker and choppier in the brief glare. I had rowed laboriously over every mile of the lake; it was a mild sort of pleasure to see those backbreaking distances beautifully elided by the Chris-Craft. For Dad had gunned the motors again and we were sitting once more on our high, thundering throne. We passed a point where the clipped lawns of an estate flowed down from a white mansion and its lit, curtained windows. Late last Sunday afternoon, as I was pulling hard through the turbulent water at the point, I'd seen a young man in a seersucker suit and a girl in a party dress. They had sauntered up the hill away from me, he slightly in the lead, she swinging her arms high in an exaggerated way, as though she were a marionette. The sun found a feeble rainbow in the mist above a sprinkler and made the grass as green and uniform as baize. The light gave the couple long, important shadows.

All around me—at the post office where we had a box, in the general store, on docks, sailboats and water skis—young people with iodine-and-baby-oil tans, trim bodies and faultless teeth were having fun. A boat would glide across the setting sun, the shadow of a broad-shouldered teen inhabiting the white sail. At the village dock I'd look up from my outboard to see two young men walking past, just a sliver of untanned skin visible under the hems of their shorts. As I sat high up the hill on our porch swing, reading, I'd hear them joking as they sunned on the white diving raft below. I'd see them up close at the country club suppers—the boy with the strong chin and honey-brown hands, in blazer and white cotton pants, seating his mother, her nose like his but pointier, her hair as blonde but fogged with gray. These were the women who wore navy blue and a single piece of woven yellow and pink gold, whose narrow feet were shod in blue and white spectators, who drove jaunty station wagons, who drank martinis on porches with rattan furniture and straw rugs and whose voices were lower than most men's. Up close they smelled of gin, cocoa butter and lake water; we sometimes sat next to such a woman and her family at a communal table. Or I'd see these women at the little branch of Saks Fifth Avenue in a town not far away. They pretended they were bored or exasperated by their children's comings and goings: "Don't even bother to tell me when you'll be home, Scott, you know you've never kept your word yet." I saw it all and envied those sons their parents and those parents their sons.

My father was never tan. He had a huge belly; his glasses weren't horn-rim or translucent pink plastic (the two acceptable styles) but black with bronze metallic wings; he seldom drank cocktails; he didn't act as if he were onstage—he had no attractive affectations. Although my stepmother had risen socially as high as one could rise in that world, she'd done so on her own. My father never took her anywhere; she was as free as a spinster and as respectable as a matron. When she was with us at the cottage during the summer, she forgot about society and helped my father with his steps or his painting, she read as much as I did, arranged for good meals and rusticated. Once in a while, one of her elegant friends would drop by for lunch, and suddenly the house was electrified by the energy of those women—their excitement, their approval, their laughter, their thrilling small talk, an art as refined (and now as rare) as marquetry. My father would beam at these guests and pat their hands and pour them thimblefuls of brandy after their doll-size luncheons. Then they'd limp away in a broken-down car, millionairesses in old cardigans covered with cat hairs, their wonderful vibrant voices their only badge of breeding.

My father was courtly but dim. I was even dimmer. I read so much in the house (on the bed in my room, on the couch in the living room, on the shaded bench at the foot of the dock) that I hadn't gotten a tan. At least my clothes were right (my sister had seen to that), but I felt all dressed up with no place to go.

Unlike my idols I couldn't play tennis or baseball or swim freestyle. My sports were volleyball and Ping-Pong, my only stroke the sidestroke. I was a sissy. My hands were always in the air. In eighth grade I had appeared in the class pageant. We all wore togas and marched solemnly in to a record of Schubert's *Unfinished*. My sister couldn't wait to tell me I had been the only boy who'd sat not cross-legged on the gym floor but resting on one hand and hip like the White Rock girl. A popular quiz for masculinity in those days asked three questions, all of which I flunked: (1) Look at your nails (a girl extends her fingers, a boy cups his in his upturned palm); (2) Look up (a girl lifts just her eyes, a boy throws back his whole head); (3) Light a match (a girl strikes away from her body, a boy toward—or perhaps the reverse, I can't recall). But there were less esoteric signs as well. A man crosses his legs by resting an ankle on his knee; a sissy drapes one leg over the other. A man never gushes; men are either silent or loud. I didn't know how to swear: I always said the final *g* in *fucking* and I didn't know where in the sentence to place the *damn* or *hell*.

My father was just a bit of a sissy. He crossed his legs the wrong way. He was too fussy about his nails (he had an elaborate manicuring kit). He liked classical music. He was not an easygoing guy. But otherwise he passed muster: he was courageous in a fight; he was a strong, skilled athlete; not many things frightened him; he had towering rages; he knew how to swear; he was tirelessly assertive; and he had a gambler's good grace about losing money. He could lose lots of it in business and walk away, smiling and shrugging.

KEVIN WAS the sort of son who would have pleased my father more than I did. He was captain of his Little League baseball team. On the surface he had good manners, but they were born of training, not timidity. No irony, no superior smirks, no fits of longing or flights of fancy removed him from the present. He hadn't invented another life; this one seemed good enough. Although he was only twelve, he already throbbed with the pressure to contend, to be noticed, to be right, to win, to make others bend to his will. I found him rather frightening, certainly sexy (the two qualities seemed linked). Because I was three years older, I guessed he expected me to be ahead of him in most ways, and that first night in the boat I was silent in order not to disillusion him. I wanted him to like me.

Kevin may have been cocky, but he wasn't one of those suave country club boys. He wasn't well groomed and I don't think he thought about such things; he didn't date girls yet and he wore clothes unironed out of the dryer until they got dirty and his mother threw them back into the washer. He still watched cartoons on television before an early supper and when he was sleepy he leaned against his father, eyes blinking and registering nothing. His seven-year-old brother, Peter, was a nervous boy, morbidly eager to be just like Kevin.

As my father barked commands, Kevin and Peter and I secured the Chris-Craft to the dock and covered it with canvas. We climbed the many steps up to the house, Old Boy blazing the trail, then darting back to urge my father on. The house was brilliant with lights. Kevin's parents had bumped me from my upstairs room, the place where last week I had read *Death in Venice* and luxuriated in the tale of a dignified grown-up who died for the love of an indifferent boy my age. That was the sort of power I wanted over an older man. And I awakened to the idea that a great world existed in which things happened and people changed, took risks—more, took notice: a world so sensitive, like a grand piano, that even a step or a word could awaken vibrations in its taut strings.

Since the house was built on a very steep hill, the basement wasn't underground, though its cinder-block walls did smell of damp soil. There were only two rooms in the basement. One was a "rumpus room" with a semicircular glass-brick bar that could be lit from within by a pink, a green and an orange bulb (the blue had burned out).

The other room was long and skinny, the wall facing the lake broken by two large windows. Ordinarily a Ping-Pong table was set up in here, its green net never quite taut. Under the overhead lamp my father would lunge and swear and shout and slam or stretch to the very edge of the net to tap the ball delicately into the enemy's court (for his opponent was inevitably "the enemy," challenging his wind, strength, skill, prowess). Whenever my sister, a champion athlete, was at the cottage, she enjoyed this interesting power over Dad, while my stepmother and I sat upstairs and read, curled up in front of the fire with Herr Pogner the Persian cat (named after my harpsichord teacher). The cat dozed, feet tucked under her chest, though her raised ears, thin enough to let the lamplight through, twitched and cocked independently of one another with each "Damn!" or "Son of a bitch!" or "Gotcha, young lady, *got* you there" floating up through the hot-air vents in the floor. My sister's fainter but delighted reproaches ("Oh, *Daddy*," or "Really, Daddy") didn't merit even the tiniest adjustment of those feline ears. My stepmother, deep in her Taylor Caldwell or Jane Austen (she was a compulsive, unselective reader), was never too mesmerized by the page not to know when to hurry to the kitchen to present the inevitable victor—drawn, grinning—with his pint of peach ice cream and box of chocolate grahams, which my father would eat in his preferred way, a pat of cold butter on each cracker.

Tonight there was no game. The grown-ups were sitting around the fire sipping highballs. Downstairs the table had been replaced by three cots for us boys. Kevin's parents sent their sons to bed but I was allowed to stay up for another half hour. I was even given a weak highball of my own, though my stepmother murmured, "I'm sure he would rather have orange juice."

"For Chrissake," my father said, smiling, "give the fella a break." I was grateful for this unusual display of chumminess and, to please him, said nothing and nodded a lot at what the others said.

Kevin's parents, especially his mother, were unlike any other grown-ups I'd met. They were both Irish, she by origin, he by derivation. He drank till he became drunk, his eyes moist, his laugh general. He had a handsome face projected onto too much flesh, black hair that geysered up at the end of the formal walkway of his part, large red hands that went white at the knuckles when he picked something up (a glass of whiskey, say) and a tender, satirical manner toward his wife, as though he were a lazy dreamer who'd been stirred into action by this spit-fire.

She said *damn* and *hell* and drank whiskey and had two moods—rage (she was always shouting at Kevin) and mock rage, an appealingly ardent sort of simmering, Virtue Stymied: "All right then, be gone with you," she'd say, feisty and submissive, or "Of course you'll be having another drink."

It was all playacting and intended to be viewed as such. She had "temperament" because she was Irish and had been trained as an opera singer. If she wandered into a room and found Kevin's T-shirt balled and hurled in a chair, she'd start bellowing, "Kevin O'Malley Cork, get in here and get in here *now*. Look alive!" Nothing could restrain these outbursts, not even the knowledge that Kevin was out of earshot. Her arms would stiffen, her clenched fists would dig into her slim flanks and bunch up her dress, her nose would pale and her thin hair, the color of weathered bricks, would seem to go into shock and rise to reveal still more of her scalp. Because of her operatic training, her voice penetrated every corner of the house and had an alto after-hum that buzzed on in the round metal tabletop from Morocco. During the mornings she chain-smoked, drank coffee and sat around in a silk robe that revealed and highlighted her bony body. With her freckled face, devoid of makeup, rising above this slippery red sheen, she looked like an angry young man trapped in travesty as a practical joke.

This couple, with their liquor and cigarettes and roguish, periodic spats, struck my stepmother as "cheap." Or rather, the woman was cheap (men can't be cheap). The husband, my father later decided, wasn't "stable" (their money was by no means secure). Though they lived in a mansion with a swimming pool and antique furniture, they rented it, probably the furniture as well.

The Corks were both "climbers," he in business, she in society; they seemed to me fascinating shams. I especially admired the way Kevin's mother, so obviously a bohemian, hard drinker and hell-raiser, had toned down her exuberance enough to win invitations to a few polite "functions," those given by the

Women's Club if not by the Steinway Club (the Steinway pretended to be nothing but a little gathering of ladies who liked to play four-hand versions of "Mister Haydn's" symphonies, though it was in fact the highest social pinnacle). In pursuit of such heights, Mrs. Cork had reduced her *damns* and *hells* by the end of the week with us to *darns* and *hecks*. I had to admire the way Mrs. Cork was pretending to be shocked by the innocent improprieties that so excited my stepmother. I could tell Mrs. Cork had palled around with real screwballs, even unwed couples—it was just a sense I had. When I took her out one day in a motorboat alone, she and I happily discussed opera. We cut the motor and drifted. I relaxed and became animated to the point of effeminacy; she relaxed and became coarser. "Oh, my boy," she promised me in her brogue, "you want to hear fine singing, I'll play you my John McCormack records, make you weep your damn eyes out of their bloody sockets. That 'Luce-van le stelle,' it'll freeze your balls." I shrieked with delight— we were conspirators who'd somehow found ourselves stranded together here in a world of unthrillable souls. I dreamed of running off and becoming a great singer; I walked through the woods and vocalized.

Tonight we had not yet made our rapport explicit, but I was already wise to her. She had through circumstance ended up not on the La Scala stage but in this American cottage, married to an affable, overweight businessman. Now her job was to ingratiate herself with people who would help her husband in his career (lawyer for industry); she was retaining just enough brogue and temperament to be a "character." Characters—conventional women with minor eccentricities—flourished in our world, as Mrs. Cork had no doubt observed. But she'd failed to notice that the characters were all old, rich and pedigreed. Newcomers, especially those of moderate means, were expected to form an attractive but featureless chorus behind our few madcap divas.

"Time for bed, young fella," my father said at last.

Downstairs I undressed by the colored light of the glass-brick bar and, wearing just a T-shirt and jockey shorts, hurried into the dark dormitory and slipped into my cot. Nights on the lake are cold even in July; the bed had two thick blankets on it that had been aired outside that day and smelled of pine needles. I listened to the grown-ups; the metal vents conducted sound better than heat. Their conversation, which had seemed so lively and sincere when I had witnessed it, now sounded stilted and halting. Lots of fake laughter. Silences became longer and longer. At last everyone said good night and headed upstairs. Another five minutes of moaning pipes, flushing toilets and padding feet. Then long murmured consultations in bed by each couple. Then silence.

"You still awake?" Kevin called from his bed.

"Yes," I said. I couldn't see him in the dark but I could tell his cot was at the other end of the room; Peter was audibly asleep on the cot between.

"How old are you?" Kevin asked.

"Fifteen. And you?"

"Twelve. You ever done it with girls?"

"Sure," I said. I knew I could always tell him about the black prostitute I'd visited. "You?"

"Naw. Not yet." Pause. "I hear you gotta warm 'em up."

"That's correct."

"How do you do it?"

I had read a marriage manual. "Well, you turn the lights down and kiss a long time first."

"With your clothes on?"

"Of course. Then you take off her top and play with her breasts. But very gently. Don't get too rough—they don't like that."

"Does she play with your boner?"

"Not usually. An older, experienced woman might."

"You been with an older woman?"

"Once."

"They get kinda saggy, don't they?"

"My friend was beautiful," I said, offended on behalf of the imaginary lady.

"Is it real wet and slippery in there? Some guy told me it was like wet liver in a milk bottle."

"Only if the romantic foreplay has gone on long enough."

"How long's enough?"

"An hour."

The silence was thoughtful, as though it were an eyelash beating against a pillowcase.

"The guys back home? Guys in my neighborhood?"

"Yes?" I said.

"We all cornhole each other. You ever do that?"

"Sure."

"What?"

"I said sure."

"Guess you've outgrown that by now."

"Well, yeah, but since there aren't any girls around . . ." I felt as a scientist must when he knows he's about to bring off the experiment of his career: outwardly calm, inwardly jubilant, already braced for disappointment. "We could try it now." Pause. "If you want to." As soon as the words were out of my mouth I felt he wouldn't come to my bed; he had found something wrong with me, he thought I was a sissy, I should have said "Right" instead of "That's correct."

"Got any stuff?" he asked.

"What?"

"You know. Like Vaseline?"

"No, but we don't need it. Spit will"—I started to say "do," but men say "work"—"work." My penis was hard but still bent painfully down in the jockey shorts; I released it and placed the head under the taut elastic waistband.

"Naw, you gotta have Vaseline." I might be knowledgeable about real sex, but apparently Kevin was to be the expert when it came to cornholing.

"Well, let's try spit."

"I don't know. Okay." His voice was small and his mouth sounded dry.

I watched him come toward me. He, too, had jockey shorts on, which appeared to glow. Though bare-chested now, he'd worn a T-shirt all through Little League season that had left his torso and upper arms pale; his ghost shirt excited me, because it reminded me he was captain of his team.

We pulled off our shorts. I opened my arms to Kevin and closed my eyes. He said, "It's colder than a witch's tit." I lay on my side facing him and he slipped in beside me. His breath smelled of milk. His hands and feet were cold. I kept my lower arm scrunched under me, but with the upper one I nervously patted his back. His back and chest and legs were silky and hairless, though I could see a tuft of eiderdown under his arm, which he'd lifted to pat my back in reciprocation. A thin layer of baby fat still formed a pad under his skin. Beneath the fat I could feel the hard, rounded muscles. He reached down under the sheet to touch my penis, and I touched his.

"Ever put them together in your hand?" he asked.

"No," I said. "Show me."

"You spit on your hand first, get it real wet. See? Then you—scoot closer, up a bit—you put them together like this. It feels neat."

"Yes," I said. "Neat."

Since I knew he wouldn't let me kiss him, I put my head beside his and pressed my lips silently to his neck. His neck was smooth and long and thin, too thin for the size of his head; in this way, too, he still resembled a child. In the rising heat of our bodies I caught a slight whiff of his odor, not pungent like a grown-up's but faintly acrid, the smell of scallions in the rain.

"Who's first?" he asked.

"Cornholing?"

"I think we need some stuff. It won't work without stuff."

"I'll go first," I said. Although I put lots of spit on him and me, he still said it hurt. I'd get about half an inch in and he'd say, "Take it out! Quick!" He was lying on his side with his back to me, but I could still look over and see him wince in profile. "Jesus," he said. "It's like a knife all through me." The pain subsided and with the bravery of an Eagle Scout he said, "Okay. Try it again. But take it easy and promise you'll pull out when I say so."

This time I went in a millimeter at a time, waiting between each advance. I could feel his muscles relaxing.

"Is it in?" he asked.

"Yep."

"All the way in?"

"Almost. There. It's all in."

"Really?" He reached back for my crotch to make sure. "Yeah, it is," he said. "Feel good?"

"Terrific."

"Okay," he instructed, "go in and out, but slow, okay?"

"Sure."

I tried a few short thrusts and asked if I was hurting him. He shook his head.

He bent his knees up toward his chest and I flowed around him. Whereas face to face I had felt timid and unable to get enough of his body against enough of mine, now I was glued to him and he didn't object—it was understood that this was my turn and I could do what I liked. I tunneled my lower arm under him and folded it across his chest; his ribs were unexpectedly small and countable, and now that he'd completely relaxed I could get deeper and deeper into him. That such a tough, muscled little guy, whose words were so flat and eyes so without depth or humor, could be so richly taken—oh, he felt good. But the sensation he was giving didn't seem like something afforded by his body, or if so, then it was a secret gift, shameful and pungent, one he didn't dare acknowledge. In the Chris-Craft I'd been afraid of him. He had been the usual intimidating winner, beyond excitement—but here he was, pushing this tendoned, shifting pleasure back into me, the fine hair on his neck damp with sweat just above the hollows the sculptor had pressed with his thumbs into the clay. His tan hand was resting on his white hip. The ends of his lashes were pulsing just beyond the line of his full cheek.

"Does it feel good?" he asked. "Want it tighter?" he asked, as a shoe salesman might.

"No, it's fine."

"See, I can make it tighter," and indeed he could. His eagerness to please me reminded me that I needn't have worried, that in his own eyes he was just a kid and I a high school guy who'd done it with girls and one older lady and everything. Most of the time I had dreamed of an English lord who'd kidnap me and take me away forever; someone who'd save me and whom I'd rule. But now it seemed that Kevin and I didn't need anyone older, we could run away together, I would be our protector. We were already sleeping in a field under a sheet of breezes and taking turns feeding on each other's bodies, wet from the dew.

"I'm getting close," I said. "Want me to pull out?"

"Go ahead," he said. "Fill 'er up."

"Okay. Here goes. Oh, God. Jesus!" I couldn't help kissing his cheek.

"Your beard hurts," he said. "You shave every day?"

"Every other. You?"

"Not yet. But the fuzz is gettin' dark. Some guy told me the sooner you start shavin', the faster it comes in. Do you agree?"

"I think so. Well," I said, "I'm pullin' out. Your turn."

I turned my back to Kevin and I could hear him spitting on his hand. I didn't particularly like getting cornholed, but I was peaceful and happy because we loved each other. People say young love or love of the moment isn't real, but I think the only love is the first. Later we hear its fleeting recapitulations throughout our lives, brief echoes of the original theme in a work that increasingly becomes all development, the mechanical elaboration of a crab canon with too many parts. I was aware of the treacherous air vents above us, conducting the sounds we were making upstairs. Maybe my dad was listening. Or maybe, just like Kevin, he was unaware of anything but the pleasure spurting up out of his body and into mine.

MY FATHER had started his own business fifteen years earlier in order to make money, be his own boss and keep his own hours. These were imperatives, not simple wishes, and whenever they were set aside he suffered, even physically. Money was for him the air superior people needed to breathe; wealth and superiority coincided, though when he said someone was from a "good" family, he meant rich first and only secondarily respectable or virtuous. But his real reason for wanting money, I imagine, was that it was a distinction as absolute as genius and as solitary; any other thing people think is worth getting would have struck him as too arbitrary and congenial. Too sociable.

His need for independence was less explicit, more shaded but just as strong. Independence conferred upon him feudal rights of the purse and gavel and allowed him to dictate his fate and ours. The fate he chose for himself was misanthropic and poetic. He slept all day, rose at three at the earliest or five at the latest and by six, when the winter sky was already dark, he was sitting down to a breakfast of a pound of bacon, six scrambled eggs and eight slices of toast freighted with preserves. He took no lunch but at three or four in the morning ate a supper of a plate-size steak, three vegetables, a salad, more bread and a dessert, preferably sugared strawberries over vanilla ice cream. His only drink was spring water delivered to the house in big glass jugs, tinted a faint blue, inverted above an office-style electric water cooler. Before bedtime he had his snack of buttered chocolate grahams. Then he'd brush Old Boy in the basement and take him out for a long dawn walk; he talked to the dog in a man-to-man but deeply solicitous way, somewhat as though the animal were a great man gone senile. His hours gave Dad the cool and silence of the night and took away the populated disorder of the day.

He worked all night at his desk, wielding a calculating machine and slide rule and printing page after page of specifications and instructions. At home he sat in his office at the top of his house, which had been built to resemble a Norman castle, and from his windows he could survey the floodlit lawn. On the wall behind him hung a big, bad painting of waves crashing in the moonlight. He smoked cigars until the last hour before bedtime, when he switched to a pipe. Its sweet smoke filtered through the central heating or air-conditioning into every corner of the sealed house. The pipe hour was the time to approach him for a favor or just a few pleasant words; I'd sit on the loveseat beside his blond mahogany desk and watch him work.

Hour after hour he wrote with an onyx fountain pen in lower-case block letters that had the angle and lean elegance of Art Deco design; his smoke drifted up through the rosy light cast by the matching red shades on floor stands that flanked the desk.

Even at the cottage he would set up an office and work till dawn when he wasn't outdoors doing manual labor under artificial light, his "hobby." But now a houseful of guests had forced him to modify his hours and habits. Had Mrs. Cork been a beauty he might have suffered the presence of her family more gladly; he was a great fancier of women and they brought out in him a courtliness as rich and old as the best port. His irritable misanthropy vanished in the presence of a beautiful woman. She could even be a child, a lovely little girl; she would still excite gallantry in him. Once a ten-year-old charmer who was staying with us announced at midnight that she wanted chocolate and my father drove fifty miles to a nearby town, dragged the owner of a candy store out of bed and paid a hundred dollars for twenty opera creams. He once gave the same amount as a tip to a full-bodied, glossy-lipped singer in an Italian restaurant who had serenaded him with a wobbling but surprisingly intimate rendition of "Vissi d'arte" to an accordion accompaniment executed by a hunchback with Bell's palsy freezing half his face while the other half modestly winked and smiled.

The only part of his customary life my father could maintain during the Corks' visit was filling every waking moment with what used to be called "classical" music, though most of it was romantic, Brahms in particular. He had always had hundreds of records, which he played on a Meissen phonograph that stood as a separate, massive piece of furniture in one corner of his office.

I mention the constant music because, to my mind at least, it served as an invisible link between my father and me. He never discussed music beyond saying that the *German Requiem* was "damn nice" or that the violin and cello concerto was "one hell of a piece," and even these judgments he made with a trace of embarrassment; for him, music was emotion, and he did not believe in discussing feelings.

His real love was the late Brahms, the piano *Intermezzi* and especially the two clarinet sonatas. These pieces, as unpredictable as thought and as human as conversation, filled the house night after night. He could not have liked them as background music to work to, since their abrupt changes of volume and dynamics must have made them too arresting to dismiss. I never showered with my dad, I never saw him naked, not once, but we did immerse ourselves, side by side, in those passionate streams every night. As he worked at his desk and I sat on his couch, reading or daydreaming, we bathed in music. Did he feel the same things I felt? Perhaps I ask this only because now that he's dead I fear we shared nothing and my long captivity in his house represented to him only a slight inconvenience, a major expense, a fair to middling disappointment, but I like to think that music spoke to us in similar ways and acted as the source and transcript of a shared rapture. I feel sorry for a man who never wanted to go to bed with his father; when the father dies, how can his ghost get warm except in a posthumous embrace? For that matter, how does the survivor get warm?

Kevin hated music. When he was horsing around with his little brother, he'd fall back into the silliness of boyhood. Like all boys, they loved cracking stupid jokes that became funnier and funnier to them the more they were repeated. The opera singers especially tickled them (strangely enough, considering their mother was a singer) and they'd jounce along with warbling falsettos, holding their right hands on their stomachs and rolling their eyes. I was chagrined by this clowning because I'd already imagined Kevin as a sort of husband. No matter that he was younger; his cockiness had turned him into the Older One. But this poignantly young groom I couldn't reconcile with the brat he had become today. Perhaps he wanted to push me away.

IN THE afternoon everyone except Kevin and me left on a boat ride. We went swimming off the dock. Clouds had covered the sun, gray clouds with black bellies and veins of fiery silver. After a while they blew away and released the late sun's warmth. We were standing side by side. I was at least half a foot taller than Kevin. We both had erections and we pulled our suits open under the cold water and looked down at them. Kevin pointed out that there were two openings at the head of his penis, separated by just the thinnest isthmus of flesh. I touched his penis and he touched mine. "Somebody might see us," I said, backing away. "So what," he said.

For quite a while we lolled on the deck. One opulent drop of water rolled down his high, compact chest into the hollow between his nipples, the right one still small and white from the cold, the left fuller and just beginning to color. The other drops were not so heavy; studding his body impressionistically with light, they didn't move; they slowly evaporated. His sides and childishly rounded stomach dried faster than the glossy epaulets on his shoulders. For a second a diamond depended from his nose. Three or four houses away, little kids were screaming in the water. One was impersonating a motorboat, another had comically lowered her voice. An older boy was trying to scare the younger ones; he was a bomber, they helpless civilians, and his way of imitating a plane was really very good. The kids were thrilled and squealed. Some of them were laughing, though their laughter contained no warmth, no irony and no humor.

Kevin was restless; he belly-flopped into the water, spraying me, stood, turned and scudded more water at me with the heel of his hand. I knew I should shout "Geronimo!" and leap in after him, clamber up on his back and push him under. The horseplay would dissolve the tension and sexual melancholy; my body would become not a snare but a friendly sort of weapon. But I couldn't go against the decorum of my own fantasies, which were all romantic.

Kevin swam freestyle away from me, way out to the white diving raft. I watched, then rested my head on the board beside my arm. A tiny ant shaped like a dumbbell crawled through the flaring, glittering hairs on my forearm. The water flowing through the pylons under me gurgled. I propped myself up on my elbow and watched Kevin diving. After a bit he found what looked like the pink plastic lid of a bucket. He tossed it again and again into the air and swam to retrieve it. The late sun, masked once more by clouds, did not send its path across the water toward us but hollowed out beneath it a golden amphitheater. The light was behind Kevin; when he held up the disk it went as pale and seductive as a pink hibiscus. His head was about the same size as the lid. When he turned his face my way it was dark, indistinguishable; his back and shoulders were carving up strips of light, carving them this way and that as he twisted and bobbed. The water was dark, opaque, but it caught the sun's gold light, the waves dragon scales writhing under a sainted knight's halo. At last Kevin swam up beside me; his submerged body looked small, boneless. He said we should go down to the store and buy some Vaseline.

"But we don't really need it," I said.

"Let's get it."

In the distance two gray-mauve clouds, like the huge rectangular sails of caravels, hung darkly, becalmed, immanent, behind mist. Kevin's lips were blue and he was covered with goose bumps as he vaulted up onto the dock. His legs were smooth except for the first signs of hair above his ankles (the first place an old man's legs go bald). He dried himself and put on a shirt. We took the outboard to the village. I went into the store with him, though I made him ask for the Vaseline. I was blushing and couldn't raise my eyes. He pulled it off without a trace of guilt, even asked to see the medium-size jar before settling for the small one. Outside, a film of oil opalesced on the water under a great axle of red light rolling across the sky from azimuth to zenith. That little round jar of grease would be a clue for my father or his to find. Worse, it was the application of method to sex, the outward betrayal of what I wanted to consider love, the inward state. At last the sun went down and the lake seemed colder and bigger and the two of us seemed bereft.

THAT NIGHT the two families, all of us, went out to dinner at a restaurant thirty miles away, a place where the overweight ate iceberg lettuce under a dressing of ketchup and mayonnaise, steaks under A.1. sauce, feed corn under butter, ice cream under chocolate, where a man wearing a black toupee and a madras sports jacket bounced merrily up and down an electric organ while a frisky couple lunged and dipped before him in cloudy recollections of ancient dance steps. The waitress was at once buddy ("How we doing here?") and temptress ("C'mon, go on"). She had meticulously carded bronze hair, an exuberant hankie exploding above a name tag ("Susie"), a patient smile and, hanging on a chain, lunettes that she wore only when writing an order or totaling the check. In one corner a colorful canopy hung over a round bar, just so the whole place could be called "The Big Top." No one was sitting at the bar. On its tiered glass shelves, lit from below, stood rank after rank of liquor bottles, soldiers at attention and glowing with fiery spirits from within. Everything smelled of the kerosene heater and the pine-scented Air Wick wafting out of the toilets. Except for the circus theme, the dominant motif seemed to be hunting, demonstrated by the rifles and glassy-eyed, dusty-antlered deer heads on the wall.

The place was smelly and oppressive, but the grown-ups, their tongues loosened by martinis, settled in for a long stay. The two women, seated next to each other, talked Paris fashions and assured each other *no one* would wear the Parachute. Mr. Cork, more Republican than the republic, was discerning a Communist conspiracy in every national mishap. I could see my father wasn't convinced, least of all by Mr. Cork's ardor; Dad took off his glasses, rubbed his eyes and nodded rhythmically through the harangue, his polite way of shielding himself from a loudmouth, of immigrating inward. Little Peter had turned a celery stalk from the relish tray into an Indian canoe and Kevin was sniping at it from the chalky promontory of a flour-dusted dinner roll; the massacre was carried out in whispered sound effects. "Kevin O'Malley Cork, how many times must I tell you not to play with your food!" "Aw, Maw."

On and on the meal devolved. The organist's pale forehead glittering under his black wig, his teeth bared, he moved from a pathetic "Now Is the Hour" with copious vibrato into a "Zip-a-Dee Doo-Dah" with a Latin beat. The waitress tempted everyone with pie—stewed apples and cinnamon enclosed in envelopes of pastry that looked like pressed Leatherette, each wedge, of course, à la mode. Coffee for the grown-ups, more milk for the kids. The bill. The argument over it. The change. The second cigar. The mints. The toothpicks. The crème de menthe frappés and the B and B's. More coffee. The tip. "Good night, folks. Hurry back!" Another tip for the organist, who nods grateful acknowledgment while staying right in there with "Kitten on the Keys."

All seven of us squeezed into my father's Cadillac and rolled off into a chilly night gray-blue and streaked with the smell of burning wood. My stepmother, Mrs. Cork and Kevin and I were in the backseat; Peter was soon sleeping on his father's shoulder up front, as my father drove. The dinner had left me bleak with rage. Something (books, perhaps) had given me a quite different idea of how people should talk and feed. I entertained fancy ideas about elegant behavior and cuisine and friendship. When I grew up I would always be frank, loving and generous. We'd feast on iced grapes and wine; we'd talk till dawn about the heart and listen to music. *I don't belong here,* I shouted at them silently. I wanted to run through surf or speed off with a brilliant blond in a convertible or rhapsodize on a grand piano somewhere in Europe. Or I wanted the white and gold doors to open as my loving, true but not-yet-found friends came toward me, their gently smiling faces lit from below by candles on the cake. This longing for lovers and friends was so full within me that it could spill over at any provocation—from listening to my own piano rendition of a waltz, from looking at a reproduction of two lovers in kimonos and tall clogs under an umbrella shielding them from slanted lines of snow or from sensing a change of seasons (the first smell of spring in winter, say).

Once, when I was Kevin's age, I'd wanted my father to love me and take me away. I had sat night after night outside his bedroom door in the dark, crazy with fantasies of seducing him, eloping with him, covering him with kisses as we shot through space against a night field flowered with stars. But now I hated him and felt he was what I must run away from. To be sure, had he pulled the car off the highway right now and turned to say he loved me, I would have taken his hand and walked with him away from the stunned vehicle that creaked as it cooled, our only spoor the sparks flying from Dad's cigar.

Kevin took my hand. He was sitting next to me in the dark. I had scooted forward on the cushion to give the others more room. Now our linked hands were concealed between his leg and mine. Just as I'd almost given up on him with his Vaseline, he placed that hot hand in mine. I could feel the calloused pads on his palm where he'd gripped the bat. Outside, the half-moon sped through the tall pines, spilled out across a glimpse of water, hid behind a billboard, twinkled faintly in the windows of a train, one window still lit and framing the face of a woman crowned by white hair. Dogs barked, then stopped as the trees came quicker and quicker and pushed closer to the winding road. Only here and there could a house light be seen. Now none. We were in the deep forest. The change from scattered farms to dense trees felt like an entry into something chilled and holy, a packed congregation of robed and mitered men whose form of worship is to wait in a tense, century-long silence. Kevin had made me very happy—a gleeful, spiteful happiness. Here we were, right under the noses of these boring old grown-ups, and we were two guys holding hands. Maybe I wouldn't have to run away. Maybe I could live here among them, act normal, go through the paces—all the while holding the hand of this wonderful kid.

Back in the basement, we three undressed under the glaring Ping-Pong light. Peter stumbled out of his clothes, which he left in a puddle on the floor. His shoulders were bony, his waist tiny, his penis a pale blue snail peeping up out of its rounded shell. He mumbled something about the cold sheets and turned his face to the wall. Kevin and I, at either end of the long, narrow room, undressed more deliberately, said nothing and scarcely looked at each other. Lights out. Then the long wait for Peter's breathing to slow and thicken. The silence was thoughtful, like a pulse heard in an ear pressed to the mattress. Peter said, "Because I don't *want* to . . . squirrel . . . yeah, but you . . ." and was gone. Still Kevin waited, and I feared he too had gone to sleep. But no, here he was, floating toward me, the ghost T-shirt on his torso browner from today's sun. With the Vaseline jar in hand. The cold jelly with its light medicinal odor, which warms quickly to body temperature. As I went in him, he said straight out, as clear as a bell, "That feels really great." It had never occurred to me before that sex between two men can please both of them at the same time.

THE NEXT afternoon my father, painfully patient but haggard from these unusual daytime hours, took us kids water-skiing. Again I walked on the lacquered deck, pushing us away from the dock with the long pole, my movements stiff, almost arthritic with fright. Again my father shouted orders that betrayed his own anxiety: "Kids, I smell something burning. The engine's on fire! Goddamn it, quick, young fellow, open those doors." "Nothing, sir, everything's fine." "You sure?" "Yes sir. Positive." "Sure?" "Yes." I was clinging to the windshield with claws of fear—and I caught a glimpse of Kevin and Peter smirking at each other. They thought my father and I were fools.

Skiing off the boat wasn't simple. The velocity of such a massive, powerful vessel almost pulled your arms out of your sockets. The wake fanning out on either side of you once you were aloft seemed mountainous and to jump over it foolhardy, if not suicidal. Kevin, of course, handled it all beautifully, though he'd never skied before. Soon he was clowning around and lifting first one ski and then the other, and he raced over the wake from side to side with great speed. I was in the bucket seat watching him. If we lost him I was supposed to signal Peter up ahead, who was to relay the message to the captain—but Kevin fell only once. We went past the diving raft and its company of teenage swimmers; I was pleased that our boat was pulling someone as athletic as Kevin. In our family the virtues were all invisible to a stranger's eye. My stepmother's social eminence, my dad's dough—they couldn't be seen. But Kevin's body as he crouched and jumped over the wake, *that* could be seen. When at last he became tired he waited till we went past our house and then released the rope and slowly sank ten paces from our dock.

That night he came to my bed again, but I irritated him by trying to kiss him. "I don't go for that," he said brusquely, though later, when we stood together in the maid's half-bathroom washing up, he looked at me with an expression that could have been weariness or tenderness, I couldn't tell. In the morning he went swimming with his father. I watched the two of them joking with each other. Kevin gave his father a hand and pulled him up on the deck. They were obviously friends, and I felt all the more rebuffed.

That afternoon Peter, Kevin and I went fishing in the little outboard. The weather was hot, muggy, clouded over, and we waited in vain for a bite. We'd dropped anchor in a marsh where hollow reeds surrounded us and scratched the metal sides of the boat. I was sweating freely. Sweat stung my right eye. A mosquito spoke in my ear. The smell of gasoline from the engine (tilted up out of the shallow water) refused to lift and float away. The boys were threatening each other with dead worms out of the bait jar and Peter's calls and pounding feet had scared off every fish in the lake. When I asked them to sit still, they gave each other that same smirk and started mocking me, repeating my words, their voices sliding up and down the scale, "You *could* be more considerate." After a while the joke wore thin and they moved on to something else. Somehow—but at what precise moment?—I had shown I was a sissy; I replayed a moment here, a moment there of the past days, in an attempt to locate the exact instant when I'd betrayed myself. We motored back over the glassy, steaming lake; everything was colorless and hot and drained of immediacy. In such a listless, enfeebled world the whine of the motor seemed particularly cruel, like a scar on the void. I went for a walk by myself.

I plodded up and down the hills on the narrow road that passed the backs of cottages, which turned their faces to the lake. An old car full of black maids sputtered past. It was Wednesday evening; tomorrow was their day off. Tonight they'd stay at a Negro resort twenty miles away and dance and laugh far into the night, eat ribs, wear gowns, talk louder and laugh harder than they could the rest of the week in the staid houses where they served. Most of the time they were exiled, dispersed into the alien population; only once a week did the authorities allow the tribe to reconvene. They were exuberant people forced to douse their merry flames and maintain just the palest pilot light. At that moment I really believed I, too, was exuberant and merry by nature, had I the chance to show it.

In the silence that ebbed in behind the departing car, the air was filled with the one-note chant of crickets. Their song seemed like the heartbeat of loneliness, a beat that sang up and down the wires of my veins. I was desolate. I toyed again with the idea of becoming a general. I wanted power so badly that I had convinced myself I already had too much of it, that I was an evil schemer who might destroy everyone around me through the poison seeping out of my pores. I was appalled by my own majesty. I wanted someone to betray.

Kevin and his family stayed on three more days. Mr. Cork became incoherent with drink one night and cracked the banister as he reeled up to bed. Mrs. Cork exploded the next morning and told my stepmother she *loathed* eggs "swimming in grease." Katy, the Hungarian cook, locked herself in her room and emerged red-eyed and sniffling two hours later. Kevin and Mrs. Cork argued with each other, or rather she nagged him and he ridiculed her; when they made up, their embrace was shockingly intimate—prolonged, wordless nuzzling. On a rainy afternoon the boys roughhoused until Peter overturned the table and smashed one of the hand-painted tiles set into the top; his parents seemed almost indifferent to the damage and allowed the pushing and shoving to continue. Mrs. Cork's way of conspicuously ignoring the pandemonium was to vocalize, full voice. Each night Kevin came to my bed, though now I no longer elaborated daydreams of running away with him. I was a little bit afraid of him; now that he knew I was a sissy, he could make fun of me whenever he chose to. Who knew what he'd do? After witnessing his vituperation against his mother, followed by the weird nuzzling, I could not continue to think of him as the boy next door. The last night I tried kissing him again, but he turned his head away.

On the afternoon they left, Mrs. Cork flushed a deep, indignant red and chased Kevin halfway up the stairs. He crouched and shouted, his face contorted, "You scumbag, you old scumbag," and pushed her down the stairs. My father was furious. He lifted the woman from the floor and said to Kevin, "I think you've done enough for one day, young man." Mr. Cork, not completely sober, kept counting the pieces of luggage. He pretended he hadn't noticed the outbreak. His wife took on an injured silence as though in heavy mourning. She barely said good-bye to us. But once she had gone through the door and was on the steps to the garage, I saw her flash a crooked little smile at her son. He rushed into her open arms and they nuzzled and stroked each other.

At last they were gone. My father and stepmother were lighthearted with relief, as was I. My stepmother, ever fastidious, had found them almost savagely dirty and cited lots of evidence, beginning with pint bottles under the bed and ending with the used ear swabs smoldering in the bathroom ashtray. My father said they were all "screwballs" and their boys more fit for a reformatory than a house. And that Cork fellow talked too much about Commies, and drank too much and knew too little and seemed unstable; Dad thought Cork would not do well in business—nor did he, as it turned out. I said the sons struck me as "babyish." My stepmother apologized to Katy for the rude guests and reported back to us that they had not left Katy a tip; my father recompensed her for the extra bother she'd been put to.

Then we all rushed into solitude, my stepmother and I to our books and Dad to his puttering. My father now seemed to like me better. I might not be the son he thought he wanted, but I was what he deserved—someone patient, appreciative, as addicted to books as he was to work, as isolated by my loneliness as he was by his misanthropy, someone he could speak to only in the best if least direct way through the recorded concert that filled the house deep into the night, even until dawn.

I was moved back into my room. We ate very late and gave ourselves to the sonorous, spacious night. My father did desk work. We were three dreamers, each musing happily in a different cubicle. The sound of the calculating machine, jumping on its metal wheels. The aroma of burning pine logs. The remarkable fairness and good humor with which the piano and clarinet took turns singing the melody. At last, the sweet smell of the pipe. My father was in the basement, which had been restored to his dog. Through the air filter I could hear him: "What is it, Old Boy? Tell me. You can tell me."

Then, unexpectedly, he invited me to join them for their walk. It was strangely chilly, the first reminder of autumn, and my father had put on a ridiculous blue cap with a bill and earflaps and a baggy tan car coat that zipped up the front. Wherever we stopped we were enveloped in a cloak of sweet smoke, like the disguised king and his favorite who've slipped out of the palace to visit the peasants' fair. Nothing could hurry my father or Old Boy along. We stopped at every bush and every overflowing garbage can behind every silent, darkened cottage. We went all the way down to the deserted village: the store, the post office, the boat works. A speedboat, its bottom leprous and in need of sanding and painting, was turned upside down on trestles. A chain rattled against the flagpole in front of the post office. A woman wearing a nurse's white cap drove past, the only car we'd seen.

We retraced our steps. As daybreak came closer, the birds began to twitter and the leaves on birches fluttered in the rising breeze. Down the sloped shore the lake slowly took on shape, then color. Behind a door an unseen dog yapped at us, and Old Boy became frantic with curiosity. "What is it? Tell me. You can tell me. What is it, Old Boy?"

As the sun, like life returning to a body, stole over the world, the beam from my father's flashlight grew less and less distinct until it had been absorbed in the clarity of something that was new yet again.

# TWO

When I was fourteen, the summer before I went to prep school, a year before I met Kevin, I worked for my father. He wanted me to learn the value of a dollar. I did work, I did learn and I earned enough to buy a hustler.

The downtown of the city Dad lived in was small, no larger than a few dozen blocks. Every morning my stepmother drove me into town from our house, the fake Norman castle that stood high and white on a hill above the steaming river valley; we'd go down into town—a rapid descent of several steep plunges into the creeping traffic, the dream dissolves of black faces, the smell of hot franks filtered through the car's air-conditioned interior, the muted cries of newspaper vendors speaking their own incomprehensible language, the somber look of sooted façades edging forward to squeeze out the light. Downtown excited me: so many people, some of them just possibly an invitation to adventure or escape.

As a little boy I'd thought of our house (the old Tudor one, not this new Norman castle) as the place God had meant us to own, but now I knew in a vague way that its seclusion and ease had been artificial and that it had strenuously excluded the city at the same time we depended on the city for food, money, comfort, help, even pleasure. The black maids were the representatives of the city I'd grown up among. I'd never wanted anything from them—nothing except their love. To win it, or at least to ward off their silent, sighing resentment, I'd learned how to make my own bed and cook my own breakfast. But nothing I could do seemed to make up to them for the terrible loss they'd endured.

In my father's office I worked an Addressograph machine (then something of a novelty) with Alice, a woman of forty who, like a restless sleeper tangled in sheets, tossed about all day in her fantasies. She was a chubby but pert woman who wore pearls to cover the pale line across her neck, the scar from some sort of surgical intervention. It was a very thin line, but she could never trust her disguise and ran to the mirror in the ladies' room six or seven times a day to reevaluate the effect.

The rest of her energy went into elaborating her fantasies. There was a man on the bus every morning who always stationed himself opposite her and arrogantly undressed her with his dark eyes. Upstairs from her apartment another man lurked, growling with desire, his ear pressed to the floor as he listened through an inverted glass for the glissando of a silk slip she might be stepping out of. "Should I put another lock on my door?" she'd ask. Later she'd ask with wide-eyed sweetness, "Should I invite him down for a cup of coffee?" I advised her not to; he might be dangerous. The voraciousness of her need for men made me act younger than usual; around her I took refuge in being a boy, not a man. Her speculations would cause her to sigh, drink water and return to the mirror. My stepmother said she considered this woman to be a "ninny." My family and their friends almost never characterized people we actually knew, certainly not dismissively. I felt a gleeful shame in thinking of my colleague as a "ninny"—sometimes I'd laugh out loud when the word popped into my head. I found it both exciting and alarming to feel superior to a grown-up.

Something about our work stimulated thoughts of sex in us. Our tasks (feeding envelopes into a trough, stamping them with addresses, stuffing them with brochures, later sealing them and running them through the postage meter) required just enough attention to prevent connected conversation but not so much as to absorb us. We were left with amoeboid desires that split or merged as we stacked and folded, as we tossed and turned. "When he looks at me," Alice said, "I know he wants to hurt me." As she said that, her sweet, chubby face looked as though it was emerging out of a cloud.

Once I read about a woman patient in psychoanalysis who referred to her essential identity as her "prettiness"; my companion—gray-eyed, her wrists braceleted in firm, healthy fat, hair swept up into a brioche pierced by the fork of a comb, her expression confused and sweet as she floated free of the cloud—she surrounded and kept safe her own "prettiness" as though it were a passive, intelligent child and she the mother, dazed by the sweeping lights of the world.

She was both afraid and serene—afraid of being noticed and more afraid of being ignored, thrillingly afraid of the sounds outside her bedroom window, but also serene in her conviction that this whole bewildering opera was being staged in order to penetrate the fire and get to her "prettiness." She really was pretty—perhaps I haven't made that clear: a sad blur of a smile, soft gray eyes, a defenseless availability. She was also crafty, or maybe willfully blind, in the way she concealed from herself her own sexual ambitions.

Becoming my father's employee clarified my relationship with him. It placed him at an exact distance from me that could be measured by money. The divorce agreement had spelled out what he owed my mother, my sister and me, but even so, whenever my mother put us kids on the train to go visit him (one weekend out of every month and for long periods every summer), she invariably told us, "Be nice to your father or he'll cut us off." And later, when my sister was graduated from college, he presented her with a "life bill," the itemized expenses he'd incurred in raising her over twenty-one years, a huge sum that was intended to discourage her from thoughtlessly spawning children of her own.

Since Dad slept all day, he seldom put in an appearance at the office before closing time, when he'd arrive fresh and rested, smelling of witch hazel, and scatter reluctant smiles and nods to the assembly as he made his way through us and stepped up to his own desk in a large room walled off from us by soundproof glass. "My, what a fine man your father is, a real gentleman," my colleague would sigh. "And to think your stepmother met him when she was his secretary—some women have all the luck." We sat in rows with our backs to him; he played the role of the conscience, above and behind us, a force that troubled us as we filed out soon after his arrival at the end of the workday. Had we stayed late enough? Done enough?

My stepmother usually kept my father company until midnight. Then she and I would drive back to the country and go to bed. Sometimes my father followed us in his own car and continued his desk work at home. Or sometimes he'd stay downtown till dawn. "Late at night—that's when he goes out to meet other women," I once overheard my real mother tell my sister. "He was never faithful. There was always another woman, the whole twenty-two years we were married. He takes them to those little fleabag hotels downtown. I know." This hint of mystery about a man so cold and methodical fascinated me—as though he, the rounded brown geode, if only cracked open, would nip at the sky with interlocking crystal teeth, the quartz teeth of passion.

Before the midnight drive back home I was sometimes permitted to go out to dinner by myself. Sometimes I also took in a movie (I remember going to one that promised to be actual views of the "orgies at Berchtesgaden," but it turned out to be just Eva Braun's home movies, the Führer conferring warm smiles on pets and children). A man who smelled of Vitalis sat beside me and squeezed my thigh with his hand. I had my own spending money and my own free time.

I hypothesized a lover who'd take me away. He'd climb the fir tree outside my window, step into my room and gather me into his arms. What he said or looked like remained indistinct, just a cherishing wraith enveloping me, whose face glowed more and more brightly. His delay in coming went on so long that soon I'd passed from anticipation to nostalgia. One night I sat at my window and stared at the moon, toasting it with a champagne glass filled with grape juice. I knew the moon's cold, immense light was falling on him as well, far away and just as lonely in a distant room. I expected him to be able to divine my existence and my need, to intuit that in this darkened room in this country house a fourteen-year-old was waiting for him.

Sometimes now when I pass dozing suburban houses I wonder behind which window a boy waits for me.

After a while I realized I wouldn't meet him till years later; I wrote him a sonnet that began, "Because I loved you before I knew you . . ." The idea, I think, was that I'd never quarrel with him, nor ever rate his devotion cheap; I had had to wait too long. I'd waited so long I was almost angry, certainly vengeful.

My father's house was a somber place. The styleless polished furniture was piled high and the pantry supplies were laid in; in the fullness of breakfront drawers gold flatware and silver tea things remained for six months at a time in mauve flannel bags that could not ward off a tarnish bred out of the very air. No one talked much. There was little laughter, except when my stepmother was on the phone with one of her social friends. Although my father hated most people, he had wanted my stepmother to take her place in society, and she had. She'd become at once proper and frivolous, innocent and amusing, high-spirited and reserved—the combination of wacky girl and prim matron her world so admired.

I learned my part less well. I feared the sons of her friends and made shadows among the debs. I played the piano without ever improving; to practice would have meant an acceptance of more delay, whereas I wanted instant success, the throb of plumed fans in the dark audience, the glare off diamonded necks and ears in the curve of loges. What I had instead was the ache of waiting and the fear I wasn't worthy. Before dressing I'd stand naked before the closet mirror and wonder if my body was worthy. I can still picture that pale skin stretched over ribs, the thin, hairless arms and sturdier legs, the puzzled, searching face—and the slow lapping of disgust and longing, disgust and longing. The disgust was hot, penetrating—nobody would want me because I was a sissy and had a mole between my shoulder blades. The longing was cooler, less substantial, more the spray off a wave than the wave itself. Perhaps the eyes were engaging, there was something about the smile. If not lovable as a boy, then maybe as a girl; I wrapped the towel into a turban on my head. Or perhaps need itself was charming, or could be. Maybe my need could make me as appealing as Alice, the woman who worked the Addressograph machine with me.

I was always reading and often writing but both were passionately abstract activities. Early on, I had recognized that books pictured another life, one quite foreign to mine, in which people circled one another warily and with exquisite courtesy until an individual or a couple erupted and flew out of the salon, spangling the night with fire. I had somehow stumbled on Ibsen and that's how he struck me: oblique social chatter followed by a heroic death in a snowslide or on the steeple of a church (I wondered how these scenes could be staged). Oddly enough, the "realism" of the last century seemed to me tinglingly far-fetched: vows, betrayals, flights, fights, sacrifices, suicides. I saw literature as a fantasy, no less absorbing for all its irrelevance—a parallel life, as dreams shadow waking but never intersect it.

I thought that to write of my own experiences would require a translation out of the crude patois of actual slow suffering— mean, scattered thoughts and transfusion-slow boredom—into the tidy couplets of brisk, beautiful sentiment, a way of at once elevating and lending momentum to what I felt. At the same time I was drawn to . . . What if I could write about my life exactly as it was? What if I could show it in all its density and tedium and its concealed passion, never divined or expressed, the dull brown geode that eats at itself with quartz teeth?

The library downtown had been built as an opera house in the last century. Even in grade school I had haunted the library, which was in the same block as my father's office. The library looked up like a rheumy eye at a pitched skylight over which pigeons whirled, their bodies a shuddering gray haze until one bird settled and its pacing black feet became as precise as cuneiform. The light seeped down through the stacks that were arranged in a horseshoe of tiers: the former family balcony, the dress circle, the boxes, on down to the orchestra, still gently raked but now cleared of stalls and furnished with massive oak card files and oak reading tables where unshaved old men read newspapers under gooseneck lamps and rearranged rags in paper sacks. The original stage had been demolished, but cleats on the wall showed where ropes had once been secured.

The railings around the various balconies still described crude arabesques in bronze gone green, but the old floors of the balconies had been replaced by rectangular slabs of smoked glass that emitted pale emerald gleams along polished, beveled edges. Walking on this glass gave me vertigo, but once I started reading I'd slump to the cold, translucent blocks and drift on ice floes into dense clouds. The smell of yellowing paper engulfed me. An unglued page slid out of a volume and a corner broke off, shattered—I was destroying public property! Downstairs someone harangued the librarian. Shadowy throngs of invisible operagoers coalesced and sat forward in their see-through finery to look and listen. I was reading the bilingual libretto of *La Bohème*. The alternating columns of incomprehensible Italian, which I could skip, made the pages speed by, as did the couple's farewell in the snow, the ecstatic reconciliation, poor little Mimi's prolonged dying. I glanced up and saw a pair of shoes cross the glass above, silently accompanied by the paling and darkening circle of the rubber end of a cane. The great eye of the library was blurred by tears.

Across the street the father of a friend of mine ran a bookstore. As I entered it, I was almost knocked down by two men coming out. One of them touched my shoulder and drew me aside. He had a three days' growth of beard on his cheeks, shiny wet canines, a rumpled raincoat of a fashionable cut that clung to his hips, and he was saying, "Don't just rush by without saying hello."

Here he was at last, but now I knew for sure I wasn't worthy—I was ugly with my sissy ways and the mole he'd find between my shoulder blades. "Do I know you?" I asked. I felt I did, as if we'd traveled for a month in a train compartment knee to knee night after night via the thirty installments of a serial but plotless though highly emotional dream. I smiled, embarrassed by the way I looked.

"Sure you know me." He laughed and his friend, I think, smiled. "No, honestly, what's your name?"

I told him.

He repeated it, smile suppressed, as I'd seen men on the make condescend to women they were sizing up. "We just blew into town," he said. "I hope you can make us feel at home." He put an arm around my waist and I shrank back; the sidewalks were crowded with people staring at us curiously. His fingers fit neatly into the space between my pelvis and the lowest rib, a space that welcomed him, that had been cast from the mold of his hand. I kept thinking, these two guys want my money, but how they planned to get it remained vague. And I was alarmed they'd been able to tell at a glance that I was the very one who would respond to their advances so readily. I was so pleased the handsome stranger had chosen me; because he was from out of town he had higher, different standards. He thought I was like him, and perhaps I was, or soon would be. Now that a raffish man—younger and more handsome than I'd imagined, but also dirtier and more condescending—had materialized before me, I wasn't at all sure what I should do: my reveries hadn't been that detailed. Nor had I anticipated meeting someone so crosshatched with ambiguity, a dandy who hadn't bathed, a penniless seducer, someone upon whose face passion and cruelty had cast a grille of shadows. I was alarmed; I ended up by keeping my address secret (midnight robbery) but agreeing to meet him at the pool in the amusement park the next day at noon (an appointment I didn't keep, though I felt the hour come and go like a king in disguise turned away at the peasant's door).

The books in the bookstore shimmered before my eyes as I worked through a pile of them with their brightly colored paper jackets bearing photographs of pensive, well-coiffed women and middle-aged men in Irish knit sweaters with pipes and profiles. Because I knew these books were by living writers I looked down on them; my head was still ringing with the full bravura performance of history in the library–opera house. Those old books either had never owned or had lost their wrappers; the likenesses of their unpictured authors had been re-created within the brown, brittle pages. But these living writers—ah! life struck me as an enfeeblement, a proof of dimmed vitality when compared to the energetic composure of the dead whose busts, all carved beards and sightless, protuberant eyes, I imagined filling the empty niches above the opera doors under a portico, which was now home to sleeping bums and stray cats but once the splendid approach across diamonds of black-and-white-marble pavement to black-and-gilt doors opening on the brilliant assembly, the fans and diamonds and the magic fire circling the sleeping woman.

At home I heard the muted strains of discordant music. One night my stepmother, hard and purposeful, drove back downtown unexpectedly to my father's office after midnight. Still later I could hear her shouting in her wing of the house; I hid behind a door and listened to my father's patient, explaining drone. The next morning Alice, my colleague, broke down, wept, locked herself in the ladies' room. When she came out, her eyes, usually so lovely and unfocused, narrowed with spite and pain as she muttered a stream of filth about my stepmother and my father (he'd tried to lure her to one of those fleabag hotels). On the following morning I learned she'd been let go, though by that time I knew how to get the endless mailings out on my own. She'd been let go—into what?

That man's embrace around the waist set me spinning like a dancer across the darkened stage of the city; my turns led me to Fountain Square, the center. After nightfall the downtown was nearly empty. A cab might cruise by. One high office window might glow. The restaurants had closed by eight, but a bar door could swing open to impose on me the silhouette of a man. Shabby city of black stone whitened by starlings, poor earthly progeny of that mystic metal dove poised on the outstretched wrist of the goddess of the fountain.

Men from across the river sat around the low granite rim of the basin—at least, I guessed they were hillbillies from their accents, a missing tooth, greased-back hair, their way of spitting, of holding a Camel cupped between the thumb and third finger, of walking with a hard, loud, stiff-legged tread across the paved park as though they hoped to ring sparks off the stone. Others sat singly along the metal fence that enclosed the park, an island around which traffic flowed. They perched on the steel rail, legs wide apart, bodies licked by headlights, and looked down, into the slowly circling cars.

At last a driver would pause before a young man who'd hop down and lean into the open window, listen—and then the young man would either shake his head or spit or, if a deal had been struck, swagger around to the other side and get in. Look at them: the curving windshield whispers down the reflection of a blinking neon sign on two faces, a bald man behind the wheel whose glasses are crazed by streaks of green light from the dashboard below, whose ears are fleshy, whose small mouth is pinched smaller by anxiety or anticipation. Beside him the young man, head thrown back on the seat so that we can see only the strong white parabola of his jaw and the working Adam's apple. He's slumped far down and he's already thinking his way into his job. Or maybe he's embarrassed by so much downtown between fantasy and act. They drive off, only the high notes from the car radio reaching me.

That night, however, I had no comfortable assumptions about who these men were and what they were willing to do. I crossed the street to the island, ascended the two steps onto the stone platform—and sat down on a bench. There were policemen nearby. I had a white shirt on, a tie at half-mast, seersucker pants from a suit, polished lace-up shoes, clean nails and short hair, money in my wallet. I was a polite, well-spoken teen, not a vagrant or a criminal—the law would favor me. My father was nearby, working in his office; I was hanging around, waiting for him. Years of traveling alone on trains across the country to see my father had made me fearless before strangers and had led me to assume the unknown is safe, at least reasonably safe if encountered in public places. I set great store by my tie and raised the knot to cover the still-unbuttoned collar opening. No one could tell me to leave this bench.

It was hot and dark. The circling cars were unnerving—so many unseen viewers looking at me. Although this was the town where I'd been born and spent every summer, I'd never explored it on my own. The library, the bookstore, Symphony Hall, the office, the dry cleaner's, the state liquor commission, the ball park, my school, the department stores, that glass ball of a restaurant perched high up there—these I'd been to hundreds of times with my father and stepmother, but I'd always been escorted by them, like a prisoner, through the shadowy, dangerous city.

And yet I'd known all along it was something mysterious and anguished beyond my experience, if not my comprehension. We had a maid, Blanche, who inserted bits of straw into her pierced ears to keep the holes from growing shut, sneezed her snuff in a fine spray of brown dots over the sheets when she was ironing and slouched around the kitchen in her worn-down, backless slippers, once purple but now the color and sheen of a bare oak branch in the rain. She was always uncorseted under her blue cotton uniform; I pictured her rolling, black and fragrant, under that fabric and wondered what her mammoth breasts looked like.

Although she had a daughter five years older than I (illegitimate, or so my stepmother whispered significantly), Blanche sounded like a young girl as she hummed to a Negro station. When she moved from one room to the next, she unplugged the little Bakelite radio with the cream-colored grille over the brown speaker cloth and took it with her. That music excited me, but I thought I shouldn't listen to it too closely. It was "Negro music" and therefore forbidden—part of another culture more violent and vibrant than mine but somehow inferior yet no less exclusive.

Charles, the handyman, would emerge from the basement sweaty and pungent and, standing three steps below me, lecture me about the Bible, the Second Coming and Booker T.

Washington and Marcus Garvey and Langston Hughes. Whenever I said something, he'd laugh in a steady, stylized way to shut me up and then start burrowing back into his obsessions. He seemed to know everything, chapter and verse—Egyptians, Abyssinians, the Lost Tribe, Russian plots, Fair Deal and New Deal—but when I'd repeat one of his remarks at dinner, my father would laugh (this, too, was a stylized laugh) and say, "You've been listening to Charles again. That nigger just talks nonsense. Now don't you bother him, let him get on with his work." I never doubted that my father was right, but I kept wondering how Dad could *tell* it was nonsense. What mysterious ignorance leaked out of Charles's words to poison them and render them worthless, inedible? For Charles, like me, haunted the library; I watched his shelf of books in the basement rotate. And Charles was a high deacon of his church, the wizard of his tribe; when he died his splendid robes overflowed his casket. That his nonsense made perfect sense to me alarmed me—was I, like Charles, eating the tripe of knowledge while Dad sat down to the steak?

I suppose I never wondered where Blanche or Charles went at night; when it was convenient to do so, I still thought of the world as a well-arranged place where people did work that suited them and lived in houses appropriate to their tastes and needs. But once Blanche called us in the middle of an August night and my father, stepmother and I rushed to her aid. In the big Cadillac we breasted our way into unknown streets through the crowds of naked children playing in the tumult of water liberated from a fireplug ("Stop that!" I shouted silently at them, outraged and frightened. "That's illegal!"). Past the stoops crowded with grown-ups playing cards and drinking wine. In one glaring doorway a woman stood, holding her diapered baby against her, a look of stoic indignation on her young face, a face one could imagine squeezing out tears without ever changing expression or softening the wide, fierce eyes, set jaw, everted lower lip. The smell of something delicious—charred meat, maybe, and maybe burning honey—filled the air. "Roll up your windows, for Chrissake, and lock the doors," my father shouted at us. "Dammit, use your heads—don't you know this place is dangerous as hell!"

A bright miner's lamp, glass globe containing a white fire devoid of blues and yellows, dangled from the roof of a vendor's cart; he was selling food of some sort to children. Even through the closed windows I could hear the babble of festive, delirious radios. A seven-foot skinny man in spats, shades, an electric-green shantung suit and a flat-brimmed white beaver hat with a matching green band strolled in front of our car and patted our fender with elaborate mockery. "I'll kill the bastard," Dad shouted. "I swear I'll kill that goddamn ape if he scratches my fender."

"Oh-h-h . . ." my stepmother sang on a high note I'd never heard before. "You'll get us all killed. Honey, my heart." The man, who my father told us was a "pimp" (whatever that might be), bowed to unheard applause, pulled his hat down over one eye like a Parisian and ambled on, letting us pass.

We hurried up five flights of dirty, broken stairs, littered with empty pint bottles, bags of garbage and two dolls (both white, I noticed, and blonde and mutilated), past landings and open doors, which gave me glimpses of men playing cards and, across the hall, a grandmother alone and asleep in an armchair with antimacassars. Her radio was playing that Negro music. Her brown cotton stockings had been rolled down below her black knees.

Blanche we found wailing and shouting, "My baby, my baby!" as she hopped and danced in circles of pain around her daughter, whose hand, half lopped off, was spouting blood. My father gathered the girl up in his arms and we all rushed off to the emergency room of a hospital.

She lived. Her hand was even sewn back on, though the incident (jealous lover with an ax) had broken her mind. Afterward the girl didn't go back to her job and feared even leaving the building. My stepmother thought the loss of blood had somehow left her feeble-minded.

In the hospital parking lot my father fussed over the blood on his suit and on the Cadillac upholstery, though I wondered if

his pettiness wasn't merely a way of silencing Blanche, who
kept kissing his whole hand in gratitude. Or perhaps he'd found
a way of reintroducing the ordinary into a night that had
dipped disturbingly below the normal temperature of tedium he
worked so hard to maintain. Years later, when Charles died, my
father was the only white man to attend the funeral. He wasn't
welcome, but he went anyway and sat in the front row. After
Charles's death my father became more scattered and apprehen-
sive. He would sit up all night with a stopwatch, counting his
pulse.

That had been another city—Blanche's two rooms, scrupu-
lously clean in contrast to the squalor of the halls, her parrot
squawking under the tea towel draped over the cage, the
chromo of a sad Jesus pointing to his exposed, juicy heart as
though he were a free-clinic patient with a troubling symptom,
the filched wedding photo of my father and stepmother in a
nest of crepe-paper flowers, the bloody sheet torn into strips
that had been wildly clawed off and hurled onto the flowered
Congoleum floor.

IN MY naïveté I imagined that all poor people, black and white,
liked each other and that here, through Fountain Square, I
would feel my way back to the street, that smell of burning
honey, that blood as red as mine and that steady, colorless flare
in the glass chimney . . . These hillbillies on the square with
their drawling and spitting, their thin arms and big raw hands,
nails ragged, tattoos a fresher blue than their eyes set in long
sallow faces, each eye a pale blue ringed by nearly invisible
lashes—I wove these men freely into the cloth of the powerful
poor, a long bolt lost in the dark that I was now pulling through
a line of light.

I opened a book and pretended to read under the weak streetlamps, though my attention wandered away from sight to sound.
"Freddy, bring back a beer!" someone shouted. Some other men
laughed. No one I knew kept his nickname beyond twelve, at
least not with his contemporaries, but I could hear these guys
calling each other Freddy and Bobby, and I found that hearten-

ing, as though they wanted to stay, if only among themselves, as chummy as a gang of boys. While they worked to become as brutal as soon enough they would be, I tried to find them softer than they'd ever been.

Boots approached me. I heard them before I saw them. They stopped, every tan scar on the orange hide in focus beyond the page I held that was running with streaks of print. "Curiosity killed the damn pussy, you know," a man said. I looked up at a face sprouting brunet sideburns that swerved inward like cheese knives toward his mouth and stopped just below his ginger mustaches. The eyes, small and black, had been moistened genially by the beers he'd drunk and the pleasure he was taking in his own joke.

"*Mighty* curious, ain't you?" he asked. "Ain't you!" he insisted, making a great show of the leisurely, avuncular way he settled close beside me, sighing, and wrapped a bare arm—a pale, cool, sweaty, late-night August arm—around my thin shoulders. "Shit," he hissed. Then he slowly drew a breath like ornamental cigarette smoke up his nose, and chuckled again. "I'd say you got Sabbath eyes, son."

"I do?" I squeaked in a pinched soprano. "I don't know what you mean," I added, only to demonstrate my newly acquired baritone, as penetrating as an oboe; the effect on the man seemed the right one: sociable.

"Yessir, Sabbath eyes," he said with a downshift into a rural languor and rhetorical fanciness I associated with my storytelling paternal grandfather in Texas. "I say Sabbath 'cause you done worked all week and now you's resting them eyeballs on what you done made—or might could make. The good things of the earth." Suddenly he grew stern. "Why you here, boy? I seed you here cocking your hade and spying up like a biddy hen. Why you watching, boy? *What* you watching? Tell me, what you watching?"

He had frightened me, which he could see—it made him laugh. I smiled to show him I knew how foolish I was being. "I'm just here to—"

"Read?" he demanded, taking my book away and shutting it.

"Shi-i-i . . ." he hissed again, steam running out before the *t*. "You here to meet someone, boy?" He'd disengaged himself and turned to stare at me. Although his eyes were serious, militantly serious, the creasing of the wrinkles beside them suggested imminent comedy.

"No," I said, quite audibly.

He handed the book back to me.

"I'm here because I want to run away from my father's house," I said. "I thought I might find someone to go with me."

"Whar you planning to run to?"

"New York."

There was something so cold and firm and well spoken about me—the clipped tones of a businessman defeating the farmer's hoaxing yarn—that the man dropped his chin into his palm and thought. "What's today?" he asked at last.

"Saturday."

"I myself taking the Greyhound to New Yawk Tuesday mawning," he said. "Wanna go?"

"Sure."

He told me that if I'd bring him forty dollars on Monday evening he'd buy me my ticket. He asked me where I lived and I told him; his willingness to help me made me trust him. Without ever explicitly being taught such things, I'd learned by studying my father that at certain crucial moments—an emergency, an opportunity—one must act first and think later. One must suppress minor inner objections and put off feelings of cowardice or confusion and turn oneself into a simple instrument of action. I'd seen my father become calm when he'd taken Blanche's daughter to the hospital. I'd also watched him feel his way blindly with nods, smiles and monosyllables toward the shadowy opening of a hugely promising but still-vague business deal. And with women he was ever alert to adventure: the gauzy transit of a laugh across his path, a minor whirlpool in the sluggish flow of talk, the faintest whiff of seduction. . .

I, too, wanted to be a man of the world and dared not question my new friend too closely. For instance, I knew a train ticket could be bought at the last moment, even on board, but I was willing to assume either that a bus ticket had to be secured in advance or that at least he thought it did. We arranged a time to meet on Monday when I could hand over the money (I had it at home squirreled away in the secret compartment of a wood tray I'd made the previous year in shop). Then on Tuesday morning at six he'd meet me at the corner near but not in sight of my house. He'd have his brother's car and we'd proceed quickly to the 6:45 bus bound East—a long haul to New Yawk, he said, oh, say twenty hours, no, make that twenty-one.

"And in New York?" I asked timidly, not wanting to seem helpless and scare him off but worried about my future. Would I be able to find work? I was only sixteen, I said, adding two years to my age. Could a sixteen-year-old work legally in New York? If so, doing what?

"Waiter," he said. "A whole hog heaven of resty-runts in New Yawk City."

Sunday it rained a hot drizzle all day and in the west the sky lit up a bright yellow that seemed more the smell of sulfur than a color. I played the piano with the silencer on lest I awaken my father. I was bidding the instrument farewell. If only I'd practiced I might have supported myself as a cocktail pianist; I improvised my impression of sophisticated tinkling—with disappointing results.

As I took an hour-long bath, periodically emptying an inch of cold water and replacing it with warm, I thought my way again through the routine: greeting the guests, taking their orders, serving pats of butter, beverages, calling out my requests to the chef . . . my long, flat feet under the water twitched sympathetically as I raced about the restaurant. If only I'd observed waiters all those times. Well, I'd coast on charm.

As for love, that, too, I'd win through charm. Although I knew I hadn't charmed anyone since I was six or seven, I consoled myself by deciding people out here were not susceptible to the petty larceny of a beguiling manner. They responded only to character, accomplishments, the slow accumulations of will rather than the sudden millinery devisings of fancy. In New York I'd be the darling boy again. In that Balzac novel a penniless young man had made his fortune on luck, looks, winning ways. New Yorkers, like Parisians, I hoped and feared, would know what to make of me. I carried the plots and atmosphere of fiction about with me and tried to cram random events into those ready molds. But no, truthfully, the relationship was more reciprocal, less rigorous—life sang art's songs, but art also took the noise life gave and picked it out as a tune (the cocktail pianist obliging the humming drunk).

Before it closed I walked down to a neighborhood pharmacy and bought a bottle of peroxide. I had decided to bleach my hair late Monday night; on Tuesday I'd no longer answer the description my father would put out in his frantic search for me. Perhaps I'd affect an English accent as well; I'd coached my stepmother in the part of Lady Bracknell before she performed the role with the Emerald City Players and I could now say *cucumber sandwich* with scarcely a vowel after the initial fluty *u*. As an English blond I'd evade not only my family but also myself and emerge as the energetic and lovable boy I longed to be. Not exactly a boy, more a girl, or rather a sturdy, canny, lavishly devout tomboy like Joan of Arc, tough in battle but yielding before her visionary Father. I wouldn't pack winter clothes; surely by October I'd be able to buy something warm.

A new spurt of hot water as I retraced my steps to the kitchen, clipped the order to the cook's wire or flew out the swinging doors, smiling, acted courteously and won the miraculously large tip. And there, seated at a corner table by himself, is the English lord, silver-haired, recently bereaved; my hand trembles as I give him the frosted glass. In my mind I'd already betrayed the hillbilly with the sideburns who sobbed with dignity as I delivered my long farewell speech. He wasn't intelligent or rich enough to suit me.

When I met him on Monday at six beside the fountain and presented him with the four ten-dollar bills, he struck me as ominously indifferent to the details of tomorrow's adventure which I'd elaborated with such fanaticism. He reassured me about the waiter's job and my ability to do it, told me again where he'd pick me up in the morning—but, smiling, dissuaded me from peroxiding my hair tonight. "Just pack it—we'll bleach you white whin we git whar we goan."

We had a hamburger together at the Grasshopper, a restaurant of two rooms, one brightly lit and filled with booths and families and waitresses wearing German peasant costumes and white lace hats, the other murky and smelling of beer and smoke—a man's world, the bar. I went through the bar to the toilet. When I came out I saw Alice, the woman I'd worked with, in a low-cut dress, skirt hiked high to expose her knee, hand over her pearl necklace. Her hair had been restyled. She pushed one lock back and let it fall again over her eye, the veronica a cape might pass before an outraged bull: the man beside her, who now placed a grimy hand on her knee. She let out a shriek—a coquette's shriek, I suppose, but edged with terror. (I was glad she didn't see me, since I felt ashamed of the way our family had treated her.)

I'd planned not to sleep at all but had set the alarm should I doze off. For hours I lay in the dark and listened to the dogs barking down in the valley. Now that I was leaving this house forever, I was tiptoeing through it mentally and prizing its luxuries—the shelves lined with blocks of identical cans (my father ordered everything by the gross); the linen cupboard stacked high with ironed if snuff-specked sheets; my own bathroom with its cupboard full of soap, tissue, towels, hand towels, washclothes; the elegant helix of the front staircase descending to the living room with its deep carpets, shaded lamps and the pretty mirror bordered by tiles on which someone with a nervous touch had painted the various breeds of lapdog. This house where I'd never felt I belonged no longer belonged to me, and the future so clearly charted for me—college, career, wife and white house wavering behind green trees—was being exchanged for that eternal circulating through the restaurant, my path as clear to me as chalk marks on the floor, instructions for each foot in the tango, lines that flowed together, branched and joined, branched and joined . . . In my dream my father had died but I refused to kiss him though next he was pulling me up onto his lap, an ungainly teen smeared with Vicks VapoRub whom everyone inexplicably treated as a sick child.

When I silenced the alarm, fear overtook me. I'd go hungry! The boardinghouse room with the toilet down the hall, blood on the linoleum, Christ in a chromo, crepe-paper flowers—I dressed and packed my gym bag with the bottle of peroxide and two changes of clothes. Had my father gone to bed yet? Would the dog bark when I tried to slip past him? And would that man be on the corner? The boardinghouse room, yes, Negro music on the radio next door, the coquette's shriek . . . As I walked down the drive I felt conspicuous under the blank windows of my father's house and half expected him to open the never-used front door to call me back.

I stood on the appointed corner. It began to drizzle but a water truck crept past anyway, spraying the street a darker, slicker gray. No birds were in sight but I could hear them testing the day. A dog without a collar or master trotted past. Two fat maids were climbing the hill, stopping every few steps to catch their breath. One, a shiny, blue-black fat woman wearing a flowered turban and holding a purple umbrella with a white plastic handle, was scowling and talking fast but obviously to humorous effect, for her companion couldn't stop laughing.

The bells of the Catholic school behind the dripping trees across the street marked the quarter hour, the half hour. More and more cars were passing me. I studied every driver—had my friend overslept? The milkman. The bread truck. Damn hillbilly. A bus went by, carrying just one passenger. A quarter to seven. He wasn't coming.

When I saw him the next evening on the square he waved at me and came over to talk. From his relaxed manner I instantaneously saw that he'd duped me and I was powerless. To whom could I report him? Like a heroin addict or a Communist, I was outside the law—outside it but with him, this man.

We sat side by side on the same bench. A bad muffler exploded in a volley and the cooing starlings perched on the fountain figure's arm flew up and away leaving behind only the metal dove. I took off my tie, rolled it up and slipped it inside my pocket. Because I didn't complain about being betrayed, my friend said, "See those men yonder?"

"Yes."

"I could git you one for eight bucks." He let that sink in; yes, I thought, I could take someone to one of those little fleabag hotels. "Which one do you want?" he said.

I handed him the money and said, "The blond."

# THREE

Until I was seven my parents, my sister and I lived in a Tudor-style house at the end of a lane in the city where my father remained after the divorce. Our house and three others formed a wooded, almost rural enclave set down in the midst of an old, poor section of the city. I could never quite situate our enclave in the world outside; I remember my astonishment the day I roamed through the hollow behind our place, climbed up the far hill, pushed aside branches—and stared out at a major four-lane thoroughfare I'd been driven down countless times but had never suspected ran so close to our property. Certainly not *behind* it, of all things. To me the city lay entirely in front of our gates in a dirty, busy antechamber. I consulted with my sister. She was four years older, could read, went to school and knew everything. "Sure, dumbbell," she said. "Of course it's behind the house. Where'd you think it was?" She screwed her fingertip into her temple and said, "Duh."

She began to chant a colorless litany of "Dumbbells." I stopped my ears with my hands and ran, crying, back into the house.

My sister had friends she'd met at Miss Laughton's School for Girls who came home to play with her some afternoons. They all belonged to a club my sister had started. She was the captain. Her success as a leader could be attributed to the methodical way she worked out her ideas: her approach lent an adult, step-by-step orderliness to projects that otherwise might have seemed wild and incomprehensible.

One afternoon she ordered each of her team members to steal

a belt from her father that night and bring it with her tomorrow. Of course every girl must be clever in stealing and hiding the belt; if caught, she must be even more resourceful in denying the real reason for filching it. The next afternoon the girls gathered in the hollow and presented their booty to my sister, who lashed each girl with her own father's belt. In one case her zeal left welts, which led to parental questions and eventually exposure of the whole drama. My sister, at that time a tall, taut platinum blonde who didn't like grown-ups, answered my mother's furious questions with indignant yeses and noes, lowered eyes and a set jaw. She was afraid of my mother, the interrogation alarmed her, but not for a moment did she feel guilty or question what she had done. She was the queen of her tribe of girls.

My sister resented the interest some of the girls took in me and banned me from the meetings held beside the empty swimming pool choked with dead leaves. When I disobeyed her and toddled smilingly into the assembly, she spanked my bare legs with a hairbrush. My father, resolved that his son should hold his own, pinioned my sister's arms behind her and ordered me to switch her on the back of her legs with a stinging branch. But I knew that soon enough he would disappear again, my mother drive off, the maids look away; I dropped the branch, howled and clattered up the stairs to my room. I think I also knew that my father preferred my sister to me and that his interest in me was only abstract, dynastic.

My sister was his true son. She could ride a horse and swim a mile and she was as capable of sustained rages as he. Still better, she was as blonde as his mother. My grandmother had not wanted my father, as she told him, she'd pummeled her stomach with her fists every day while she was bearing him. Nonetheless, my father somehow got born and survived to serve his mother humbly and lovingly, washing the family's sheets in the bathtub when he was still only a child and brushing out her blonde hair every night. One night, soon after my grandmother died, I stole into my father's study and found him standing behind my sister's chair, brushing her hair and crying.

Right now I'm looking at an ancient photograph of my sister and me. I'm three and she's seven, both of us bundled up for winter and posed against a door under an ominously black Christmas wreath. She's much taller than I. My sister is dressed in a fashionably cut camel's-hair coat belled out above black leggings. She's sporting a matching hat bordered in brown piping, the front brim flipped up and the whole thing placed rakishly far back on her head. She's smiling a thin-lipped, obviously forced smile. Her eyes, so blue they're bottomless and white, express the pain of an unhealed convalescent, as do the shadows, like bruises below her temples—bruises forceps might have left.

Because my sister tormented me and I loved her but feared her, I turned away from her to imaginary playmates. There were three of them. Cottage Cheese, the girl, was older than I, sensible and bossy but my ally. She and I tolerated our good-natured younger sidekick, Georgie-Porgie, a dimwit we fussed over for his own good. We felt nothing of this benign condescension toward Tom-Thumb-Thumb, the hellion who roamed the woods beyond the barbed-wire fence guarding the neighbor's property, off limits to us and to him too, I'm sure, though he ignored this rule and all others. He was just a rustle of dried leaves, a panting of quick hot breath behind the honeysuckle, a blur of tanned leg and muddy knees or a distant hoot and holler—an irrepressible male freedom (all the freer because he was a boy and not a man). He needed no one, he'd listen to no reprimand. One time Cottage Cheese and I cornered him (we'd taken him by surprise as he was furtively pawing my father's untouchable tools in the garage) and we lectured him at length, but his eyes, the whites flashing wonderfully clear and bright through the matted hair, never stopped darting back and forth looking for an escape route—and then he was off, leaving behind him only the resonance of the concrete vault and our voices calling Tom, calling, calling out to him, Tom, to behave, to be good, Tom, as good as we had to be.

He never cared for me. Cottage Cheese and I, determined that naïve Georgie-Porgie should not fall under Tom's spell, made a great show of listing Tom's faults—but privately I worried about Tom and at night I wondered where he was sleeping, was he dry, was he warm, hungry. I even envied his sovereignty, though the price of freedom—total solitude—seemed more than I could possibly pay.

Tom's independence and Georgie's dependence rendered them both unsatisfactory as playmates. If the family was going on a trip, I gladly left the boys behind so long as I could take Cottage Cheese with me. My mother made sure there was always a place for Cottage Cheese beside me in the backseat of the pale blue Chrysler with its royal blue upholstery, its delicate chrome ashtray tilting out from the quilted rear panel of the front seat and its translucent celluloid knobs on the window cranks—although once Cottage Cheese, in an uncharacteristically willful moment, insisted on riding the exterior running board as I held her hand through the lowered window. Her skirts flew up and her taffeta hair ribbons bobbed crazily behind her until she looked as windswept as the silver figurine on the hood.

Ordinarily Cottage Cheese was a calm, sensible girl content to wander with me through the endless days as we surveyed our world and sententiously described it to ourselves: "Now here's that slippery log, make sure you don't slip on the slippery log, step over it, that's right—oh, look, there are the poisonous red berries, don't eat them, they're poison." She took my afternoon naps with me, a deflating heap of dry, hot organdy and drooping white stockings as she settled on the bed beside me, only the feeblest ectoplasm when I first awakened until I was able to pump life and body back into her.

She was not a pretty girl. She had freckles, big black glasses and ears that kept poking their tips out through limp hanks of straight hair. She was something of a tomboy, not by being athletic (she was as afraid of sports as I) but by being straightforward, hearty, confiding. I prized her companionship and liked it when she told me to brush my teeth or flush the toilet. She liked to bathe with me but, I am pleased to say, never undressed to do so.

And yet I didn't really like my imaginary friends precisely because they were so irritatingly vague and unreal. My mother went to great lengths to respect my whim—in fact, she may have known how to deal with my imaginary playmates better than with some of my other more disturbing vagaries. And I might have held on to these friends longer than need be precisely because they earned me a certain deference. A place was laid at the table for Cottage Cheese and my parents inquired after her often. But the imaginary friends were almost, at times, less real to me than to my indulgent mother—the imagination is not the consolation people pretend. It can even be regarded as the admission of some sort of failure.

And yet on my third birthday a professional marionette troupe performed *Sleeping Beauty* in our living room before an audience of my mother's lady friends' children, imported for the occasion. The plates from which we kids had eaten cake and vanilla ice cream were collected and the curtains drawn, creating night in day, a magic trick I associated only with afternoon naps. It was a warm, sniffling, giggling audience. A little raised stage framed in blue cloth had been erected at one end of the room. The toe of a big brown shoe protruding from beneath the hem of the proscenium draperies kept in mind real dimensions only for a few more minutes; soon the reduced scale of the stage had engulfed me, as though I'd been precipitated through a beaker and sublimated into another substance altogether. I had never heard the story before. The curse of Carabosse, the Princess's mishap in the Rose Garden, her long sleep and the funny, frozen postures of the courtiers, the arrival of the Prince and the joyous nuptials all transported me to a world of boldly modeled faces from which character could be readily deduced, a world in which menace foreshadowed disaster, evil was defeated and love crowned. In this lighted cube my emotions coalesced because they were given a firm bounding line and because things devolved with the logic of art, not life.

For if the imaginary playmates were insubstantial, the overly material people who surrounded me were opaque. Now only these miniature figures—with a hooked nose punctuated by a wart, a skein of lustrous blond hair, lace cuffs, velvet trains—only they seemed lit from within and legible as they floated up out of the bottomless floor, gestured wildly, gazed as though blind in only the general direction of an interlocutor, shook with tearless sobs, growled or piped, then flew at one another for hearty, back-slapping embraces until they were whipped up into the wings. *That* was the secret of the imagination—its creations were feeble only to the maker but stronger than life itself to the observer. When the curtains were opened again and the puppeteers—balding husband and bespectacled wife—emerged with shy grins and joined the party, a deep sadness sounded inside me.

When I was seven my mother divorced my father. My sister and I, aroused by the declamatory tone of the grown-ups downstairs, sat in pajamas on the front stairs and listened to the speeches. How odd and thrilling that where we'd live and go to school could be decided in this manner. My father, my mother and the woman who'd eventually be my stepmother took turns giving speeches, although my father was mostly silent unless prodded into murmurs by the women. My mother was saying, "If she is the one you really want, then far be it from me to stand in the way of your happiness, yet if I might speak in my own behalf . . ." The complex sentences with their unfamiliar locutions sometimes tripped my mother up, as though she were a debutante in her first long dress.

Everything about the conference seemed dramatic—the late hour, the formal tone, even the notion that something momentous could or should be decided all at once. Soon my sister and I, sitting in the bleachers of the dark stairwell and peering down into the brightness, had sworn our own complicity by dissembling: both of us were excited by the prospect of living in a new city and shedding our difficult father, but we both pretended to be grief-struck.

The real excitement, of course, lay in learning that a life could be changed and that one could enter a brand-new, better world ("I shall move wherever the children will have the cultural and eductional advantages of a major metropolis," our mother was saying). That a life could be changed posited the still more thrilling notion that one had a thing called a *life*, a wonderful being that was growing silently inside like an infant. How its body would be formed and what its temperament would be like would surely remain unknown—along with the color of its eyes, the cubits of its height and the beauty of its face—up to the moment of birth. Until I heard the three adults discussing their lives and our lives ("I cannot lead my life in this way," "The children have their whole lives before them") I had never suspected that I'd been impregnated with this "life," this tragic embryo. The divorce, for me, was primarily an accession into self-consciousness.

It was also a deliverance from my father. Since he slept all day, I seldom saw him. But sometimes my mother would say, "Your father's awake. Why don't you go in and rub his back?" Reluctantly I'd enter the bedroom, in which the drawn curtains stained the late-afternoon light. On the bed, facedown, lay my naked father under sheets, like a sea monster beached and sick in a tide pool of foam. The mingled smells of night sweat and stale cigar smoke awed me; I toddled out and told my mother he was still sleeping. "No, no," she said, smiling and guiding me back in. I looked around the room from which I was usually barred. Everything was silent except for his breathing and the tick of his gold pocket watch on the night table beside him. Within my father's half-closed closet I could see his shoes. I intuited one shoe from no more than a single burning vertical line of light that followed me by traveling glassily across the black leather rondure above the heel. Floating up there, high above the shoes, hung a smoky cashmere Olympus of all his discarded but potential selves: his suits. Now to the bed.

I sat beside him and lightly patted his back. He murmured encouragingly and I worked my way up the thickly padded torso to the shoulders. The pores looked huge, some of them specked with black. A film of sweat seemed to be methodically seeping out of him; I sniffed my right hand; it smelled funny. My job seemed to be to creep over him as a lone climber, with nothing but rope and crampons, might assault a glacier. If he was fully awake he didn't let on, as though a state of torpor were all a father owed a very little son—or at least all the son would accept from such a massive father.

He was entirely naked but shrouded up to the waist in sheets. Whereas my sheets were small, sufficient for my cot where I slept in the governing shade and disturbingly intimate smell of my black nurse, these sheets were sculpturally white, vast and twisted, testimony to adult nights of passion or strife.

Later, an hour later, he'd descend to his squire's breakfast, shaved and dressed in a white shirt, silk tie and double-breasted suit, his eyes young, sharp and intelligent in a head I'd seen earlier from an odd, wounded angle. He was now polite to the cook, deferential to my mother and lighthearted and cutting with my sister and me—he who'd been nothing but a felled deity exuding a cold sweat an hour before. This transformation of the mystery man in the tangle of sheets into the bantering gentleman I attributed to the rites of the bathroom mirror and the bracing smell of carbolic soap and witch hazel. How he'd study himself in that mirror, both taps running full blast, as though out of the haze on the glass his true identity might emerge under a swipe of the towel—a cutting of the self if not the full blossoming branch.

Dad had a friend of sorts—to him possibly a very minor business associate—whom my sister and I worshipped because he gave us money. "Dollar Bill," we called him, since he was William and always gave us a dollar each. Though we wanted for nothing and we dimly sensed that our way of living cost many, many dollars, this unseen cash meant nothing to us compared to the actual loot Dollar Bill handed over. If the Devil or Hitler had offered us even a single dollar for our parents' heads, we would have cut them off and presented the bloody, bulky packages in happy exchange. How greedy we were, we who'd learned so early the value and sinister glory of the dollar. How we'd fawn on Dollar Bill, hugging his legs and kissing his neck. How we'd squeal with excitement when we spied him coming down the walk. The grown-ups would guffaw in chorus over our gold-digging antics, pleased to see us miming their own sentiments—much as one might be pleased to see chimps mounting or presenting in inflated purple imitation a human desire less colorful but no less persistent.

In a sense all of our daddy's dollars were casters on which the furniture of our lives glided noiselessly; every dollar was assigned a function and kept out of sight. Dollar Bill, however, liberated two dollars a week from invisible utility. We loved him more than anyone we knew.

Once my mother became so exasperated with me that she asked my father to beat me with a strap. He marched me into his bedroom; the bed was now neatly covered by a fitted pale yellow satin spread, an antique mirror so shiny it reflected lights and shadows if not coherent figures. "Drop your pants," my father said. I had already started a sort of gasping, an asthmatic gasping, in anticipation of a pain that seemed impossibly cruel because I had no idea when it would descend on me nor how long it would last. My lack of control over the situation was for me the worst punishment, and I gasped and gasped for air and escape and justice, or at least mercy. Panic lit up everywhere within me; I longed to run or disappear in a burst of chemical smoke and reappear as a white, frightened animal from under a top hat, gently nibbling at the fumes. I thought I could win my father over; I said with sullen candor (I had nothing but candor to work with), "I'll never do it again. I'm sorry."

But he was angry now. His hate, more intense than any other feeling he'd ever had for me, was making his face younger and younger. His eyes no longer had that veiled, compounded look of adults who stare at blank spots on walls or get tangled up in the tulle of thought. Now his eyes were simple and curious, eyes I recognized as those of another child. A scream caught up with me and outraced me. I felt myself inhabited by this scream that was registered in a voice bigger, more released than anything I had ever heard—a scream that seemed even bigger than my fear. It took me over and wouldn't stop. It was a cry of outrage against a violation at the hands of a child no older than I but much less appeasable—a heartless boy.

He tugged my pants down and pushed me forward into the

glossy spread. The belt fell again and again, much too long and much too harshly to my mind, which had suddenly turned strangely epicurean. The solace of the condemned is scorn, especially scorn of an aesthetic stripe. In that moment the vital energies retreated out of my body into a small, hard gland of bitter objectivity, a gland that would secrete its poison through me for the rest of my life. At last my mother, conveniently tardy, rushed in and asked for mercy; she even had the satisfaction of accusing my father of being unduly harsh.

While the divorce was still pending and the school year still in session, our mother moved my sister and me to a hotel in a community that had been built to resemble a Tudor village, all half-timbered stucco. That entire spring it seemed to rain. Every day after school I went walking for hours through unknown streets that were nearly empty. The intense, pure colors of traffic signals burned through the rain and cast long edible smears on the wet pavement. Green, yellow, red. A click in the box. Then red, yellow, green. I found a church, ivied and squat, with rounded arches and murky painted windows and, inside, the smell of floor polish. I walked down the resonant deserted aisles and came upon a carved wood door behind and to one side of the altar. A sign indicated that this was the minister's office. I knocked on the door. A pleasant man in a dark business suit opened it. "Yes?"

"Are you the minister?"

"Yes."

"Do you mind if I talk to you? I have a problem."

"That's what I'm here for. Come in."

The office seemed efficient with its typewriters and files and fluorescent ceiling lamps and water cooler; it struck a reassuringly practical note of business. He indicated I should sit in a green leather chair. He then sat down and faced me across the desk.

"Are you busy?"

"No. I have a few minutes. What's the problem?"

"My parents are getting divorced."

"Does that disturb you?"

"Yes. Well, maybe."

"Are you going to live with your mother?"

"Yes."

"Would you rather live with your father?"

"No."

"Do you dislike your father?"

"Goodness no."

"Would you like to see your parents stay married?"

The sympathy in his eyes caused me to say, "Yes." Once I had, I realized that this single lie had made me into a character in a story—just like one of the marionettes. "I want them to—yes." I felt my face become more beautiful. I hoped the minister would invite me to his house and take care of me, or at least tell my mother how wonderful I was. I hoped the minister would tell his congregation about the wonderful little boy who had visited him one rainy afternoon. "Is there anything I can do? To bring them back together?" I asked.

"Probably not. You can pray for them, for both of them to make the best possible decision."

I lowered my eyes but thought prayer sounded rather useless. I stood and thanked him. He walked me to the door and told me to come back. I wondered if he would pick me up into his arms, but he didn't. I was small enough, but he didn't. Instead he gave me his hand to shake, which I didn't really like since I was uncertain about how to shake it. The gesture was also, I recognized, a way of treating me with respect as an independent young man. I wasn't sure that was what I wanted to be.

This precocious role I took in the world was possible only because the world seemed so unreal, the stage transected by lights, its fourth wall missing in order to afford a view to thronged but shadowy spectators. Everything I did was being watched. If I turned right rather than left, someone took careful notice. If I repeated a magic phrase, the words were recorded and obeyed. Those spectators were certainly real, though I did not know them yet, but what they were watching, this dumb show in which I played such a decisive role—it was merely a simulacrum of actual feelings. These tears were paste. What was slowly dawning on me was my extreme importance, something the audience had long ago suspected. Who were they, these spectators? I'd look up into the evening sky to see them ranked in blowing white robes, the hems wet with blood. When I had a fever I could hear them.

We moved to a city several hundred miles to the north and there we lived in a luxury hotel, sedate and respectable, a place with goldfish in a low marble pool in the lobby and a small velvet settee on the elevator. On the top floor a valet steamed and pressed clothes in a closet beside the double doors that opened onto a ballroom. The windows of the ballroom were heavily and perpetually draped and curtained, but I discovered a tiny door just two panes high that led out onto a narrow balcony. This balcony obviously was not intended to be used, just a strip of gravel over tar behind an escarpment of stone ornamental urns. In good weather I'd hide on this secret balcony and read; my favorite book was about the lost dauphin. On some days the ballroom was set up with long banquet tables bearing napery and floral arrangements between rows of gilt and velvet chairs. Other days the room would smell of stale cigarette smoke and the tables would have been stripped to their scarred wood tops and pipe-metal bases.

As a little boy I'd scarcely known my mother; she'd seldom been home and I'd been left to my nurse. Sometimes at night, after I'd gone to bed, Mother would perch beside me for a moment before she went out for the evening. She smelled of a rich, unfamiliar perfume and her face glimmered behind a full veil drawn down under her chin, the net woven here and there with dark birds in flight, her hands encased in tiny white leather gloves of a morbid softness. Then she'd sing to me in her thin, high, quavering voice, "I'll Be Seeing You in Apple Blossom Time." The birds would seem to move when she sang and in my drowsiness I imagined they, too, were serenading me.

Now I saw her much more and she became more real to me. She had wonderful brown eyes, sharp and clear, that changed with her many moods, as pearls are said to respond to the different bodies that wear them. She cried easily, when her feelings had been hurt. When she cried I became frantic and held on to her until she stopped. I wanted her to be happy, and I saved up money to buy her presents; if the gifts were ignored I felt powerless and dejected. She could also be sharp-eyed. Though she was in fact impetuous and extravagant, she would occasionally put on her glasses, stick out her chin and ponder a legal or business document for hours. She sat perfectly still on the edge of a chair, her feet barely touching the floor since she was so short.

She had no humor beyond a low country cackle at things that were silly or naughty. At such times she'd sound like her own mother, an illiterate farm woman who crowed over traveling-salesman stories, slapped her knee and then wriggled like a wet bird back into smooth-feathered sobriety. My mother had no interest in what she called "theory," by which she meant ideas. What did interest her were plans and arrangements—all the details of daily life. These elicited her full attention, and mastering them brought her the pleasant feeling that hers was a tidy life. Plans were my despair; the minute maps were drawn out of a glove compartment or a calendar was consulted, I retreated into irritable daydreams.

My mother's interest in plans and arrangements coexisted with the most peculiar notion of what those arrangements should consist of—and a wild caprice that could overturn everything she'd worked out so methodically. Naïve and proud at the time of her divorce, she wanted to conserve money but also maintain a good address. She decided the three of us should live in that expensive hotel in one furnished room with twin beds, my sister and I taking turns sleeping on the floor. For the first time in her life our mother had a job, one at which she worked long hours. At night she was going out on dates or haunting nightclubs downtown. Because she was seldom at home I ate most of my suppers alone in the hotel dining room; my sister ate at a different hour in order to avoid my company.

Before her divorce my mother had never so much as written a check. Now our fortunes teetered and careened and ground to a halt. She bought a knee-length mink but economized on food, bought a flashy Lincoln convertible but refused to send my sister to the orthodontist, packed us off to expensive summer camps but on the bus, not the train. She drank heavily and played sentimental records in the evening on the few nights she stayed home; one winter the record of "Now Is the Hour" became so worn the spindle hole grew as big as a dime, but still the voice yearned on and on. Another winter the voice, wobbling sickeningly, sang "The Tennessee Waltz."

When Mother was discouraged a smell of physical self-hatred would come off her body; she groaned her way through her self-hatred as though it were a mountain of laundry she had to wash, a dirty, physical, humiliating task. Then something nice would happen. Someone would compliment her or a man would take an interest in her—and presto, she was not only equal to other people but superior to them. The terrible laundering would be forgotten. She'd sit up very straight in her chair and smile a sort of First Lady smile.

I spent many gala nights, including my eighth, ninth and tenth birthdays, in nightclubs beside my mother. She'd split a simple pasta dish with me to save money and then order highball after highball as we'd look longingly toward the man at the bar. Had he noticed Mother? Would he send her a drink? Or would he be scared off by my presence?

My mother had met a handsome man much younger than she who wanted her to buy him a fishing camp in Kentucky; luckily his greed finally caused her to drop him. On the way down to join him one time in Kentucky, Mother kept the radio tuned to a hillbilly station, but my sister and I mocked the cornpone accents and sad lyrics. Once we were in Kentucky the handsome man, mustached and cologned, took us out fishing in a rented boat. It rained. No one caught anything. A strict silence had to be maintained when the man cast his rod as though blessing the waters. At night my sister and I slept in bunk beds in the man's sister's house. My mother wore a new, dazed expression and treated us with great politeness, as though my sister and I were guests she didn't know very well. She spoke of our accomplishments and of her own trials and powers of recuperation. The man laid a strong hand on my shoulders, but withdrew it when my mother left the room. At night his family and ours sat together; everyone visited as a bowl of pecans and a nutcracker were passed around the room from one grown-up to another on down to silent children in pajamas stained with orange juice. Our mother was betraying us into this dingy house permeated by the smell of hot grease. Mother was losing interest in me; she'd willingly hand me over to this good-looking fool.

During the night they fought. The engagement was broken off and the next morning we were in the car again, blinking and exhausted, the radio blaring, the temperature noticeably warmer, familiar plants unseasonably in bloom. Mother started reciting the litany of our lives. She questioned us once more about our father and how he behaved toward his new wife. Each twisted or colored fact we gave her she plaited into a heavy weave. Then she tore that up and started again. He would soon leave his wife or he would never leave her, he was being blackmailed by that woman, no he loved her, he was a man of honor, no he was a man without principle, he had failed us, no he stayed true, he'd tire of her, no she was a born fascinator, this was just an adventure, it was a life, she made him feel superior, she made him feel cheap, he'd soon be back or he'd never return—oh, my mother was a tedious Penelope weaving her tales and tearing them up.

I listened to everything, smiling and in possession of my secret power.

And then there were her other men—the one in California with all the money, who was Catholic and brought brandy alexanders to Mama's bedside in the morning. Or the captain in the army with the sports car whom she'd met at Hot Springs, Arkansas. Or the Jew in Chicago with the sailboat, the Camel cigarettes and the skin that tanned so easily. We'd analyze their motives hour after hour as the towns and countryside sped past. We'd sing songs. We'd listen to the news. We'd point out sights to one another. But soon we'd be talking again about Herb or Bill or Abe. Did he miss our mother? What were his intentions? Was he dating anyone else? Should Mom play harder to get?

Mother gained weight, sighed beside the phone, cried, hypothesized, thought up schemes of seduction or revenge, and all her technique—that is, all her helplessness—made my sister more and more ashamed of her. We were losers who talked a winning game. No wonder honesty came to mean for my sister saying only the most damaging things against herself. If she *began* by admitting defeat, then something was possible: sincerity, perhaps, or at least the avoidance of appearing ludicrous.

My mother's helplessness filled my sister with confusion and shame. She was confused after Mother had talked her way with conviction and obsessive tenacity all the way around the circumference of an absence. Mother would say Abe was just stringing her along, he had dozens of women, she was just another gal—one burdened, moreover, with two brats. Within half an hour she'd convinced herself that he thought so much of her he was afraid of her. She was too cultured, too intelligent, too genteel, too dynamic for him. She frightened him.

I wasn't ashamed. I was coldly indifferent as my mind closed its locks and slowly flooded with dreams. I was a king or a god.

How my mother longed for that phone to ring. When my sister was old enough to date, she, too, waited by the phone. The negligence of men toward women struck me as past belief; how could these men resist so much longing?

All this waiting, of course, was a petri dish in which new cultures of speculation were breeding. Was he not calling to prove a point? His independence, perhaps? Men hated feeling trapped. His own desirability? Or had he found someone else? Or was he shy and himself waiting for a call? I half wanted to be a man, a grown-up man, but a gallant one who could finally put an end to all this suffering. My other half wanted to have a man; I thought I'd know better how to get one and keep him. Or else how to punish him for his neglect.

And all this speculation, I noticed, was occurring beside the obstinately mute telephone—brilliant, glittering black proof of the inefficacy of yearning. No thought, no architecture of thoughts no matter how intricate, could make that phone ring.

Only beauty, youth, charm, money—only those things worked. The rest (goodness, worthiness, the conjuring of desire) was a pitiable substitute for the brute fact of glamour.

And then my mother would turn her hardworking, always shifting, tumbling scrutiny on me. She and I enjoyed a perfect communication, or so she said. I was a man far more mature than the riffraff she was dating. I was beautifully sensitive to the slightest shift in her moods. If I weren't her son, I'd be her best friend—or she'd marry me.

And yet (the wheels whirred faster and faster) without a man to emulate I was in danger of developing abnormally. I mustn't be a mama's boy, I mustn't become effeminate. I mustn't lean on her too much. That was the real reason she was so eager to remarry, to provide me with a suitable male role model. Children of broken homes were known to grow up wounded, their sexuality damaged. "Are you developing normally?" she asked when I was ten.

I told her something that astounded her, though I thought it would please her: "I don't want to go through puberty." I cited my sister. "She's already acting like a nut. I see myself standing on a hill above a lonesome valley I'll never be able to cross. I'll probably never be this calm again."

My sister, my mother and I—three unhappy people, and yet my mother's ceaseless optimism didn't even grant us the dignity of suffering. "Kids," she said, driving us away from school on a weekday, "we're going on vacation. Isn't that wonderful! We're off to Florida! Isn't that exciting?" In every way we had more fun than other people and were superior to them. At Christmastime Mother would count up her cards as though they were a precise numerical rendering of her worth; if someone neglected to send her a card, she'd worry about it, question herself, seem wounded—and then she'd dismiss the offender from her thoughts, even her life ("He wasn't much of a friend. I don't know why I hang around such crummy people").

My sister and I have been left alone in the hotel room all day. Mother is off on a date after work. We've been instructed to take our meals in the dining room downstairs ("I'll be home when I'm home—don't worry about me"). I'm ten, my sister is fourteen. She's interested in being a nurse. She has "sterilized" Mom's scissors and tweezers under hot tap water. Out of her allowance she's bought some gauze in a long roll. She convinces me to lie down and play sick. "You poor guy," she says in a sweet, unfamiliar voice, "just look at this burn!" She is the consoling, sympathetic nurse.

"Yeah, it really hurts. You see, I was boiling some water—"

"Sh-h-h!" she urges me. In real life she's always shutting me up; in the fiction of the hospital she's silencing me in the interest of my recovery. "You'll feel much better once I change your dressing. Please be quiet. I won't hurt you."

We're both bored. It's six on a December night and the sky outside the filmy hotel curtains (they smell of coal smoke) has long been dark. The phone hasn't rung all day—none of us is popular, that's evident. Not my sister, not me, not Mom. "Ouch!" I whine. "That bandage is too tight!"

"It's not!"

"It is so."

"It's not."

"I'm telling you it is so."

"Well, just play with yourself," my sister says. "I don't want to play with you. You wanna know why? Do you? Wanna know why?"

I'm sitting up in bed now, uneasy, wishing I hadn't complained about the bandage.

"I'll tell you why: you smell bad. You do." My sister sticks her face right into mine. One of her barrettes has come loose without her noticing, and suddenly an unexpectedly adult sweep of hair frames her face and caresses her shoulder. She's so close that some of her hair grazes my cheek.

"I do not," I mumble uncertainly. Perhaps I do smell bad. But where is the bad smell coming from? My mouth? My bottom? My feet? I long to creep into the bathroom, to cup a hand over my mouth and nose and test my breath for foulness, then to examine my underwear for skid marks. Or is the bad smell inside me, the terrible decaying Camembert of my heart?

"You do. You smell bad and I hate you. Wherever you go you smell bad, you stink up the place, how do you think I like having people think you're my brother? And look at your big nostrils. And you're such a big sissy, you can't even throw a baseball, you throw like a girl, you can't even walk right, you're a gimp. You are. I'm not kidding."

Now it all seems too true. I'm an embarrassment—to my mother, my sister, most of all to myself. I haven't a right to take up the space I occupy. I poison every room I enter.

"Look at your nails," my sister says, grabbing my hand and holding it under my nose for inspection. "You've got black gook under there. You're icky. You really are. It's probably poop. Do you play with your poop. You play with your poop, you play with your poop, you play with your poop . . ."

I can't get her to shut up or to release my hand. Now she's grabbed a pillow and stuffed it in my face. "Whatsa matter, can't you take it, can't you take it, play with your poop," she's chanting. I turn my head to breathe but she's right there, applying the pillow to my face in this new position. Her terrible words continue, though the pillow muffles the sound. She's planted a knee in my chest to hold me down.

Terrified of suffocating, I push her off in a frantic burst of energy. I grab the nail scissors and stab her in the hand. Blood leaps out. I drop the scissors; they fall to the floor. I'm aghast, an Indian hopping around on one foot with horror, hooting a little war hoot of anguish: "Oh! Oh! Oh!" But she is transformed into a scientist, a doctor. She watches the blood pulse, pool in her palm, finally coagulate. "Neat," she whispers with awe.

By the time our mother returns, I'm exhausted by my tears of repentance. I've been sobbing on the bed, sobbing and sobbing with guilt and fear of punishment. When I hear the door click, I look up. "It was an accident!" I shout. "I hurt her, but it was an accident."

"Oh no, what now! What's going on here?" Mother shouts, throwing her packages on the foot of the bed. My sister alone seems calm. She has bandaged her hand and pinned back her hair and donned a fresh nightgown. She's sitting peacefully under a lamp, reading. She's proud of her wound; it's made her important.

"My baby!" my mother shouts, rushing to my sister's side.

The wound is unbound and revealed. I can tell my mother is confused, since ordinarily I'm the one who's tormented by my sister. I'm ordinarily the sweet soul, too good for this world, too kind for my own good, too gentle, a little lamb. To discover the wolf cub in lamb's skin doesn't suit my mother's preconceptions, the story of our lives she's telling herself. She sits on the edge of the bed, magisterial, coldly rational, suffering disappointment but resolved to appear fair. "Start at the beginning. Tell me everything that happened."

My sister and I compete, we try to outshout each other ("You did, I did not, Yes, you did"). Mother opens a bottle of bourbon and calls room service, ordering ice and seltzer water.

At last our anger and my fear and my sister's spite are spent. We subside into silence. It's my turn to sleep on the floor; tonight my sister and mother will have the twin beds. Defeated, silent, embarrassed, all three of us take turns in the bathroom. Mother is sad. "If only you kids could behave. Just one night. Is it too much to ask? Why do you hate each other so much? Do you hate yourselves? Do you miss your daddy? I miss him. I don't see how a fine man like him could have left me for that cheap—that common, that cheap woman."

As the bottle slowly empties, its brown liquid, like kerosene fueling a lamp, radiates, in words and more words, the intense heat of despair.

The next morning Mother has decided that we all deserve a treat to pick up our defeated spirits, something cultural, something uplifting. My sister complains about her hand and refuses to leave the room. "Well, if you're going to be such a baby, then I'll just take your brother. He has an open mind, an adventurous mind. He wants to learn."

Together my mother and I drive downtown to a museum. On the way we dial in a classical music station. We try to guess the composer; she votes for Haydn, I for Mozart. Neither of us is right—it's early Beethoven. She asks me to read to her. "You know I learn best auditorily," she mentions. The book she has brought along is something uplifting, inspirational. At every insight or poetically phrased generalization, my mother and I exclaim, "Isn't that wonderful!" "I'd like to memorize that." "Turn down the page, we'll come back to that." "Where does an author find such beautiful phrases?"

By the time we reach the museum we're both glowing with wisdom and a lofty love of culture and humanity. I've forgotten that I smell bad. In fact, by now I smell wonderful, I'm a paschal lamb, but one rendered in cake and icing. We stand in front of a gloomy masterpiece of the Spanish Renaissance, a Christ whose wounds are shockingly deep and black and whose skin is livid; Christ seems less a god and more an addict tossed here, in the public morgue, after a fatal overdose, the puncture marks still open but no longer bleeding.

My mother trembles. "I don't like depressing things," she confides, and hurries us to the French Impressionists.

Outside, in the feeble winter sunlight, she grabs my hand and says, "I feel you're such a perfect companion. When I'm with you I feel such total spiritual union that I sometimes forget I'm with you. I think we're two halves of the same soul, don't you?"

I look her deep in the eyes and tell her, "Yes. I've never felt so close to anyone."

MY CALM was restored—but the calm was sepulchral. When a psychologist gave me the inkblot test, I saw no people in the abstract shapes, only cemeteries, diamonds and ballrooms. I thought I was Jupiter or his disguised and only seemingly powerless incarnation. We lived one year in a suburb so new it was still being built in fields of red clay: a neat grid of streets named after songbirds was being dropped like a lattice of dough over a pie. Up and down Robin and Tanager and Bluebird I raced my bike; in a storm I pedaled so fast I hoped to catch up with the wind-driven rain. As I sped into the riddling wet warmth I shook my right hand according to a magical formula of my own. The universe, signaled by its master, groaned, revolved, released a flash of lightning. At last the imagination, like a mold on an orange, was covering the globe of my mind.

In the sand I built castles that took on a splendor only the sea could fathom. In the winter I re-created my royal residences and processions in the snow. The ruler was an empress—isolated and superb—and she wandered sleeplessly through miles of gray, dilapidated corridors. You see, something new with a mansard roof had been provided for her, but she felt herself drawn instead to the much older rooms that lay behind and beyond, the low-ceilinged rooms lit by icon candles and filled with smoke in which such terrible things had been done, in which history had been born or butchered. Half-numb with the cold, my fingers and toes burning, my nose running and eyes tearing, I hovered over my dingy kremlin for yet another half hour although the light was failing and a stray dog had just yellowed the coronation chapel. The tuppity-tuppity-tuppity of snow chains on passing car tires was the only sound in the evening air. Blooms of mild radiance suddenly opened within the glass globes of streetlamps. Headlights coming around the curve transected me, so crystalline had I become, a transparence dancing attendance on my imperial insomniac. She penetrated farther and farther into the unmapped mysteries of her palace; tuppity, tuppity; she pushed aside a leather curtain, entered the surprisingly small old throne room. There on a raised chair sat a skeleton, bracelets like manacles on its wrists and a gold hat eating its way into the tiny brown skull.

I was three people: the boy who smelled bad when I was with my sister; the boy who was wise and kind beyond his years when I was with my mother; but when I was alone not a boy at all but a principle of power, of absolute power.

# FOUR

Like a blind man's hands exploring a face, the memory lingers over an identifying or beloved feature but dismisses the rest as just a curve, a bump, an expanse. Only *this* feature—these lashes tickling the palm like a firefly or this breath pulsing hot on a knuckle or this vibrating Adam's apple—only this feature seems lovable, sexy. But in writing one draws in the rest, the forgotten parts. One even composes one's improvisations into a quite new face never glimpsed before, the likeness of an invention. Busoni once said he prized the most those empty passages composers make up to get from one "good part" to another. He said such workmanlike but minor transitions reveal more about a composer—the actual vernacular of his imagination—than the deliberately bravura moments. I say all this by way of hoping that the lies I've made up to get from one poor truth to another may mean something—may even mean something most particular to you, my eccentric, patient, scrupulous reader, willing to make so much of so little, more patient and more respectful of life, of a life, than the author you're allowing for a moment to exist yet again.

When I was eleven I started going every day after school to a bookshop which was near the hotel where my mother and sister and I lived. I was fascinated by a woman who worked there. She moved and talked and even sang as though she were on a big stage and not in a very small store. I had seen an overweight and coquettish diva portray Carmen, and this woman seemed just as ready for the role—a peasant blouse worn off the shoulders and so low as to reveal the tops of large breasts; black hair drawn back into a ponytail that hopped almost of its own accord from her back up onto her shoulder, where it would perch like a pet as she nuzzled it with her cheek; a tiny waist sadistically cinched in by a stout black belt that laced up the front; ample hips in rolling motion under a long skirt that swirled in meticulously ironed pleats around her; and small flat feet with painted nails in sandals she remained true to even on snowy days. She bathed herself in a heavy, ruttish perfume that suggested neither a girl nor a matron but rather the overripe coquette, the sort of imposing beauty one could imagine a weak nineteenth-century king taking on as his mistress. This scent, as shameless as her half-naked body, billowed to conceal or shrank to disclose her other abiding odor, the smell of burning cigarettes. She could sit for hours on a high stool behind the counter with an open book and kick her pleated skirt with a dangling leg and stab out one cigarette after another into a small black ashtray from a restaurant in New York. On television I'd seen the host of a New York nightclub introduce the viewing public to celebrities; some of this glamour now attended the woman's smoking. Each of her butts was lavishly smeared with bloodred lipstick; the growing mound of smoldering butts resembled an open grave, ghastly trough of quartered torsos.

As she smoked she hummed throatily, then exhaled, coughed, paused; her eyebrows shot up, her trembling upper lip curled back on one side to reveal a big, red-flecked front tooth, her jaw dropped, her spine grew, her massive shoulders shook—and out came a high, high head tone. Then a snatch of nasal Gounod tossed off saucily, scales sung in muted vocalese ripped open here and there to full volume (dark sleeves slashed with crimson silk), then a bit of hey-nonny-nonny. . . She turned a page in the novel and blindly reached for the smoking ashtray.

The low scabrous radiator that ran the length of the display window clanked and hissed. Someone came in as the bell rang out merrily. The cold air cut the angled, floating panels of blue smoke to ribbons. The woman put her book down and dashed lightly to greet the customer. Her body, which in repose appeared leviathan, in motion took on a balletic lightness. She cocked her head to one side and smiled. In the cold winter daylight I could see the thick layer of pancake makeup covering her face and neck but stopping short of her shoulders. The makeup was so evidently painted on and of such an unlikely hue that I gasped: this woman must be very old, I thought, to need such a disguise.

Everything about her intrigued me and I returned day after day just to be near her. I watched her so hard that I forgot I existed; she provided me with a new, better life. For hours I stood in front of one bookcase or another reading as the dirty snow melted off my boots and left black tracks on the wood floor. First I'd remove the cap with earflaps and stuff it in a pocket; ten minutes later I'd unwind the maroon scarf. The coat came off and fell in a heap on the floor; then a sweater threw its twisted body onto the coat: clumsy wrestlers. The woman hummed and placed a small nickel-coated pot on the hot plate. The upper third of each windowpane was steamy; as a result, a passing man was striated into blurred and clear zones, his neck detailed down to the stubble but his face an embryo's still streaming within the caul. Although it was only four the light was already dying; the world creaked from the cold and hugged itself hopelessly. Blue mounds of snow cast bluer shadows, but inside, everything was cheery and animated. The woman, whom the new customer called Marilyn, was laughing at his long, murmured story and her laugh was lovely.

By the third long afternoon I'd spent there I'd fallen into conversation with Marilyn. She made some comment or other on the book I'd been holding for half an hour as I kept stealing glances at her and eavesdropping on her snatches of song and remarks to customers. She said to me, "I noticed you're intrigued by the set of Balzac. It's a very good buy—the complete works for just forty dollars. That's about a dollar a volume. You can't beat that. And it's a handsome edition, the titles in gold stamped on leather, which may or may not be real. Turn of the century."

I was not a fast reader. Months could go by before I'd finish a single book. The project of reading all of Balzac would obviously absorb the rest of my life. Was I prepared to make that commitment before I'd read even one of his novels?

"How interesting," I said, as I'd been trained to say to everything, even the grossest absurdity. "Who was Balzac?"

She smiled and said, to spare my pride, "Ah, now there's a good question. We'll wait till Fred comes. He can tell us both."

Fred, it turned out, owned the store. He was a tall man with ragged red hair streaked prematurely gray and acne-pitted skin and work clothes that weren't quite clean and hundreds of scraps of odd knowledge he stored in his head just as he secreted (in the pockets of his faded blue shirt or his baggy chinos or the blue vest from one secondhand suit or the brown jacket from another) tiny slips of paper on which he jotted notes for his stories. The slips were of five different pastel shades; whether this variety followed a system or merely injected random color into cerebrations so exalted they would otherwise have been uniformly gray I have no way of knowing—certainly at that age I had no way of judging him, only of gazing at him with awe.

His eyes, magnified by thick glasses, never met mine. When he spoke to me he scrutinized a point precisely a foot to the left of my head. His voice was so soft and low and expressionless that one might have ignored him had Marilyn not listened to him with such deference. Since everything she did was theatrical, "listening" also had to be pantomimed: she stood like a schoolgirl and her hands, pointing down, were pressed together in inverted prayer. Her mouth was pursed, her head lowered; at a certain moment in Fred's mutterings her head would start to bob wildly and those strange tones of assent that can only be transcribed as "Mmnn" would issue forth from her throat on a high, surprised note and then on lower, affirming ones—even, finally, on a very low grunt that bore the unintentionally rude message "Of course. Everyone knows that. Get on with it." None of this was subtle. It was really quite ridiculously overdone—or would have been had Marilyn been concerned at all with the impression she was making on other people. As it happened, she wanted only to conform to a role she was simultaneously writing and reciting.

The exact dimensions of that role became clear only as the years went by. She saw herself, I was to learn, as the grisette in a nineteenth-century opera—as Mimi or Violetta or Manon. Like them she was impulsive, warm-hearted, immoral and pious. Like them she must remain eternally young—hence her flamboyant clothes and gestures and hectic displays of energy (the middle-aged imagine the young are energetic).

Later, much later, when I was sixteen and eighteen and twenty, I'd meet her downtown where she worked at a museum and we'd go off in the middle of a dim winter afternoon to a deserted bar and drink manhattans (I remember because they were the first drinks I ever ordered). Another afternoon I attended a madrigal concert she sang in at the public library, something planned in conjunction with an exhibition of one page from the hand of that monster Gesualdo. There she was, breasts half-exposed and working, eyes turned inward, trembling upper lip rising on one side until it had suddenly been everted, her face painted an unlikely yellow and her hair dyed a brittle blue-black, her clothes still "youthful" but now so out of date that the few members of the audience under twenty-five would have had no idea what she was signifying. They might have thought that she was an émigré wearing the national costume of Estonia and that these songs—these gliding transits, startling rhythms and suave, uncomfortable harmonies—were folk songs in need of a pitch pipe. One afternoon over manhattans I confessed to Marilyn I was gay and she told me she was, too, and that she and Fred had known all along that I would be, even when I was eleven.

"And Fred? Was he gay?"

"Oh yes. Didn't you know? I thought we all knew about each other," Marilyn said as she redrew her eyes in the compact mirror.

"Well, I knew you both liked me and that I felt good with you, better than with most grown-ups."

"Then why did you stop coming by the shop? Waiter, another round."

"Because my mother told me I couldn't see you anymore.

The old ladies in our hotel told my mother that you and Fred were Communists and living in sin."

Marilyn laughed and laughed. "Of course the truth is we're both Catholics and gay and never touched each other. Perhaps those ladies even knew the truth but—but"—shriek of laughter— "assumed that Communism and living in sin, that those two things together equaled being gay."

I was wearing a Brooks Brothers sack suit of black and brown twill that ran on the diagonal and a soft felt fedora from Paris, and this getup, which seemed so stylish to me, cast our conversation into the light of an excited urbanity, as did the cocktails, no doubt. Elevated tracks ran outside above the bar, and whenever a train passed by, our table trembled under our elbows and the glasses, accidentally touching each other, registered the shock in a muted chime. The light in the bar was as murky as old water in an aquarium dimmed by storms of fish food beat up by lazy fins. I could peer out through it onto a sidewalk bright with mica chips and frost, the permanent glitter and the passing. A radio played a rumba.

I asked her news of Fred, and Marilyn said she'd lost touch with him, that the last she had heard he was still living with an Indian tribe in the Yucatán, where he'd gone to write his stories. And I recalled that when I was thirteen I'd run into him at the public library after not seeing him for a year. But he was no longer contained in his blue vest and brown jacket with his hair tousled but cut—no, now he was a wild man, something strapped with hemp to his back, his hair and beard flowing red and gray over his shoulders, his calves wrapped up to the knees in orange and red rags, feet shod in boots with cleats, eyes still big and averted behind glasses now mended with tape and his hands much redder and bigger and flatter somehow, as though he'd hammered each finger flat. I didn't recognize him, but he touched me on the shoulder; and when I looked up into those eyes peering a foot to one side of me and saw the acne scars above the sprouting whiskers and heard his dull, mechanical and very soft voice, the sound of a voice choking on its own phlegm—well, then I knew him but didn't want to, so drastically transformed was he. If he'd had an iguana on his shoulder he couldn't have been more exotic. He told me he'd been in Mexico for a few months and was heading back there soon, that he had no money but lived by doing odd jobs—that this precariousness was necessary to his art. Before, in the shop, his dull muttering and his magnified, frozen eyes had seemed pitiable signs of shyness, but such an interpretation had fitted him only in his scruffy bourgeois guise, had fitted the sound of the clanking radiator and the smell of reheated coffee. Now that he was released out of his confining shop and had turned himself into a gaudy fetish, into a hank of streaked hair and bright rags, now his gaze seemed paralyzed by grandeur and his voice remote only because it was the sound of divinity.

As a little boy I'd recognized that my imaginary playmate, Tom, was free but only by virtue of enduring total isolation; now Fred (but was this huge, mumbling, godlike bum really Fred?), now this new Fred was telling me mendicancy was the price of making art.

And what finally became of him and his stories? Was he absorbed one day into the Yucatán jungle? I've been told that in some Indian villages in Mexico homosexual men live in a separate compound where they take care of the tribe's children; is Fred still living as some ancient nanny respectably obscured by pure white veils of beard and hair, his glasses long since broken and abandoned, his constant murmur unheard below the squeal of warm, naked toddlers who clamber over him as though he were nothing but a weathered garden god half-sunk into the creepers and vines, his notebook of handwritten stories open to the elements to scatter its pages as the leaves of a calendar in old movies fly away to indicate the passage of years, even decades?

And Marilyn? The last time I saw her the color of her makeup had gone iodine, her lips had thinned, her hair had become a spiky black cap and her large, rolling eyes no longer seemed a coquette's but those of a virgin martyr, protuberant, cast up, the whites wept clean, the lower lids sooty with despair. She told me that for the last two years she'd been living in a boardinghouse in a room next to that of a young violinist whom she loved and who loved her fraternally but, alas, not passionately. He was planning to become a Benedictine and she thought she'd follow him into Holy Orders. "This is the great love of my life—not a woman as always before but a beautiful young man who doesn't want me. How ironic! We met through music. His beauty, his music, his indifference—don't you see?"

"Not exactly."

She smiled the hazardous, hard-won smile of the lover determined to have found a consolation: "He was sent to me to awaken in me an appetite only God can feed. I've been such a sinner—waiter, another round—but I never became coarse or jaded or thick-skinned. I was ready for God's gift." Her hair didn't satisfy her. She studied it in her compact mirror, shifting the small round glass from side to side, top to bottom; a macula of light searched her face intensely and dissected it inch by inch, swerving here, hovering there, highlighting the withered cheek, the crepey neck, the hard, jutting chin. It moved where the glance of the contemptuous beloved would go. She propped the compact up between the oil and vinegar cruets and her fingertips touched her hair with wonderful delicacy as the reflection glowed steadily in her right eye and even seemed to travel surgically through it. At last she blinked and snapped the glass shut. "I still feel like a young girl, as though everything is about to happen. And don't you see"—her dry, rough hand with the painted nails seized mine—"I *am* a sort of spiritual debutante."

In our imaginations the adults of our childhood remain extreme, essential—we might say *radical* since they are the roots that feed luxuriant later systems. Those first bohemians, for instance, stay operatic in memory even though were we to meet them today—well, what would we think, we who've elaborated our eccentricities with a patience, a professionalism they never knew?

Soon after I first met Fred and Marilyn they decided I must learn German in order to read the novels of Hermann Hesse, at that time still largely untranslated. Hesse's mix of suicide, mysticism and sexual ambiguity had launched them into a thrilling

void; reading him, they said, was like being in an airplane above
the breathable stratosphere. He wasn't healthy. In fact, a smell
of taint seeped off his pages. He wasn't right or even wise, but
they never stopped to check his words against what they knew
to be true since they adored him precisely as an exit out of experience and an entrance into the magic theater of sensations
wholly invented. In place of the torpor of everyday life Hesse
called them to a disciplined quest—even if the Grail he offered
was vaporous and poisoned.

The teacher they'd selected for me was a part-time professor
at the university. He lived in one room in a huge pile thrown up
as faculty and graduate-student housing. He had a double bed
that pulled down out of the wall; by day it hid behind two
white doors with cut-glass doorknobs. When he greeted me for
my first lesson I was overwhelmed by his size. He was six foot
four and brawny and I looked up into chestnut hair sprouting
from his nostrils; my hand was lost in his. He was at once formal and hearty and spoke with a strong German accent. Our
lessons followed an exact system and began and ended at fixed
times without interludes or chitchat. By the same token the professor bounded about in a shirt open to his navel, his sleeves
rolled up above his massive biceps, and on his desk I saw a photograph of him in a swimsuit at the beach holding his girlfriend aloft with just one hand. Like many athletes he found it
impossible to sit still, and his grammatical points and pronunci-
ation tips were underscored with a ceaseless tattoo. He slapped
his knees. He rocked back and forth in his straight-backed
chair. He shot his hand up in a menacing *Sieg Heil*—but only to
reach back to scratch between his shoulder blades, a difficult
feat for someone so muscle-bound. As I sat beside him (I almost
said *within* him, so totally did he surround me) I became more
and more feeble. He'd stride up and down the small room, kick-
ing the baseboard of each wall when he reached it as if to
protest the insult of such a small cage for such a mighty lion.
Before I met him I could have imagined someone huge and stupid and taciturn; I could just as readily have pictured a brilliant
tiny chatterbox, bald pate and soft curls fringing it, a midget

dynamo who read everything and played the cello when depressed. But a giant with calluses on his palms at the base of each finger, someone who breathed in a conscious, voluntary way as I tentatively recited my lesson and who stood and folded a huge paw over his jaw before delivering a judgment about my performance—such a man was so new to me that he confused me, he thrilled me.

One winter Friday afternoon at four he didn't answer his door. Desperation seized me. I hadn't realized how devoted to him I'd become. Our sessions didn't call for devotion. I'd simply show up, obey his commands and sink into a desire to please him that could only have been called devotion. But things didn't go that far, there wasn't the absence necessary for adoration until that afternoon when he didn't open his door. For some reason I was convinced that he was inside but in bed with his girlfriend, that lithe, tiny woman in the black swimsuit whom the Herr Professor had held so effortlessly aloft last summer, a simple smile on his face. He was in that bed which, when pulled down, no doubt filled his whole room and there he was heartily rolling on his tiny but acrobatically receptive partner. Soon enough it would be time to push the bed back behind its white doors, to gnaw on a sausage and quaff a beer and then, in his lordly way, open the door to his ridiculously young pupil. I didn't knock very loudly because I didn't want to break his concentration or rhythm; the only question was, had I calibrated my knock so as to indicate my presence but not to annoy him?

And yet—what if he wasn't at home at all? What if he had forgotten our lesson? As long as I thought his closed door was barring me from those deep invasions of a fragile body, just so long was I content to stand in that shabby, windowless corridor. Waiting for my teacher was no burden to me (wasn't Hesse himself teaching me the value of a patient apprenticeship?). But what made me frantic was the fear that no one was behind the door. No bed, no lazily smiling German face, no huge hand stroking a pale, engorged pelvis—nothing, an unlit room devoid of everything but a ticking clock and a refrigerator that groans and goes dead, groans and goes dead.

And I was terrified someone would ask me what I was doing in the hall. A great deal of time had already gone by. People had begun to cook supper and the overheated corridor was filling with the smells of food. I had peeled off my coat, scarf and sweater. I sat on them and leaned against a wall. In the distance I could hear the elevator doors opening and closing. An old woman shouted into a telephone. Another woman was giving instructions to a child. This corridor was a sort of catch basin for the domesticity trickling down around me. The smells. The irritations. The complicated lives of absolutely everyone.

My professor didn't come that day. Of course he phoned the next with a reasonable excuse. Of course I should have anticipated just such a hitch and explanation, but my need, though usually held in check or released only on imaginary beings, could, if turned on someone real, devour him. I had worshipped my teacher, I'd even forgiven him for not loving me—but now I hated him. I dreamed of revenge. In the past I'd been protected from humiliating rejection because I so seldom asked anything of anyone. The gods were my company; the lilac in flower embraced me; books did all the talking but only when I permitted the monologue to begin. They were transparent companions whose intentions were never in doubt. Gods, flowers, words— why, I could see right through them! Nor did they waver into or out of focus or leave even an inch of the surround blank. Whereas people batted thoughts and feelings like badminton birdies at you, a whir that might take you by surprise, that you might not even see but that you were expected to return until the air began to go white, the gods made no such demands. They propped themselves up on gold elbows and lazily turned their wide, smiling faces down on you. When their glance locked with yours their eyebeams lit up. In an instant you were they, they you, gods mortal and mortals divine, the mutual regard a reflecting pool into which everything substantial would soon melt and flow.

WHEN I was twelve, the year after I began my German classes, the boys I knew started playing a violent game called Squirrel ("Grab his nuts and run"). Guys who'd scarcely acknowledged me until now were suddenly thrashing, twisting muscles in my arms, their breath panting peanut butter right up into my face, my hands sliding over their silky skin just above the rough denim . . . and now his gleaming crotch buttons were pressing down on me as his knees burned into my biceps and I put off shouting "Uncle" one more second in order to inhale once again the terrible smell of his sweat.

Or the light was dying and piles of burning leaves streaked the air with the smoky breath of the very earth. My hands were raw with cold, my nose was running, I was late for supper, my shirt was torn, but still I called him back again and again by shouting, "I'm not sorry. I just said that. I'm not sorry, I'm—"

"Look, you little creep"—his voice was much lower, he was a year older, he came at me, really mad this time, I didn't want his anger, just his body on top of me and his arms around me.

Or Harold, the minister's son—that small, athletic blond with the pompadour preserved in hair lotion and the black mole on his full, hairless cheek, that boy who strutted when he walked, preferred his own company to everyone else's and who had a reputation among adults for being "considerate" that was directly contradicted by his cheerfully blind arrogance—he was someone with whom I could play Squirrel in the late afternoons after his trumpet practice (he shakes the silver flood of saliva out of the gold mouth and snaps open the black case to reveal its purple plush, worn down here to a slick, reflecting white-ness, roughed up there into a dark bruise, then he places the taut heroism of the instrument into that regal embrace and locks it shut).

Even in the winter, as winds blowing up off the lake cast nets of snow over us and the sun pulsed feebly like the aura of a mi-graine that doesn't develop, we lunged at each other, rolled in drifts, squirrels hungry for hard blue nuts in the frozen land. Suddenly fingers would be squirming and pulling, a wave of pain would shoot through me, his sapphire eye set in white faience would arc past and dip below the shadowy horizon of my nose, hot breaths would tear out of my lungs and cross his—at cross-purposes.

The summer I was twelve I was sent in a Greyhound bus to a camp for boys. We lived in tents in rows on the grounds of a famous military academy. The massive, reddish brown buildings with their green turrets and gables were closed for the season, but the adult staff—the captains and generals in perpetual uniform—stayed behind to run the camp and earn an extra income. The campers, though younger than the usual cadets, were nevertheless submitted to the same military discipline. In fact our camping activity, beyond nature hikes and swimming lessons in a chlorinated indoor pool, consisted of nothing but drill and inspection. We learned to make a bed with hospital corners and to stretch the rough flannel blanket so taut a coin would bounce on it. Everyone owned precisely the same gear, stowed away in precisely the same manner. Shoes were placed just under the cot, each pair four inches from the next, each shoe of a pair two inches from its mate. Trumpets awakened us and sent us to bed. We marched to the mess hall where we were served cold mashed potatoes and boiled cabbage; more horribly at breakfast we ate bacon in congealed grease and scrambled eggs floating on hot water. After breakfast we marched double-time back to our tents, where we had an hour to prepare our quarters for white-glove inspection. Our captain saw everything and forgave nothing. He could find that single pair of kneesocks at the bottom of a steamer trunk that wasn't properly rolled and he would hand out to the offender enough demerits to fill all his free time for the rest of the summer.

He was a small, wiry man with black eyebrows so full that if they weren't pressed or combed into place they would stick out in disconcerting clumps like brittle, badly cared for paintbrushes or could droop down over an eye in a droll effect at odds with the commands he was barking. His skin was a tan mask clapped over a face that always appeared seriously exhausted; the dark circles and drained, bloodless cheeks could be seen through the false health of his tan. I ascribed his weariness to irritation. In fact he was much older than the other instructors. He may even have been close to retirement age. He might have been ill and in pain and perhaps his irritation was due to his ailment.

After lights-out he became someone new. Although he was still in uniform his tie was loosened, his voice seemed to have dropped an octave and a decibel, he had scotch mysteriously and pleasantly on his breath, and his regard had grown gentle beneath its thatch of drooping eyebrows. He stopped by each tent, sat on the edge of each cot and spoke to each boy in a tone so intimate that the roommate couldn't eavesdrop. My roommate was a tall, extremely shy and well-bred redhead from a small town in Iowa: someone who seemed not at all eager to confide in me or to seek my friendship or even comments, as though he recognized that *this* life, at least, was worth enduring only if it remained unexamined. And yet his silences did not guarantee that he was altogether without thought or feeling. At unexpected moments he'd blush or stutter or in midsentence his mouth would go dry—and I could never figure out what had prompted these symptoms of anxiety.

One night, after our captain had lingered longer than usual in his cloud of scotch and then passed on to the next tent, I asked my rommate why the captain always stayed longer beside him than me.

"I don't know. He rubs me."

"What do you mean?"

"Doesn't he rub you?" the boy whispered.

"Sometimes," I lied.

"All over?"

"Like how?" I asked.

"Like all"—his voice went dry—"down your front?"

"That's not right," I said. "He shouldn't do that. He shouldn't. It's abnormal. I've read about it."

A few nights later I woke up with a fever. My throat was so sore I couldn't swallow. My sheets were wet and cold with sweat. Even when I lay still I could feel the blood running through my veins; a metronome was ticking loudly within me and with each tick an oar of sensation cut into the water and pulled against it. No, now I could detect a line of divers jumping off the prow to the right, the left, right, left—the columns of marching boys advanced across the floor of the chlorinated pool. I closed my eyes and felt my heartbeat pluck a string in the harp of my chest. Was the night really so cold? I had to get help; the infirmary; otherwise pneumonia. My roommate was propped up on his elbow speaking giddy nonsense to me ("I like, I like, I like the Lackawanna") until I opened my eyes and saw him serenely asleep, his face the cutting edge of the prow as it parted a sea of liquid mercury. The flow, clinging to itself, boiling but cold, had swept me overboard with a chipmunk who was singing snatches from the Top Ten through the painful red hole in his neck—I sat up. I could barely swallow. I whispered my roommate's name.

When he didn't respond I put on my regulation cotton robe and regulation black slippers and walked up and down the raw clay roads between the rows of tents. Was that the first streak of dawn or the lights of a town? Should I wait till reveille? Or should I wake our captain up now?

I walked and walked and watched the night sky phosphoresce like plankton in the August sea. Gold would glimmer at the horizon and then feed its way up through delicate glass circuits into the main switchboard, where it would short out in a white explosion that would settle into a fine jeweler's rouge. Were those bats overhead? I'd heard that bats lived in the school towers. Here they were: blind, carnivorous and getting closer, lacing their way from eye to eye up the tongue.

At last the captain heard my knock and came to the door. He had a whole tent to himself, I could see, and he was still awake with a mystery novel and a bottle of scotch. He appeared confused—at least he didn't know who I might be. When he'd unraveled my identity and figured out I was ill, he urged me to spend the rest of the night with him. We'd go to the infirmary first thing in the morning, he said to me. We'd go together. He'd take care of me. I had to insist over and over again on the urgency of my seeing a nurse now ("I'm really sick, sir, it can't wait") before he finally relented and led me to the infirmary. Even as I was pleading with him I was wondering what it would be like to live in this spacious tent with him. But why hadn't he noticed me before? Why hadn't he tried to rub me? Was I inferior to my roommate in some way? Less handsome? At least I wasn't abnormal, I said to myself, glancing over at his haggard unshaven face, at his profile with its shelf of eyebrows in the darkness bright with mercury.

The next summer I refused to go to camp until my mother lied and told me I'd be a junior counselor in charge of dramatics at a lovely place in the northern woods where practically no discipline existed and what there was would be waived in my case. I rode up north before the season began with the owner of the camp, who humored me ("Yes, well, you'll have to decide which plays you'll want to stage—you *are* the dramatics department"). After he said such things, he seemed to choke on his own generosity; his mouth would contract into an acidic kiss.

We were driving farther and father north. I sat in the front seat with the owner of the camp and looked out at the tall pines, so blue they were almost black against the gray spring sky. The road was the same color as the sky. When we came to the top of a gentle rise and looked down, the road below seemed forlorn and distant, enchanted into the shadows. But as we sped through the valley, the road came close and brightened and the crowns of the blue-black trees slid over the car's polished metal hood. In the backseat behind me lolled a special camper my mother, upon the advice of the owner, had warned me to avoid ("Be polite, but don't let him get you alone"). She seemed reluctant to explain what the danger was, but when I pressed her she finally said, "He's oversexed. He's tried to take advantage of the younger boys." She then went on to assure me that I mustn't despise the poor boy; he was, after all, braindamaged in some way, under medication, unable to read. If God had gifted me with a fine mind, He'd done so only that I might serve my fellow man.

In this brief parting word of warning, my mother had managed to communicate to me her own fascination with the wild boy. The day had turned cool and the car windows were closed. The motor ran so smoothly that the ticking of the dashboard clock could be heard. When I cracked the vent open I heard volleys of birdsong but the birds themselves were hiding. In the valley below, empty of all signs of humanity except for the road, a mist was curling through the pines. I didn't really know the owner of the camp, and so I felt awkward beside him, ready to discuss whatever he chose but afraid of tiring him with my chatter. I sat half-rigid with expectation, a smile up my sleeve. And I felt the sex-crazed boy behind me who was half stretched out on the backseat, the sunlight from between the passing pines rhythmically stroking his body.

After it got dark we stopped for gas and a snack. Ralph, the special camper, said he was cold and wanted to sit up front with us just to keep warm. There was nothing affectionate or come-on-ish in his manner to me in the coffee shop; I could tell desire and affection had not clasped hands across *his* heart. He was alone with his erection, which I could see through the thin fabric of his summer pants. It was something he carried around with him wherever he went, like a scar. In the dark interior of the car, brushed here and there by a dim, firefly glow from the panel, Ralph's leg pressed mine. I was forced to return the pressure lest I lean against the driver and cause comment. When I caught sight of Ralph's face in the magnesium explosion of passing headlights, he looked exhausted, mouth half-open, a thirsty animal whose eyes had turned inward with craving.

The camp, when we finally arrived at midnight, was a sad, cold, empty place. The owner had to unlock a thick rusted chain that stretched from tree to tree across the narrow dirt road. When we reached an open field our car waded slowly, slowly through grasses as tall as the roof and wet and heavy with dew. At the foot of the hill glimmered the lake through a mist—more a chill out of the ground than a lake, more an absence, as though this fitful, shifting dampness was what was left in the world after everything human had been subtracted from it. I was given a bunk in a cold cabin that smelled of mildewed canvas; Ralph was led off somewhere else. As I tried to fall asleep I thought of him. I pitied him, as my mother wanted me to. I pitied him for his dumb animal stare, for his helpless search after relief—for his burden. And I thought about the plays I would direct. In one of them I'd be a dying king. In my trunk I'd brought some old 78s of *Boris Godounov*. Perhaps I'd die to those tolling bells, the Kremlin surrounded by the forces of the pretender, his face red and swollen with desire.

There was a week to go before the other campers were due to arrive. Some local men with scythes swept their way through the overgrown grasses. Someone else repaired the leaking roof in the main house. Stocks of canned food were delivered. The various cabins were opened and aired and swept out. A wasp's hive above the artesian well was bagged and burned. The docks were assembled and floated between newly implanted pylons. The big war canoes came out of winter storage and were seasoned in the cold lake. I worked from the first light to the last—part of my duty as a junior counselor. Ralph had no chores. He stayed in his cabin and came out just for his meals, led wherever he trudged by the big implacable bulge with the wet tip in his trousers.

Every afternoon I was free to go off on my own. The chill still rose off the lake but at high noon the sun broke through its clouds like a monarch slipping free of his retinue. The path I took girdled the hills that rimmed the lake; at one point it dipped and crossed a bog that looked solid and dry, planted innocently in grasses, but that slurped voluptuously under my shoes. I'd race across and look back as my footprints filled with cold, clear water. A hidden bullfrog makes a low gulp and repeats the same sound but more softly each time under the steady high throb of spring peepers in full chorus. A gray chipmunk with a bright chestnut rump scurries past, his tail sticking straight up. Canoe birches higher up the hill shiver in a light breeze; their green and brown buds are emerging from warty, dark brown shoots. A hermit thrush, perched on a high branch, releases its beautiful song while slowly raising and lowering its tail.

I came to know every turn in the path and every plant along the way. One day, late in the summer, I pushed farther into the woods than I'd ever ventured before. I clambered through brambles and thick undergrowth until I reached a logger's road sliced through the wilderness but now slowly healing over. I followed that road for several miles. I entered a broad field and then a smaller clearing surrounded by low trees, although high enough to cut off all breezes. The sun burned hotter and hotter, as if someone were holding a magnifying glass over me. I took off my T-shirt and felt the sweat flow down my sides to my stomach as I bent over to pick blueberries from low bushes. The ground was wet. A huge bee hung buzzing, motionless, in the air.

I was so happy alone and in the woods, away from the dangers posed by other people. At first I wanted to tell someone else how happy I was; I needed a witness. But as the great day revolved slowly above me, as the scarlet tanager flew overhead on his black wings to the distant high trees, as an owl, hidden and remote, sounded a hoot as melancholy as winter, as the leaves, ruffled by the wind, tossed the sun about as though they were princesses at play with a golden ball, as the smell of sweet clover, of bruised sassafras leaves, of the mulch of last year's duff flowed over me, as I crushed the hot, sweet blueberries between my teeth and then chewed on an astringent needle from a balsam, as I sensed the descent of the sun and the slow decline of summer—oh, I was free and whole, safe from everyone, as happy as with my books.

For I could thrive in the expressive, inhuman realm of nature or the expressive, human realm of books—both worlds so exalted, so guileless—but I felt imperiled by the hidden designs other people were drawing around me. The tender white bells of the flower by the rotting stump, the throbbing distillation of blue in the fringed gentian, the small, bright green cone of the Scots pine—these were confidences nature placed in me, wordless but as trusting as a dog's eyes. Or the pure, always comprehensible and sharply delineated thoughts and emotions of characters in fiction—these, too, were signs I could read, as one might read a marionette's face. But the vague menace of Ralph with his increasingly haggard face, this boy at once pitiable and dangerous, who had already been caught twice this summer attempting to "hypnotize" younger campers and was now in danger of expulsion, who studied me at meals not with curiosity, much less with sympathy, but with crude speculation (Can I get him to do it? Can he relieve me?)—this menace was becoming more and more intense.

After the other campers appeared and the summer's activities had been under way for a week, I understood that I'd been betrayed. There wouldn't be any plays for me to put on, and I had exhausted myself for no good reason with all-night fantasies of the rehearsals, the performances, the triumphs. My mother's promises had just been a way of getting me out of the house for the summer. A few miles away my sister—shy to the point of invisibility in the winter, unpopular, pasty, overweight—had emerged once again into her estival beauty. She was Captain of the Blues, bronzed and muscular, her hair a gold cap, her enthusiasm boundless, her manner tyrannical ("Get *going*, you guys"), as though all she needed to flower was the complete absence of men and the intense, sentimental adoration of other girls. She'd always been able to command other girls, even when she had been a child and had ordered them to bring her belts for their own chastisement.

Once my sister and I were out of the house, our mother was free to pursue her amorous career; would she present us with a new stepfather on Labor Day, someone too young and handsome to seem quite respectable?

One afternoon, while the other boys were off on a canoe trip, my counselor showed me some "art photographs" he'd taken, all of a naked young man on a deserted beach. The cabin was quiet, the light dim as it filtered down through the old pines and the half-closed shutters, the blanket on Mr. Stone's bed rough under my bare legs as I sorted through the large, glossy prints. I'd never seen a naked adult man before; I became so absorbed in the pictures that the cabin vanished and I was there before the model on that clean white sand. My eyes were drawn again and again to his tanned back and narrow, intricate, toiling white hips as he ran away from me through a zone of full sunlight toward a black, stormy horizon. Where was this beach and who was this man? I wondered; as though I could find him there now, as though he were the only naked man in the world and I must find him if I were to feel again this pressure on my diaphragm, this sensation of sinking, these symptoms of shame and joy I fought to suppress lest Mr. Stone recoil from me in horror as it dawned on him my reactions were not artistic. Was my fascination with the model abnormal?

Mr. Stone inched closer to me on the bed and asked me what I thought of his art photographs. I could feel his breath on my shoulder and his hand on my knee. A thrill of pleasure rippled through me. I was alarmed. I stood, walked to the screen door, made a display of casualness as I stooped to scratch a chigger bite on my ankle. "They're neat, real neat, catch you later, Mr. Stone." I hoped he hadn't noticed my excitement.

At that age I had no idea that hair could be bleached, a tan nursed, teeth capped, muscles acquired; only a god was blond, brown, strong and had such a smile. Mr. Stone had shown me a god and called it "art." Until now, my notions of art had all been about castles in the sand or snow, about remote and ruthless monarchs, about power, not beauty, about the lonely splendors of possession, not the delicious, sinking helplessness of yearning to possess. That young man pacing the beach—with knees that seemed too small for such strong thighs, with long, elegant feet, with a blur of light for a smile, a streak of light for hair, white pools of light for eyes, as though he were being lit suddenly from within that delicately modeled head poised on a slender neck above shoulders so broad he'd have to grow into them—that young man came toward me with a beauty so unsettling I had to call it love, as though he loved me or I him. The drooling adult delectation over particular body parts (the large penis, the hairy chest, the rounded buttocks) is unknown to children; they resolve the parts into the whole and the physical into the emotional, so that desire quickly becomes love. In the same way love becomes desire—hadn't I desired Fred, Marilyn, my German professor?

I went running through the woods. The day was misty; someone had seen a bear eating blueberries and I turned every time I heard a branch snap. A thread of smoke emerged from a dense stand of pine trees across the lake. After I passed the rotting stump and the white flowers beside it I felt as though I'd pressed through a valve into my own preserve and I slowed down to a walk. I stopped to breathe and I heard a woodpecker far away, knocking softly, professionally, auscultating a hollow limb. The trees, interpreting the wind, swayed above me.

Where the path crossed the logger's road, Ralph was sitting in a sort of natural hummock created by the exposed roots of an old elm. He had his pants down around his knees and was examining his erect penis with a disbelieving curiosity, a slightly stunned look emptying his face. He called me over and I joined him, as though to examine a curiosity of nature. He persuaded me to touch it and I did. He asked me to lick the red, sticky, unsheathed head and I hesitated. Was it dirty? I wondered. Would someone see us? Would I become ill? Would I become a queer and never, never be like other people?

To overcome my scruples, Ralph hypnotized me. He didn't have to intone the words long to send me into a deep trance. Once I was under his spell he told me I'd obey him, and I did. He also said that when I awakened I'd remember nothing, but he was wrong there. I have remembered everything.

# FIVE

If my sister was happy with other girls in the summer, in the winter she sat home night after night waiting for boys to ask her out on dates she dreaded. Our mother had moved us into a large apartment and furnished it luxuriously—but no one came to visit. By now my sister was certain I was the one who'd been hurting her chances. With a brother so weird, who was in no way athletic or cool or neat, no wonder she had a reputation for being out of it.

Since my sister was only four years older than I, she knew precisely what would appeal to my classmates—what sort of penny loafers, which red-and-white-checked short-sleeved shirt, what style of jeans, what manner of low-key joshing. She helped me buy the right clothes and she showed me how to wear them ("You've got to roll up the sleeves exactly three times—the folds should be tight, see?—and no more than an inch wide"). She taught me to say hi to as many people as possible in the school corridors, to notice with care who responded and to brave each blank stare with a glittery smile.

I kept a phone list of the people I thought I knew well enough to call in the afternoon and evening, and I'd work my way down systematically through all the names. Soon the list was so long, a good thirty names, that I needed three days to complete a full cycle. "Hi, it's me. What are you doing? Yeah, I mean right now—what'd you think I meant, stupid? Geez . . . chewing gum? You call that doing something? Naw . . . I'm staying in. My mom's on my back about the old homework. 'Sides, there's that weird new sci-fi thing on TV—yeah, that's the one.

You? Janey coming over to study? I like that blue sweater she had on, but the black loafers looked sort of hoody. I *know* she's not a hood—just see you two on a motorcycle, vrmm, vrmm—can you picture it? You are there: vrmm, vrmm."

And so on for hours, pure ventriloquism, nausea of small talk, a discipline nearly Oriental in its exclusion of content and its focus on empty locutions, the chatter of social fear confused with yearning, for I not only feared my friends, I also wanted to make them love me.

Until now, until this great conversion, friendship for me had been more a minor pleasure than a science. Friends had been people to sit with in the cafeteria, people who had the same hobbies or the same study hall, boys equally hopeless in gym class or girls in assembly whose last names started with the same letter as mine. I hadn't courted those acquaintances. I made no effort to draw them out, to elicit or reflect on their confidences, or to advise them. I required almost nothing of them, for if I wasn't attentive neither was I demanding. Practically anyone could be my friend. For me friendship was an innocent, unconscious habit that didn't confer prestige on anyone, that led nowhere, that scarcely bore thinking about, unremarkable as breath.

When my sister taught me ways to be popular she was teaching me something I hadn't known about. She filled a need the instant she created it. Or perhaps I should say she taught me that the loneliness I felt like a bad burn could be soothed. I most certainly had been lonely. I had ached and writhed with loneliness, twisting around and smearing it on me as though it were a tissue of shame pouring out of my body: shameful, familiar, the fell of shame. And yet the company I longed for, the radiant face smiling down into mine, the arm around my shoulders (an arm so lean every vein could be read through it, as light can be seen between marks on vellum)—in my daydreams this company came to me unbidden. The notion that I might have been able to court friends, win attention, conjure it, would have spoiled it for me. Unbidden love was what I wanted. Under my sister's tutelage I learned that love or at least friendship must be coaxed, that there are skills (listening, smiling, remembering, flattering) that lure it closer. Sometimes, as I learned, a friend is no more than someone to kill time with, a voice chattering into the receiver a litany of questions, all those lumpy sandbags—individually light but cumulatively heavy—that hang from the girdle around the balloon's suspended car to slow its ascent into cold, unbreathable solitude. But the very act of enticing friendship, of managing and conducting it, the whole politics of sentiment—well, I didn't despise it, for how could I despise what I needed so much?

While I was growing up I had never glimpsed the underbrush of kid society that lay just behind the topiary of the classroom. Dumb me—I'd just assumed the kids knew only whoever happened to be in their homeroom. Nor did I suspect some kids saw each other every day after school, and saw each other strolling under a shifting leaf spray of social lights and sexual shadows, imprints of illumination that had nothing to do with the grid of adult arrangements. A popular boy named Butch was the son of a bone surgeon; his girl was the daughter of a delivery man.

They made love every afternoon in the basement of her house. By the time they were fifteen they'd already been lovers for three years and their friends regarded them as older and wiser mentors—parents, really—to whom they could turn for advice. We'd all drop by her house around four-thirty or five. She and he would be coming up out of the basement, smiling, flushed, his fingers on his fly buttons, hers tugging her tartan skirt a quarter-circle around so that the giant safety pin would be on the right side. Then she'd bake chocolate chip cookies while he horsed around outside with a football. Our own parents had only to say a word to us to inject scalding resentment into our veins, but these lesser, better parents, matured not by years but by passion and its induction into sadness, seemed to be mild guardians, he with his chipped tooth and froth of sweat curls above his neck, she with the childhood scar that drew a silky white stitch through one eyebrow and with the melancholy smile. Even the suppers we sat down to of cold milk and hot cookies pocked with runny chocolate were wonderfully unhealthy parodies of nursery meals.

At first I didn't know how to become really popular. The other kids had grown up together and they just more or less accepted one another. Of course, some of them worked at being popular, but others preferred watching TV alone in the afternoons while drinking beer and some had special interests (sewing, dramatics, yearbook, world affairs) that drew them off into tight little groups too peripheral to count. Still others, by virtue of a sudden blossoming into physical beauty or athletic prowess, became leaders without worrying about it. But that left the whole middle ground of those of us with no strange little niche and no inherent distinction (except brains, possibly, or money, neither of which carried much weight), and for us the only way to win popularity was through "personality." Girls, of course, had personality more than boys, but some boys had personality, too, as a jester has jokes or a seducer sherry. Something bogus, that is, something shameful.

I set my sights on the most popular boy in the whole school. I figured that if I could hoodwink him into being my friend, people would have to accept me. I think my strategy, on the whole, was sound. Since I wasn't athletic, I had nothing to offer other people beside the flattering mirror of my attention, a service that suited my sweet, devious nature.

I can't really remember how I met Tommy. I recollect him first as a smooth cloche of shiny light brown hair sporting the slender plume of a cowlick, a head bent over a book in study hall belonging to someone I'd heard was captain of the tennis team, leader of the Crowd and Sally's steady; then, without transition, he was my friend and he was struggling to explain to me his theory about Sartre's *Nausea* as we kicked our way through autumn leaves. "Uh . . . uh . . ." he was crying out on a loud, high note, a sustained nasal sound, as he stopped walking and held a finger up. Then his small blue eyes, straining to see an idea in the distance, blinked, glanced smoothly up and down. The glitter of prophecy faded. He shrugged: "Lost it."

He exposed his palms and then pocketed his hands in his trousers. I held my breath and counted ten before I offered my soft, apologetic suggestion: "But aren't you really saying that Sartre thinks man is . . ." and I filled in the blank with the closest approximation I could invent, not of Sartre's thought, but of Tommy's dubious interpretation of it.

"That's it! That's it!" Tommy shouted, and again he excitedly waded out into the philosophical murk. I, who thought only of survival, had no interest in philosophical questions. The proximate ones were enough to obsess me, not as things I chose to contemplate, but as decisions rushing up at me as out of oncoming traffic. These were the things I thought about: Am I boring Tommy? Will he mind if I rest my elbow on his shoulder? Should I powder my white bucks or keep the scuff marks? How low should I let my jeans ride?

If the ultimate questions—the meaning of life, time, being— interested me now, it was only because they interested Tommy. To the extent the other kids thought of me at all they considered me to be something of a brain; certainly in their eyes Tom was a jock. Ironic, then, that he was the one who did all the thinking, who had the taste for philosophy—ironic but predictable, since his sovereignty gave him the ease to wonder about what it all meant, whereas I had to concentrate on means, not meaning. The meaning seemed quite clear: to survive and then to become popular. The game of monarch I'd played in the snow or sand or in cloud castles now became real. The princess, asleep for so many years, awakes to the taste of the prince's lips, a slightly sour taste; she stares up into a face visored in shadow.

In that old, comfortable suburb even the biggest mansions hunkered democratically down on the curb and sat right next to other dwellings. No concealing hedges or isolating parks could be seen anywhere. Even quite massive houses of many rooms and wings engulfed their plots down to the sidewalk. This conspicuousness declared a pride and innocence: we have nothing to hide, and we want to show you what we've got. Tom's house was a Mediterranean villa with six bedrooms and servants' quarters over a double garage, but its gleaming leaded panes and the front door (thick oak gouged into griffins) loomed up just ten paces from the street.

Once inside that door, however, I felt transported into another society that had ways I could never quite master. The Wellingtons were nice but not charming. The Wellingtons gave thought to everything they did. The staircase was lined with expensive, ugly paintings done from photographs of their four children. Their kids' teeth were bound in costly wires, their whims for sailboats or skis or guitars were lavishly but silently honored, they were all paraded in a stupor past the monuments of Europe, their vacations down rapids and over glaciers or up mountains were well funded—but silence reigned. No one said a word.

Dinner there was torture. A student from the university served. Mr. Wellington carved. Mrs. Wellington, a woman with a girlish spirit trapped inside a large, swollen body, made stabs at conversation, but she was so shy she could speak only in comical accents. She'd grunt in a bass voice like a bear or squeak like a mouse or imitate Donald Duck—anything rather than say a simple declarative sentence in her own fragile, mortified voice. The father terrified us all with his manners (the long white hands wielding the fork and knife and expertly slicing the joint). He radiated disapproval. His disapproval was not the martyr's blackmail but a sort of murderous mildness: if he weren't so fastidious he'd murder you. We watched him carve. We were wordless, hypnotized by the candle flames, the neat incisions and deep, bloody invasions, the sound of the metal knife scraping against the tines of the fork, the sickening softness of each red slice laid to the side and the trickle down silver channels ramifying back into a bole of blood.

The odd thing is that the father's spirit did not contaminate the house. His lair, the library, was even the sunniest, most relaxed room of all as the two little dogs, Welsh corgies, trotted from couch to front door at every disturbance, their small, shaggy feet clicking on the polished red tiles. The dogs, the children, his wife—all seemed to prosper in spite of his punitive reserve, his tight eyes, the way he sniffed with contempt at the end of every sentence someone else said. "Oh yes," he said to me, examining his overly manicured hand, "I know of your mother . . . by reputation," and my heart sank.

In this house the parents maintained a silence except for the father's dreaded little comments, the sugar substitute of his sweetness, and the whole chirping menagerie of the mother's comical voices. No one hovered over the kids. They came and went as they chose, they stayed home and studied or they went out, they ate dinner in or at the last moment they accepted the hospitality of other tables. But under this superficial ease of manner ran their dread of their father and their fear of offending him in some new way. He was a man far milder, far more (shall I say) ladylike than any other father I'd known, and yet his soft way of curling up on a couch and tucking his silk dressing gown modestly around his thin white shanks terrified everyone, as did his way of looking over the tops of his glasses and mouthing without sound the name of his son: "Tom-my"—the lips compressed on the double *m* and making a meal out of his swallowed, sorrowing disappointment. He was homely, tall, snowy-haired, hardworking, in bad health. He seemed to me the absolute standard of respectability, and by that standard I failed. My sister had coached me in some sort of charm, but no degree of charm, whether counterfeit or genuine, made an impression on Mr. Wellington. He was charm-proof. He disapproved of me. I was a fraud, a charlatan. His disapproval started with my mother and her "reputation," whatever that might refer to (her divorce? her dates? the fact she worked?). He didn't like me and he didn't want his son to associate with me. When I entered his study I'd stand behind Tom. Only now does it occur to me that Tommy may have liked me precisely because his father didn't. Was Tom's friendship with me one more way in which he was unobtrusively but firmly disappointing his father?

Once we closed Tom's bedroom door we were immersed again in the happy shabbiness of our friendship. For he was my friend—my best friend! Until now other boys my age had frightened me. We might grab each other in the leaves and play Squirrel; Ralph might have hypnotized me, but those painful stabs at pleasure had left me shaken and swollen with yearning—I wanted someone to love me. Someone adult. Someone under my power. I had prayed I'd grow up as fast as possible.

No longer. For the first time I found it exhilarating to be young and with someone young. I loved him, and the love was all the more powerful because I had to hide it. We slept in twin beds only two feet apart. We sat around for hours in our underpants and talked about Sartre and tennis and Sally and all the other kids at school and love and God and the afterlife and infinity. Tom's mother never came to his door, as mine would have, to order us to sleep. The big dark house creaked around us as we lay on our separate beds in zany positions and talked and talked our way into the inner recesses of the night, those dim lands so tender to the couple.

And we talked of friendship, of our friendship, of how it was as intense as love, better than love, a kind of love. I told Tom my father had said friendships don't last, they wear out and must be replaced every decade as we grow older—but I reported this heresy (which I'd invented; my poor father had no friends to discard) only so that Tom and I might denounce it and pledge to each other our eternal fidelity. "Jesus," Tom said, "those guys are so damn *cynical*! Jeez . . ." He was lying on his stomach staring into the pillow; his voice was muffled. Now he propped himself up on one elbow. His forehead was red where he'd been leaning on it. His face was loose from sleepiness. His smile, too, was loose, rubbery, his gaze genial, bleary. "I mean, God! How can they go on if they think that way?" He laughed a laugh on a high brass note, a toot of amazement at the sheer gall of grown-up cynicism.

"Maybe," I said suavely, "because we're not religious, we've made friendship into our religion." I loved ringing these changes on our theme, which was ourselves, our love; to keep the subject going I could relate it to our atheism, which we'd just discovered, or to dozens of other favorite themes.

"Yeah," Tom said. He seemed intrigued by this possibility. "Hold on. Don't forget where we were." He hurried into the adjoining bathroom. As I listened through the open door to the jet of water falling into the toilet, I imagined standing beside him, our streams of urine crossing, dribbling dry, then our hands continuing to shake a final glistening drop of something stickier than water from this new disturbance, this desire our lifting, meeting eyes had to confess.

No sooner would such a temptation present itself than I would smother it. The effect was of snuffing out a candle, two candles, a row of twenty, until the lens pulled back to reveal an entire votive stand exhaling a hundred thin lines of smoke as a terraced offering before the shrine. In this religion hidden lights had been declared superior to those that glared. Somewhere I was storing up merit, accumulating the credit I'd need to buy, one day, the salvation I longed for. Until then (and it was a reckoning that could be forestalled indefinitely, that I preferred putting off) I'd live in that happiest of all conditions: the long but seemingly prosperous courtship. It was a series of tests, ever more arduous, even perverse. For instance, I was required to deny my love in order to prove it.

"You know," Tom said one day, "you can stay over any time you like. Harold"—the minister's son, my old partner at Squirrel—"warned me you'd jump me in my sleep. You gotta forgive me. It's just I don't go in for that weird stuff."

I swallowed painfully and whispered, "Nor—" I cleared my throat and said too primly, "Nor do I."

The medical smell, that Lysol smell of homosexuality, was staining the air again as the rubber-wheeled metal cart of drugs and disinfectants rolled silently by. I longed to open the window, to go away for an hour and come back to a room free of that odor, the smell of shame.

I never doubted that homosexuality was a sickness; in fact, I took it as a measure of how unsparingly objective I was that I could contemplate this very sickness. But in some other part of my mind I couldn't believe that the Lysol smell must bathe me, too, that its smell of stale coal fumes must penetrate my love for Tom. Perhaps I became so vague, so exhilarated with vagueness, precisely in order to forestall a recognition of the final term of the syllogism that begins: If one man loves another he is a homosexual; I love a man . . .

I'd heard that boys passed through a stage of homosexuality, that this stage was normal, nearly universal—then that must be what was happening to me. A stage. A prolonged stage. Soon enough this stage would revolve, and after Tom's bedroom vanished, on would trundle white organdy, blue ribbons, a smiling girl opening her arms . . . But that would come later. As for now, I could continue to look as long as I liked into Tom's eyes the color of faded lapis beneath brows so blond they were visible only at the roots just to each side of his nose—a faint smudge turning gold as it thinned and sped out toward the temples.

He was a ratty boy. He hated to shave and would let his peach fuzz go for a week or even two at a time; it grew in in clumps, full on the chin, sparse along the jaw, patchy beside the deep wicks of his mouth. His chamois-cloth shirts were all missing buttons. The gaps they left were filled in with glimpses of dingy undershirt. His jockey shorts had holes in them. Around one leg a broken elastic had popped out of the cotton seam and dangled against his thigh like a gray noodle. Since he wore a single pair of shorts for days on end, the front pouch would soon be stained with yellow. He got up too late to shower before school; he'd run a hand through his fine hair but could never tame that high spume of a cowlick that tossed and bobbed above him, absurdly, gallantly.

His rattiness wore a jaunty air that redeemed everything. Faded, baggy jeans, Indian moccasins he'd owned so long the soft leather tops had taken on the shape of his toes, sunglasses repaired with Band-Aids, an ancient purple shirt bleached and aged to a dusty plum, a letter jacket with white leather sleeves and on the back white lettering against a dark blue field— these were the accoutrements of a princely pauper, a paupered prince.

We walked beside the lake at night, a spring night. As we walked we rolled gently into each other, so that our shoulders touched with every other step. A coolness scudded in off the lake and we kept our hands in our pockets. Now Tom had leaped up onto the narrow top of a retaining wall and was scampering along it in his moccasins. Although heights terrified me I followed him. The ground on both sides fell away as we crossed a canal flowing into the lake, but I put one foot in front of the other and looked not down but at Tom's back. I prayed to a God I didn't believe in to preserve me. Soon enough I was beside Tom again and my pulse subsided: that dangerous crossing was a sacrifice I'd made to him. Our shoulders touched. As usual he was talking too loud and in his characteristic way, a sustained tenor *uh* as he collected his thoughts, then a chuckle and a rapid, throw-away sentence that came almost as an anticlimax. Since Tom was the most popular boy at school, many guys had imitated his halting, then rushing way of talking (as well as his grungy clothes and haphazard grooming). But I never wanted to be Tom. I wanted Tom to be Tom for me. I wanted him to hold his reedy, sinewy, scruffy maleness in trust for us both.

We were heading toward a concrete pier wide enough for a truck to run down. At the far end people were fishing for smelt, illegal lanterns drawing silver schools into nets. We ambled out and watched the lights play over that dripping, squirming ore being extracted from the lake's mines. A net was dumped at my feet and I saw that cold life arc, panic, die. Tommy knew one of the old guys, who gave us a couple dozen fish, which we took back to the Wellingtons' place.

At midnight everyone was in bed, but Tom decided we were hungry and had to fry up our smelt right now. The odor of burning butter and bitter young fish drew Mrs. Wellington down from her little sitting room where she dozed, watched television and paged through books about gardening and thoroughbred dogs. She came blinking and padding down to the kitchen, lured by the smell of frying fish, the smell of a pleasure forbidden because it comes from a kingdom we dare not enter for long. I was certain she would be gruff—she was frowning, though only against the neon brightness of the kitchen. "What's going on here?" she asked in what must have been at last the sound of her true voice, the poor, flat intonations of the prairies where she'd grown up. Soon she was pouring out tall glasses of milk and setting places for us. She was a good sport in an unselfconscious way I'd never seen in a grown-up before, as though she and we were all part of the same society of hungry, browsing creatures instead of members of two tribes, one spontaneous and the other repressive. She seemed to bend naturally to the will of her son, and this compliance suggested an unspoken respect for the primacy of even such a young and scruffy man. My own mother paid lip service to the notion of male supremacy, but she had had to make her own way in the world too long to stay constant to such a purely decorative belief.

After the midnight supper Tommy started to play the guitar and sing. He and I had trekked more than once downtown to the Folk Center to hear a barefoot hillbilly woman in a long, faded skirt intone Elizabethan songs and pluck at a dulcimer or to listen, frightened and transported, to a big black lesbian with a crew cut moan her basso way through the blues. The People—those brawny, smiling farmers, those plump, wholesome teens bursting out of bib overalls, those toothless ex-cons, those white-eyed dust bowl victims—the People, half-glimpsed in old photos, films and WPA murals, were about to reemerge, we trusted, into history and our lives.

All this aspiration, this promise of fellowship and equality, informed Tom's songs. We worried a bit (just a bit) that we might be suburban twerps unworthy of the People. We already knew to sneer at certain folk singers for their "commercial" arrangements, their "slickness," their betrayal of the heartrending plainness of real working folks. Although we strove in our daily lives to be as agreeable and popular as possible, to conform exactly to reigning fads, we simultaneously abhorred whatever was ingratiating. We were drawn to a club where a big, scarred Negro with lots of gold jewelry and liverish eyes ruminated over a half-improvised ballad under a spotlight before a breathless, thrilled audience of sheltered white teens (overheard on the way out from the newly elected president of our United

Nations Club: "It makes you feel so damn phony. It even makes you Question Your Values").

Of course, the best thing about folk music was that it gave me a chance to stare at Tommy while he sang. After endless false starts, after tunings and retunings and trial runs of newly or imperfectly learned strums, he'd finally accompany himself through one great ballad after another. His voice was harsh and high, his hands grubby, and soon enough his exertions would make the faded blue work shirt cling to his back and chest in dark blue patches. Whereas when he spoke he was evasive or philosophical, certainly jokey in a tepid way, when he sang he was eloquent with passion, with the simple statement of passion. And I was, for once, allowed to stare and stare at him.

Sometimes, after he fell asleep at night, I'd study the composition of grays poised on the pale lozenge of his pillow, those grays that constituted a face, and I'd dream he was awakening, rising to kiss me, the grays blushing with fire and warmth—but then he'd move and I'd realize that what I'd taken to be his face was in fact a fold in the sheet. I'd listen for his breath to quicken, I'd look for his sealed eyes to glint, I'd wait for his hot, strong hand to reach across the chasm between the beds to grab me—but none of that happened. There was no passion displayed between us, and I never saw him show any feeling at all beyond a narrow range of teasing and joking.

Except when he sang. Then he was free, that is, constrained by the ceremony of performance, the fiction that the entertainer is alone, that he is expressing grief or joy to himself alone. Tom would close his eyes and tip his head back. Squint lines would stream away from his eyes, his forehead would wrinkle, the veins would stand out along his throat and when he held a high note his whole body would tremble. One time he proudly showed me the calluses he'd earned by playing the guitar; he let me feel them. Sometimes he didn't play at all but just sounded notes as he worked something out. He had forgotten me. He thought he was alone. He'd drop the slightly foolish smile he usually wore to disarm adolescent envy or adult expectation and he looked angry and much older: I took this to be his true face. As a folk singer Tom was permitted to wail and shout and moan and as his audience I was permitted to look at him.

His father invited me to go sailing. I accepted, although I warned him I was familiar only with powerboats and had had no experience as a crew member. Everything about dressing the ship—unshrouding and raising the sails, lowering the keel, installing the rudder, untangling the sheets—confused me. I knew I was in the way and I stood, one hand on the boom, trying to inhale myself into nonexistence. I heard Mr. Wellington's quick sharp breaths as reproaches.

The day was beautiful, a cold, constant spring wind swept past us, high towers of clouds were rolling steadily closer like medieval war machines breaching the blue fortress of sky. Light spilled down out of the clouds onto the choppy lake, gray and cold and faceted, in constant motion but going nowhere. Hundreds of boats were already out, their sails pivoting and flashing in the shifting beams of sunlight. A gull's wings dropped like the slowly closing legs of a draftsman's compass.

At last we were under way. Mr. Wellington, unlike my father, was a smooth, competent sailor. He pulled the boat around so that the wind was behind us and he asked me to attach the spinnaker pole to the jib sail, but I became frightened when I had to lean out over the coursing water and Tommy filled in for me, not vexed at me but, I suspect, worried about what his father would think. And what was I afraid of? Falling in? But I could swim, a rope could be tossed my way. That wasn't it. Even my vertigo I had overcome on the seawall for Tom's sake. It was, I'm sure, Mr. Wellington's disapproval I feared and invited, that disapproval which, so persistent, had ended by becoming a manner, a way of being, like someone's way of holding his head to one side, something familiar, something I would miss if it were absent. Not that he bestowed his disapproval generously on me. No, even that he withheld and dispensed in only the smallest sums.

The wind blew higher and higher and Mr. Wellington, who'd taken in sail, was holding close to it. We gripped the gunwales and leaned back out over the cold, running waves, the water brushing, then soaking the backs of our shirts. The sun solemnly withdrew into its tent of cloud, disappointed with the world. By the slightest turn of my head I could change the moan of the wind into a whistle. There we were, just a father and his teenage son and the son's friend out for a sail, but in my mind, at least, the story was less simple. For I found in this Mr. Wellington a version of myself so transformed by will and practice as to be not easily recognizable, but familiar nonetheless. He had never been handsome, I was certain, and his lack of romantic appeal shaded his responses to his glamorous son, the muted, wary adoration as well as the less than frank envy.

I'd begun to shiver. The day was turning darker and had blown all the birds out of the sky and half the boats back to harbor. I was huddling, hugging myself down in the hull, wet back to the wind. Mr. Wellington was letting out sail—the tock-tock-tock of the winch releasing the mainsheet—and he was looking at me, holding his judgment in reserve. Between us, these two tight minds, flew the great sail and Tom haunting it as he leaned back into it, pushing it, pushing until we came around, he ducked and the boom swung overhead and stopped with a shocking thud. Here was this boy, laughing and blonded by the sun and smooth-skinned, his whole body straining up as he reached to cleat something so that his T-shirt parted company with his dirty, sagging jeans and we—the father and I—could see Tom's muscles like forked lightning on his taut stomach; here was this boy so handsome and free and well liked and here were we flanking him, looking up at him, at the torso flowering out of the humble calyx of his jeans.

It seemed to me then that beauty is the highest good, the one thing we all want to be or have or, failing that, destroy, and that all the world's virtues are nothing but the world's spleen and deceit. The ugly, the old, the rich and the accomplished speak of invisible virtues—of character and wisdom and power and skill—because they lack the visible ones, that ridiculous down under the lower lip that can't decide to be a beard, those prehensile bare feet racing down the sleek deck, big hands too heavy for slender arms, the sweep of lashes over faded lapis-

lazuli eyes, lips deep red, the windblown hair intricate as
Velázquez's rendering of lace.

THAT SUMMER I spent with my father; I worked the Addressograph machine and I hired a hustler, who was as blond as Tommy.
When I returned home to my mother I was a bit smug—but also
frightened by the tenacity of my homosexual yearnings.

One fall evening Tom called me to ask if I'd like to go out on
a double date. He'd be with Sally, of course, and I'd be with
Helen Paper. Just a movie. Maybe a burger afterward. Not too
late. School tomorrow. Her regular date had come down with a
cold.

I said sure.

I dashed down the hall to tell my mother, who in a rare do-
mestic moment had a sewing basket on her lap. Her glasses had
slid down to the tip of her nose and her voice came out slow
and without inflection as she tried to thread a needle.

"Guess what!" I shouted.

"What, dear?" She licked the thread and tried again.

"That was Tom and he arranged a date for me with Helen Paper, who's the most beautiful and sophisticated girl in the
whole school."

"Sophisticated?" There, the thread had gone through.

"Yes, yes"—I could hear my voice rising higher and higher;
somehow I had to convey the excitement of my prospects—
"she's only a freshman but she goes out with college boys and
everything and she's been to Europe and she's—well, the other
girls say top-heavy but only from sour grapes. And she's the
leader of the Crowd or could be if she cared and didn't have
such a reputation."

My mother was intent upon her sewing. She was dressed to
go out and this, yes, it must be a rip in the seam of her raincoat;
once she'd fixed it she'd be on her way. "Wonderful, dear."

"But isn't it exciting?" I insisted.

"Well, yes, but I hope she's not too fast."

"For me?"

"For anyone. In general. There, now." My mother bit the

thread off, her eyes suddenly as wide and empty and intelligent as a cat's. She stood, examined her handiwork, put the coat on, moved to the door, backtracked, lifted her cheek toward me to peck. "I hope you have fun. You seem terribly nervous. Just look at your hands. You're wringing them—never saw anyone literally wring his hands before."

"Well, it's terribly exciting," I said in wild despair.

My sister wasn't home, so I was alone once my mother had gone—alone to take my second bath of the day in the mean, withholding afternoon light permeating the frosted glass window and to listen to the listless hum of traffic outside, in such contrast to my heart's anticipation. It was as though the very intensity of my feeling had drained the surroundings of significance. I was the unique center of consciousness, its toxic concentration.

I was going out on a date with Helen Paper and I had to calm myself by then because the evening would surely be quicksilver small talk and ten different kinds of smile and there would be hands linking and parting as in a square dance you had to be very subtle to hear called, subtle and calm. I wanted so badly to be popular, to have the others look back as I ran to catch up, then to walk with my left hand around his waist, the right around hers, her long hair blown back on my shoulder, pooling there for a moment in festive intimacy, a sort of gold epaulet of the secret order of joy.

I had spent so much of my childhood sunk into a cross-eyed, nose-picking turpitude of shame and self-loathing, scrunched up in the corner of a sweating leather chair on a hot summer day, the heat having silenced the birds, even the construction workers on the site next door, and delivering me up to the admonishing black head of the fan on the floor slowly shaking from left to right, right to left to signal its tedious repetition of no, no, no, and to exhale the faintly irritating vacillations of its breath. No, no, no—those were the words I repeated to myself, not with force but as a Jesus prayer of listless grief. Energy in itself is a sort of redemption. No wonder we admire Satan. But if the Devil were listless, if he were a pale man in his underwear who watched television by day behind closed venetian blinds— oh, if that were the Devil I would fear him.

That's what Being Popular seemed to promise, a deliverance from the humiliation of daily life, its geological torpor, the dailiness that rusts the blade of resolve and rots the stage curtain, that fades all colors and returns all fields to pasture. Being popular was equivalent to becoming a character, perhaps even a person, since if to be is to be perceived, then to be perceived by many eyes and with envy, interest, respect or affection is to exist more densely, more articulately, every last detail minutely observed and thereby richly rendered. I knew that my sister wasn't popular, at least not at school. She sat at home night after night and no matter how she styled her hair or wore her skirts she looked unliked, dowdy with dislike.

Our mother told us she'd been popular as a girl, but she had grown up on a farm where families did everything together. How could I explain to her how much things had changed, that we kids scarcely admitted we had parents, that to us parents were as uninteresting as the rich in novels about backstairs life; they were large naïve personages who ask irrelevant questions from time to time and from whom the truth must always be kept. In particular the logical or at least consistent standards of adults, their admiration of money, of substance, of homely virtue, were valuable to us kids precisely as rules to flout, for our preferences in clothes, music, people were rigorously whimsical.

As long as I remained unpopular I belonged wholely to my mother. I might fight with her, insult her, sneer at her, ignore her, but I was still hers. She knew that. She even had a way of swaggering around me. There was a coarseness in the speculations she made about me to my face, the way an owner might talk about a horse in its stall. At times she insisted that I had a great future ahead of me, by which she meant a job and a salary, but just as often she'd look at me and ask, "Do you think you're really bright?" Quick smile. "Of course you are.

You're very very bright." Pause. "But I wonder. *We* think you are. But shouldn't we have a second opinion? One that's more objective?"

She subjected herself to the same doubts—I was so completely hers that I had to eat what she ate, even her self-hatred, as a fetus must live off its host's blood. The great event of our household had been that my father had left us for someone else. Afterward, how could we like each other all that much, since we were all equally guilty of having driven him away? At least, we'd failed to keep him. Nor was our shared fate black as good ink or crisp as a crow's wing on snow; we hadn't been assigned clear, tragic roles we could play with any sort of despairing joy. Instead, we'd been shamed and we'd become vacant, neglected, shabby with neglect. I don't mean to say that we exhibited interesting symptoms or made trouble for anyone. But we were shadows, like the dead after Orpheus passes them on his way through the Underworld, after this living man vanishes and the last sound of his music is lost to the incoming silence. All my life I've made friends and lost lovers and talked about these two activities as though they were very different, opposed; but in truth love is the direct and therefore hopeless method of calling Orpheus back, whereas friendship is the equally hopeless because irrelevant attempt to find warmth in other shades. Odd that in the story Orpheus is lonely, too.

HELEN PAPER had a wide, regal forehead, straight dark hair pulled back from her face, curiously narrow hips and strong, thin legs. She was famous for the great globes of her breasts, as evident as her smile and almost as easy to acknowledge and so heavy that her shoulders had become very strong. How her breasts hung naturally I had no way of knowing, since in her surgically sturdy brassiere her form had been idealized into — well, two uncannily symmetrical globes, at once proud, inviting and (by virtue of their symmetry) respectable.

But to describe her without mentioning her face would be absurd, since everyone was dazzled by those fine blue eyes, harder or perhaps less informative than one would have anticipated, and by that nose, so straight and classical, joined to the forehead without a bump or transition of any sort, the nose a prayer ascending above the altar of lips so rich and sweet that one could understand how men had once regarded women as spoils in wars worth fighting. She was a woman (for she surely seemed a woman despite her youth) supremely confident of her own appeal, her status as someone desirable in the abstract, that is, attractive and practicable to anyone under any conditions at any time, rather than in the concrete, to me now as mine. She wasn't shy or passive, but to the extent she was a vessel she was full to the brim with the knowledge that she represented a prize. She was the custodian of her own beauty.

She acted as though she were royalty and being beautiful a sort of trooping the colors. At any rate, I once watched her through a window (she didn't know I was there) and she was acting very differently. She was with just one other person, a girl from school, and they were on the floor in front of the television with beers and a big bowl of popcorn. It was a summer night and it must have been very late and they were laughing and laughing. Helen Paper, wearing just shorts and halter, was sprawled on the floor sick with laughter, in a squalor of laughter. She kept saying, "Stop or you'll make me pee."

Our date was quick, unremarkable (it's the particular curse of adolescence that its events are never adequate to the feelings they inspire, that no unadorned retelling of those events can suggest the feelings). Tommy's mother collected us all in her car (we were still too young to drive) and deposited us at the theater. Green spotlights buried in fake ferns in the lobby played on a marble fountain that had long since been drained. The basin was filled with candy wrappers and paper napkins. Inside, behind padded doors each pierced by a grimy porthole, soared the dark splendors of the theater brushed here and there by the ushers' traveling red flashlights or feebly, briefly dispelled by the glow of a match held to a forbidden cigarette. The ceiling had been designed to resemble the night sky, the stars were minute bulbs, the moon a yellow crescent. To either side of the screen was a windswept version of a royal box, a gilt throne on a small carpeted dais under a great blown-back stucco curtain topped by a papier-mâché coronet. When I finally held Helen Paper's hand after sitting beside her for half an hour in the dark, I said to myself, "This hand could be insured for a million dollars."

She surrendered her hand to me, but was I really a likely candidate for it? Was this the way guys became popular? Did certain girls have the guts to tell everyone else, "Look, be nice to this guy. He's not a nerd. He's worth it. He's special"? Or was this date merely some extraordinary favor wangled for me by Tommy, something that would not be repeated? Could it be (and I knew it could) that the Star Chamber of popularity was sealed and that no one would be admitted to it—no one except some casual new prince who belonged there?

Tommy was a prince. He had a knack for demanding attention; even when he called the telephone operator for a number, he'd hold her in conversation. Once he even talked her into meeting him after work. The receptionists in offices downtown, salesladies in stores, the mothers of friends—all of them he sized up, mentally undressed, and though this appraisal might seem to be rude, in fact most women liked it. An efficient woman would be sailing past him. He'd grab her wrist. He'd apologize for the intrusion, but he'd also stand very close to her and his smile wouldn't apologize for a thing. And she, at exactly the moment I would have expected outrage, would flush, her eyes would flutter, not in an experienced way but meltingly, since he'd touched a nerve, since he'd found a way to subvert the social into the sexual—and then she'd smile and rephrase what she was saying in a voice charmingly without conviction.

After the movie we went somewhere for a snack and then I walked Helen home. Her beauty stood between us like an enemy, some sort of hereditary enemy I was supposed to fear, but I liked her well enough. Even the fiercest lovers must like each other at least once in a while. The trees arching above the deserted suburban streets tracked slowly past overhead, their crowns dark against a hazy white night sky, clouds lit up like internal organs dyed for examination, for augury . . . I spoke quietly, deliberately, to Helen Paper and I snatched glances of her famous smile rising to greet my words. Our attention wasn't given over to words but to the formal charting of that night street that we were executing. I mean we, or rather our bodies, the animal sense in us, some orienting device—we were discovering each other, and for one moment I felt exultantly worthy of her. For she did have the power to make me seem interesting, at least to myself. I found myself talking faster and with more confidence as we approached the wide, dimly lit porch of her house. Some late roses perfumed the night. A sprinkler someone had left on by mistake played back and forth over the grass. A sudden breeze snatched up the spray and flung it on the walkway ahead, a momentary darkening of the white pavement. Inside, upstairs, a room was just barely lit behind a drawn curtain. Crickets took the night's pulse.

Although I said something right out of dancing school to Helen—"Good night, it's been great to spend some time with you"—an unexpected understanding had fallen on us. Of course her allure—the sudden rise and fall of her wonderful soft breasts, the dilation of her perfume on the cool night air, the smile of a saint who points, salaciously, toward heaven—this allure had seduced me entirely. I loved her. I didn't know what to do with her. I suspected another, more normal boy would have known how to tease her, make her laugh, would have treated her more as a friend and less as an idol. Had I been expected to do something I would have fled, but now, tonight, I did love her, as one might love a painting one admired but didn't, couldn't, wouldn't own. She was completely relaxed when she took my hand and looked in my eyes, as she thanked me and bobbed a curtsy in a little-girl manner other men, I'm sure, liked better than I; sensing my resistance to anything fetching, she doubled back and intensified her gravity. By which I'm not suggesting she was playing a part. In fact, I don't know what she was doing. Because I loved her she was opaque to me, and her sincerity I doubted not at all until I doubted it completely.

I thanked her and I said I hoped I'd see her soon. For a moment it seemed as though it would be the most natural thing to kiss her on those full, soft lips (had I not seen her a moment ago covertly pop some scented thing into her mouth to prepare for just such an inevitability?). Her eyes were veiled with her awareness of her own beauty. I suppose I suddenly liked myself and I could see a light in which I'd be plausible to others. My love for Tommy was shameful, something I was also proud of but tried to hide. This moment with Helen—our tallness on the moon-lashed porch, the cool winds that sent black clouds (lit by gold from within) caravelling past a pirate moon, a coolness that glided through opening fingers that now touched, linked, squeezed, slowly drew apart—this moment made me happy, hopeful. An oppression had been lifted. A long apprenticeship to danger had abruptly ended.

After I left her I raced home through the deserted streets laughing and leaping. I sang show tunes and danced and felt as fully alive as someone in a movie (since it was precisely life that was grainy and sepia-tinted, whereas the movies had the audible ping, the habitable color, the embraceable presence of reality). I was more than ready to give up my attraction to men for this marriage to Helen Paper. At last the homosexual phase of my adolescence had drawn to a close. To be sure, I'd continue to love Tommy but as he loved me: fraternally. In my dream the stowaway in the single bunk with me, whom I was trying to keep hidden under a blanket, had miraculously transformed himself into my glorious bride, as the kissed leper in the legend becomes Christ Pantocrator.

When I got home my mother was in bed with the lights out. "Honey?"

"Yes?"

"Come in and talk to me."

"Okay," I said.

"Rub my back, okay?"

"Okay," I said. I sat beside her on the bed. She smelled of bourbon.

"How was your date?"

"Terrific! I never had such a good time."

"How nice. Is she a nice girl?"

"Better than that. She's charming and sophisticated and intelligent."

"You're home earlier than I expected. Not so hard. Rub gently. You bruiser. I'm going to call you that: Bruiser. Is she playful? Is she like me? Does she say cute things?"

"No, thank God."

"Why do you say that? Is she some sort of egghead?"

"Not an egghead. But she's dignified. She's straightforward. She says what she means."

"I think girls should be playful. That doesn't mean dishonest. I'm playful."

"_____"

"Well, I am. Do you think she likes you?"

"How can I tell? It was just a first date." My fingers lightly stroked her neck to either side of her spine. "I doubt if she'll want to see me again. Why should she?"

"But why not? You're handsome and intelligent."

"Handsome! With these big nostrils!"

"Oh that's just your sister. She's so frustrated she has to pick on you. There's nothing wrong with your nostrils. At least I don't see anything wrong. Of course, I know you too well. If you like, we could consult a nose doctor." A long pause. "Nostrils . . . Do people generally dwell on them? I mean, do people think about them a lot?" Small, high voice: "Are mine okay?"

A hopeless silence.

At last she began to snore delicately and I hurried to my own room. My sister's door, next to mine, was closed but her light was burning resentfully.

And I gave myself over to my reverie. I had a record player I'd paid for myself by working as a caddy and records I exchanged each week at the library, the music an outpost of my father's influence in this unmusical female territory.

I slipped out of my clothes as quickly as possible, though I tried to do everything beautifully, as in a movie of my life with Helen. In some way I felt it was already being filmed—not that I looked for hidden cameras but I simplified and smoothed out my movements for the lens. There were those, my mother and sister, who suffered too much and were too graceless to be film-worthy, but there were those others I aspired to join who suffered briefly, consolably and always handsomely, whose remarks were terse and for whom the mechanics of leaving a party or paying a bill had been stylized nearly out of existence in favor of highly emotional exchanges in which eyes said more than lips. Every detail of my room asked me to be solicitous. When the dresser drawer stuck I winced—this sequence would have to be reshot. I turned my sheets down as though she, Helen, were at my side. I rushed to snap off the lights.

She and I lay side by side in the narrow boat and floated downstream. The stars moved not at all and only the occasional fluttering of a branch overhead or the sound of a scraping rock below suggested our passage. The moon was the wound in the night's side from which magic blood flowed; we bathed in it. By dawn I'd made love to Helen four times. The first time was so ceremonial I had a problem molding the mist into arms and legs; all that kept flickering up at me was her smile. The second time was more passionate. I was finally able to free her breasts from their binding. By the third time we'd become gently fraternal; we smiled with tired kindness at each other. We were very intimate. At dawn she began to disintegrate. The certainty of day pulsed into being and all my exertions were able to keep her at my side only a few more moments. At last she fled.

I stumbled from class to class in a numb haze. Strangely enough, I was afraid I'd run into Helen. I didn't feel up to her. I was too tired. In homeroom I yawned, rested my head on my desk and longed for the privacy of my bed and the saving grace of night. I wanted to be alone with my wraith. In my confusion the real Helen Paper seemed irrelevant, even intrusive.

That night I wrote her a letter. I chose a special yellow parchment, a spidery pen point and black ink. In gym class as I'd stumbled through calisthenics and in study hall as I'd half dozed behind a stack of books, phrases for the letter had dropped into my mind. Now I sat down with great formality at my desk and composed the missive, first in pencil on scratch paper. If I reproduced it (I still have the pencil draft) you'd laugh at me or we would laugh together at the prissy diction and the high-flown sentiment. What would be harder to convey is how much it meant to me, how it read to me back then. I offered her my love and allegiance while admitting I knew how unworthy of her I was. And yet I had half a notion that though I might be worthless as a date (not handsome enough) I might be of some value as a husband (intelligent, slated for success). In marriage merits outweighed appeal, and I could imagine nothing less eternal than marriage with Helen. Naturally I didn't mention marriage in the letter.

A week went by before I received her answer. Twice I saw her in the halls. The first time she came over to me and looked me in the eye and smiled her sweet, intense smile. She was wearing a powder blue cashmere sweater and her breasts rose and fell monumentally as she asked me in her soft drawl how I was doing. Nothing in her smile or voice suggested a verdict either for or against me. I felt there was something improper about seeing her at all before I got her letter. I mumbled, "Fine," blushed and slinked off. I felt tall and dirty. I was avoiding Tommy as well. Soon enough I would have to tell him about my proposal to Helen, which I suspected he'd disapprove of.

Then one afternoon, a Friday after school, there was her letter to me in the mailbox. Even before I opened it I was mildly grateful she had at least answered me.

The apartment was empty. I went to the sunroom and looked across the street at the lake churning like old machinery in a deserted amusement park, rides without riders. My mind kept two separate sets of books. In one I was fortunate she'd taken the time to write me even this rejection, more than a creep like me deserved. In the other she said, "You're not the person I would have chosen for a date, nor for a summer or semester, but yes, I will marry you. Nor do I want anything less from you. Romance is an expectation of an ideal life to come, and in that sense my feelings for you are romantic."

If someone had made me guess which reply I'd find inside the envelope, I would have chosen the rejection, since pessimism is always accurate, but acceptance would not have shocked me, since I also believed in the miraculous.

I poured myself a glass of milk in the kitchen and returned to the sunroom. Her handwriting was well formed and rounded, the dots over the $i$'s circles, the letters fatter than tall, the lines so straight I suspected she had placed the thin paper over a ruled-off grid. The schoolgirl ordinariness of her hand frightened me—I didn't feel safe in such an ordinary hand. "I like you very much as a friend," she wrote. "I was pleased and surprised to receive your lovely letter. It was one of the sweetest tributes to me I have ever had from anyone. I know this will hurt, but I am forced to say it if I am to prevent you further pain. I do not love you and I never have. Our friendship has been a matter of mutual and rewarding liking, not loving. I know this is very cruel, but I must say it. Try not to hate me. I think it would be best if we did not see each other for a while. I certainly hope we can continue to be friends. I consider you to be one of my very best friends. Please, please forgive me. Try to understand why I have to be this way. Sincerely, Helen."

Well, her phrasing was less childish than her hand, I thought, as though the letter were a composition in class that concerned me in no way. Even as this attitude broke over me but before I was drawn into another, more troubling one, I had time to notice she said I was one of her very best friends, an honor I'd been unaware of until now, as who had not: I registered the social gain before the romantic loss. Unless (and here I could taste something bitter on the back of my tongue)—unless the "mature" advice ("I think it would be best if we did not see each other for a while") was actually a denial of the consolation prize, a way of keeping me out of her circle at the very moment she was pretending to invite me into it. Could it be that the entire exercise, its assured tone, the concision and familiar ring of the phrasing, figured as nothing more than a "tribute" (her word) she had piled up before the altar of her own beauty? How many people had she shown my letter to?

But then all this mental chatter stopped and I surrendered to something else, something less active, more abiding, something that had been waiting politely all this time but that now stepped forward, diffident yet impersonal: my grief.

For the next few months I grieved. I would stay up all night crying and playing records and writing sonnets to Helen. What was I crying for? I cried during gym class when someone got mad at me for dropping the basketball. In the past I would have hidden my pain but now I just slowly walked off the court, the tears spurting out of my face. I took a shower, still crying, and dressed forlornly and walked the empty halls even though to do so during class time was forbidden. I no longer cared about rules. I let my hair grow, I stopped combing it, I forgot to change my shirt from one week to the next. With a disabused eye I watched other kids striving to succeed, to become popular. I became a sort of vagabond of grief or, as I'd rather put it, I entered grief's vagabondage, which better suggests a simultaneous freedom and slavery. Freedom from the now meaningless pursuit of grades, friends, smiles; slavery to a hopeless love.

Every afternoon I'd stumble home exhausted to my room, but once there my real work would begin, which was to imagine Helen in my arms, Helen beside me laughing, Helen looking up at me through the lace suspended from the orange-blossom chaplet, Helen with other boys, kissing them, unzipping her shorts and stepping out of them, pushing her hair back out of her serious, avid eyes. She was a puppet I could place in one playlet after another, but once I'd invoked her she became independent, tortured me, smiled right through me at another boy, her approaching lover. Her exertions with other men fascinated me, and the longer I suffered, the more outrageous were the humiliations I had other men inflict on her.

I became ill with mononucleosis, ironically the "kissing disease" that afflicted so many teenagers in those days. I was kept out of school for several months. Most of the time I slept, feverish and content: exempted. Just to cross the room required all my energy. Whether or not to drink another glass of ginger ale could absorb my attention for an hour. That my grief had been superseded by illness relieved me; I was no longer willfully self-destructive. I was simply ill. Love was forbidden—my doctor had told me I mustn't kiss anyone. Tommy called me from time to time but I felt he and I had nothing in common now—after all, he was just a boy, whereas I'd become a very old man.

# SIX

The more isolated I became, the more incapable I thought I was of resisting my homosexual fate. I blamed my sister and my mother—my sister for eroding my confidence (as though homosexuality were a form of shyness) and my mother for babying me (homosexuality as prolonged infancy). At the same time I recognized that my mother was my best and truest friend, that she alone fretted over my health, listened to my term papers, waited up for my return, attempted to understand my enthusiasms.

In my immense world-weariness I decided to become a Buddhist. My mother had for years encouraged my sister and me to find a church of our own, one that answered our real needs. True to type, my sister in her burrowing if vexed drive toward normality had become a Presbyterian. The local church had the most affable, crew-cut minister (former football coach) and the most prestigious congregation (semi-believers in a heaven of jocks, a hell of brains and a purgatory of friendless stay-at-homes).

I interpreted my mother's mandate in a different way. I spent day after day at the library reading through Max Müller's *Sacred Books of the East* as one might try on clothes—but isn't Hinduism just a bit busy? Confucianism? Too sensible, no flair.

But Buddhism appealed to me. Not in its later, elaborated northern form, the Mahayana with its infinite regress of paradises, its countless bodhisattvas (those compassionate midwives), its efficacious prayers and praying effigies given over to the pornography of worship, squirming nude maidens representing the anima straddling the erect lingam of the meditating animus. No, what I liked was the earlier Hinayana, those austere instructions that lead to an extinction of desire (in Sanskrit, *nirvana* means "to extinguish," as one might blow out a candle flame). I felt a strong affinity to this curiously life-hating religion that teaches us we have no soul and that the self is merely a baggage depot where random parcels have been checked (labeled *emotions, sensations, memories* and so on) soon enough to be collected by different owners, an emptying out that will leave the room blissfully vacant. That emptiness, that annihilation is what the Christian most dreads but the Buddhist most earnestly craves—or would if craving itself were not precisely what must be extirpated. Desire—hankering after sex, money, fame, security— ties us to the world and condemns us to rebirth; "the cycle of rebirth" I pictured as a wheel on which the sinner was stretched and bound, the wheel that crushed him as it turned but cruelly failed to kill him.

I felt the need to free myself of desire. I must not want anything. I must feel no attachments. Above all, no attractions. I must give up all hope, plans, glad anticipations. I must study oblivion. I must give room and board to silence and pay tuition to the void. Even the slightest flicker of longing must be stilled. Every wire must be pulled until the console goes dead and all dials point to zero.

My mother discovered a Buddhist church some thirty miles away. She gamely drove me down to it one Sunday (*Sunday!* I mentally sniffed, already the ascetic snob; *Church!* I exclaimed, an Oriental purist). On the preceding Saturday night I dreamed of opening wicker gates, the process shot as the wizened abbot walks toward me on a treadmill, getting nowhere fast against a rear projection of a retreating, expanding universe of thickening blue sandalwood incense and swaying, saffron-robed monks.

Instead I encountered a congregation of grinning Japanese families in a former Baptist church and heard announcements of the Young Buddhists Association's annual picnic and basketball practice as well as disappointingly melodic hymns with words such as "Dearest Amida, Your Light Is Shining Through the Gloomy World of Sin" sung by us all to a wheezing organ accompaniment, then a tedious sermon on the evils of adultery. I fled, red-cheeked and offended, my puzzled mother reluctantly following me ("But I liked it, dear. It seemed so Christian, though of course they were much better dressed than your average Christian").

I desperately needed a new beginning. The thought of resuming my life made me want to end it—unless I could change it completely. If my homosexuality was due to a surfeit of female company at home (for so ran the most popular psychological theory of the day), then I should correct the imbalance by entering an all-male world. In order to become a heterosexual I decided I should attend a boys' boarding school (for so ran my wonderfully logical addendum to the theory). I phoned my father long-distance and pleaded with him to help me escape my mother. Whereas I loved her I dreaded her mysterious influence, as though she were a plant like rhubarb, stalk nourishing, leaves poisonous.

"I don't think you should talk about your mother that way, young fellow," my father said. "She's a fine woman." I heard him gasp as he drew on his cigar. I could picture him at his blond mahogany desk. Perhaps he'd rolled up a pipe cleaner into a hoop and was throwing it for his cat, Baby, to fetch while *my* cat, Herr Pogner, stretched on the sill, yawned, raised her fluffy tail and arched her feathery back, then sank down on all fours, front paws neatly tucked under her downy tortoiseshell chest. The smell of the cigar, the way my father tilted his head back so that he could watch through the close-up lenses of his bifocals as Baby batted the pipe cleaner across his desk, scattering business papers as she went, then tumbled over the edge onto the carpet, then dashed off to a corner (look down, through the upper lenses), the distant drone of a carpet sweeper a black maid was pushing downstairs—this whole dense world came rushing back toward me with his first words.

"But, Daddy," I exclaimed, my voice breaking and rising up, up the scale into a soprano delirium, "I *love* my mother."

"Like. Like," he said. "A man likes things. Girls love, men like."

"But that's just the *problem*," I wailed. "I'm too involved with Mommy. I'm not"—and here I put the decisive card on the table—"I'm not turning out . . . as I should. I need to be with men."

Long pause. The faint transmitted sound of the sweeper had died away. A click revealed to me that my stepmother had picked up on an extension phone. Three pairs of eyes blinked as three hands held three silent receivers.

"I need male role models," I said, delighted that I had remembered the very word my mother liked to use.

"Role what?" my father asked, annoyed. "To hell with that." I subsided into silence.

Then suddenly he and I were both speaking at once, both stopped, he resumed: "As I was saying, you could come live here, I suppose."

"That would never work. You're always at the office, Daddy. Last summer we were in the same house three months and I didn't spend more than an hour with you altogether. You slept all day. I was working the Addressograph machine. No, what I want is to go to a boarding school. I want to live with a bunch of guys my own age and just, well, learn sports"—could he tell how much I was lying? I ended on a rehearsed phrase—"and be with the *fellows*. You know."

"Don't say 'you know.' Poorly educated people say it all the time. It becomes a habit."

"Yes, sir." I could imagine him lighting a new cigar, twirling the brown baton for an even fire, filling the room with thick smoke that engulfed the fussy Herr Pogner on her perch, her gold eyes squinting through that noxious cloud.

"I don't want to make a decision over the phone. Put it all in writing. Can you type?"

"No, sir."

"You must learn. There are only two useful things to be learned in school, typing and public speaking. Before you're graduated I want you to study both. So, print your letter. I want it to be very neat, as neat and businesslike as you can manage, and in it you should present all your arguments for going away to school. Then go to the public library and read through the guide to private schools and pick one. Got it? I'm not promising anything but I'll consider your proposal carefully."

The guide devoted a page to each school. In each case it presented black-and-white photographs of the grounds and buildings, a portrait of the headmaster and a brief description of the "philosophy" of the institution. For hours I'd muse over this volume of future lives, weighing one possibility against another. Did I want to be a senator? Should I attend a school in Washington? A general? Military academy? A monk? I read of a school where each student served as an acolyte at least once a week, since all the priests (the teachers) had to say Mass daily. I pictured a long row of side chapels in a ruined priory on the coast of New England, the aisles invaded at vespers by mist as dense as wool and by sheep as white as mist, seagulls cooing on the hundred altars, hungrily darting forward to snatch at the Host, the surf pounding out a solemn "Dies Irae" as the funeral procession of a dead brother wound its way over fallen columns up toward the marine cemetery. Or did I need the permissiveness of a Quaker school, all plain wood in clear light, the patrician simplicity that only money can buy?

The question turned out to be, well, academic. My father chose a school for me merely because it was on the route between his winter and summer houses, a convenient stopover on the long trip for him. Right after Christmas he drove me to the deserted campus, the buildings shrouded in snow like chairs in holland cloth, the rectilinear paths treacherously iced over, the wide-open square, originally designed to resemble a piazza, now an arctic court where the snow played handball with itself, white sports whirling up off the pavement and racing to slam glittering explosions on brick walls tenoned in ice.

The architecture of the school had been conceived by a famous Finn and built by an army of Scots who'd stayed on as gardeners and maintenance men (they outnumbered the teachers). The school was nothing but reminiscence—of an Italian hill town, a French abbey, an English academy, the different sources improbably but convincingly melded into a fantasy about the classic sites of Europe as imagined by exiles from cold peripheral lands, nostalgia for someone else's past. Because the school was a fantasy and not a reality, its architecture alternated as in a dream between vague, featureless expanses of wall, the ectoplasmic surround of the action, and by contrast the places the dreamer looks at, concentrates on: maniacally detailed ornaments, chiseled gargoyle heads peering down out of the odd niche, tiled Moorish arches framing a rose garden, scriptural and classical mottoes spelled out in stone along the backs of benches. Those benches circled a deep basin surmounted by a fountain as wide as a barber pole and much taller on which was balanced a stone pineapple that expressed, depending on how literally one took the conceit, either juice or water.

The headmaster of Eton (yes, the name, too, had been borrowed) was a great shaggy and strangely yellowed man. He wore tweeds and smoked a pipe and had pale, glutinous hands—really as sticky and shiny as the gluten in kneaded bread—and yellowing white hair that shot straight back from his liver-spotted brow and huge yellow teeth that looked useless for eating though effective enough for polite baring in interviews with intimidated parents. He was tall and unctuous and unintelligent and lived in a rambling "cottage" with fieldstone walls, low black eaves that curled back under on themselves like ingrown toenails, and leaded panes that rattled decoratively in the winter winds in front of solid, modern, cryptically sealed storm windows.

He granted us a long interview in which he spoke of the need for "balance" in the training of a young mind and (looking appraisingly over the top of his glasses) of the young male body. A little later he found a way of mentioning again the sound mind that should go with the sound (raised eyebrows) body. I was terrified that what all this meant was more athletics for me, and it did. But my father was pleased, more or less. He distrusted the headmaster's English accent and melodious voice issuing from someone so obviously weak and fraudulent and American. Dad sniffed a little laugh at all the dark wood, dark sherry, crackling fire of small, evenly matched birchwood logs laid on brass andirons, the whole instant tradition of dear Eton, Anglican primroses amidst the alien corn. But even as he sniffed he nodded approval, for the pretensions were exactly what he was buying for his son, much as a cowpuncher might hire a French tutor for his children—airs fit an heir, even if distasteful to the patriarch.

The headmaster philosophized about manliness over a feminine clutter of tea things, tiny pots of marmalade, eggshell-thin cups, a linen-lined basket of warm scones and a cozy embroidered on one side with an Art Deco archer kneeling nudely in Aztec profile, crossbow aimed at a five-pointed Gentile star (the archer was the school emblem, *ad astra* the motto). My father puffed skeptically on his smelly cigar, by now a misshapen stub black with spit, and asked for a scotch and soda. For my father, sitting uncomfortably in that petit-point chair without arms, manliness was not discussable, but had it been, it would have included a good business suit, ambition, paying one's bills on time, enough knowledge of baseball to hand out like tips at the barbershop, a residual but never foolhardy degree of courage, and an unbreachable reserve; to the headmaster manliness was discussed constantly, every day, and entailed tweeds, trust funds, graciousness to servants, a polite but slightly chilly relationship to God, a pretended interest in knowledge and an obsessive interest in sports, especially muddy, dangerous ones like lacrosse or hockey or rugby that ended with great sullen lads hobbling off the field to lean on sticks at the sidelines, the orange and blue vertical stripes of their jerseys clinging to panting diaphragms, bare knees scarred, blond hair brown with sweat, an Apache streak of mud daubed across a wan, bellicose cheek.

I was starting school in the middle of the year and knew no one. Two other fourth-formers were also entering between semesters, and they became my companions. One, whose room was just next door, had a Spanish mother. I once caught a glimpse of her trim body in a black suit, her glossy, painted red lips barely visible through the bouquet of violets she was sniffing to distract herself during a dull sermon in the school chapel, her eyes lifting and hanging there like amber worry beads bright from having been told so often. Heberto had those same fine eyes and his mother's olive skin and those teeth as white as the apples he was always eating. He was just fourteen and still at times a silly kid, especially just before lights-out. We had half an hour (if you please) of "free" time after evening study hall before we had to submit to silence, a rustling, Argus-eyed silence (if Argus was a lonely, horny tribe of kids) intensified by wide-awake yearning. In that brief spasm of freedom before lights-out, competing radios would blare out, tuned to a dozen different stations, and pent-up athletes, sore from two hours of immobility at their desks, would explode into shouting football matches in the corridors. Toilets flushed, steam from showers crept out of the bathrooms into the unheated corridors. In one room five boys were sitting around in the dark lighting farts. One expert—fully clothed of course—was lying on his back, legs above his head, holding a lit match to the seat of his pants. A quick spurt of blue flame was his reward. The whole building trembled with the thundering of boys climbing up and down stairs or now shrieking in a water fight by the cooler.

Heberto was also full of energy. Look at the vein pulsing in his neck, the aimless trills his long fingers are playing, the weird ululations hooting out of his mouth—until after the fact he invents an explanation of all this spontaneity by resolving himself into an airplane, the hoots modulating into the drone of jets, his flickering hands freezing into rigid wings, the ticking vein force-feeding fuel into the engine as he runs and runs, hysterical with youth, up and down the halls. After such an outburst he could be visited. I'd sit on his bed and watch him carve bits of balsa wood with an X-Acto knife. His eyes would dart up from his task. Everything about him was high-strung, tentative, off course. I never found out why he'd been shunted off to Eton in the middle of the year.

The other newcomer, Howie, was my real companion, friend and enemy, someone whose room I couldn't resist visiting though I didn't want the other kids to see me going there.

Howie had been a bleak, sit-in-a-stupor nihilist, he told me, but now he'd ascended to the discipline and heartlessness of the Nazi Party. A real Nazi. He'd written away for the "literature" of the American Renaissance Party and proudly showed me his foot-long library of books on race, the Aryan heritage, the Führer's legacy, Communist lies about the "so-called death camps" and so on. He was almost as fat as he was tall. His eyes blinked and glowered and squinted and widened in mocking wonder behind the intense magnification of his glasses, but once denuded they lost all power of expression and seemed as pale and vulnerable as new skin under a bandage. Although he'd never traveled anywhere he was teaching himself French and of course German; he had pinned up photos of Berchtesgaden and the Riviera over his desk. He brewed espresso in a tin Napoletano that, when reversed, threw sputtering drops onto the glowing coils of the strictly forbidden hot plate, and he played over and over again his one record of Juliette Greco, the chanteuse beloved of the existentialists, the waif who'd emerged out of the ruins of war with black eyes all pupils and lyrics all plangent, tough-guy sentimentality. Howie's ties came from Charvet on the Place Vendôme because that had been Proust's haberdasher.

He and I shared the irregular, never-foreseen status of students too clever for afternoon study hall and too inept for afternoon sports. As a result we alone were free to spend those long vacant hours from two to six in the empty dorms or, when the weather was good, on walks through the baronial grounds of the estate. The weather, however, was usually polar and he and I then found our exercise in stubborn, smoldering debates about equality and democracy (I for, he against). I can still taste the bitter black coffee and hear the jolly accordion and sweeping strings of Juliette Greco's accompaniment, music we'd have sneered at as polka-Polish or Hollywood-snythetic had it not been French, but that, since it was, we relished and hummed along to though neither of us was ever quite capable of translating the words ("Something . . . something . . . if you something I'll always? *Toujours?* Is that *toujours?* Play it again").

Howie had a face only a medieval Japanese woman could have loved: perfectly round, pasty, just a wisp of fine hair above, below a dark, tiny dead rosebud of a mouth, the rudiment of a chin, like a child's hand poking through a sheet, and those eyes, so arrogant and expressive with glasses, so myopic and defenseless without.

"No, I *don't* concede your point. Not at all," he'd say, lowering his head so that the child's hand poked farther out through the sheet and his voice, naturally high and nervous, took on a swallowed, subdued tone. "In fact," he'd add, letting his features become beatifically composed, "I think you're a fool."

I could hardly breathe. And yet, calling to me across the smoking valley sang a soprano telling me how exciting all this was, this verbal game that could at any moment take a nasty turn but that as of now remained a parody of spite. Until now I'd never known anyone my own age who was so willing to flout the bland convention that held that the normal unit of conversation should be the unfunny joke and the expected response a mirthless giggle. Howie didn't want to be liked, or if he did, then only after I'd passed tests calculated to eliminate anyone with the least bit of pride.

Despite my fears and my aching loneliness, I believed without a doubt in a better world, which was adulthood or New York or Paris or love. But Howie just as stubbornly knew things wouldn't work out. He was convinced he'd die before he was twenty. He knew people weren't equal, that they were wired for hatred, that they were glandularly incapable of decency and that any semblance of goodness had to be attributed to the last vestiges of hypocrisy that fools were tearing away, like gauze from a mummy—not, as we'd been assured, perfectly preserved but rather compounded of dust and rot.

He had put on his large pale green officer's hat with the mirror-shiny black visor and the pewter swastika and now he was striding about the dorm room slapping his boots with a crop. Everything in sight—the single cot, the piles of books on the desk, the mirror above the dresser, the rugless floor, the simple muslin cloth on big wood rungs that concealed the narrow opening to the walk-in closet—everything was spotless as it had to be for morning inspections, but everything smelled of a sulfurous acne cream. Howard was striding back and forth, his glasses slipping down his nose, his pale, pudgy knuckles dimpling and paling still whiter where he grasped the crop. He was laughing in short, metallic bursts.

And yet he was someone I could talk to about Rimbaud, the poet who'd conquered Paris or at least Verlaine by age sixteen (I was fifteen—a year to go). I'd sneak into the bathroom after lights-out and sit on the toilet behind a locked stall door and read "The Drunken Boat" or "The Poet at Age Seven" or best of all "A Season in Hell" and I'd glance back and forth in my bilingual edition from the smooth French gallop to the jarring English trot, every night hoping to change magically our bony native nag for the sleek back of that Gallic charger but always falling off in midstream, unseated—or rather seated on that hardwood toilet seat, my eyes burning from the strain of reading by the light of a single dim ceiling bulb, my bare chest covered with goose bumps from the night chill and my left leg asleep, a horrible slab of dead beef to be dragged down the corridor until life sparkled back into it. Then I'd lie under covers in the darkness and conspire to be great: I must run away tomorrow, to New York, poems in hand, scorn and genius in my heart, an amiable, infatuated older lover within my grasp . . . It always disturbed me that Rimbaud was the infernal bridegroom, Verlaine the foolish virgin. Perhaps such a reversal of traditional roles shocked my bourgeois heart, or perhaps their truth came too close to my fondest if most dangerous fantasy, the one in which I'd no longer be the obliging youth but the harsh young lord, the prince with the pewter ornament stuck in his hat, my older lover helpless, betrayed . . .

Howard and I would fight and not speak to each other for a week, and then I was truly alone. Although I'd been popular for a moment back home, my suffering over Helen Paper and my bout of mononucleosis had caused me to lose my social nerve. I now looked back on those days at public school when I'd said hi to so many people as a fabulous era. I'd been rich and famous and young, before this long, bitter decline I'd entered, this threnody I'd become. Now I was living in shadow between two radiances, the mythic past and the mythic future, the past the dreamlike, confusing story of injured love, the future a cheerful, perfectly crisp fable of love about to be crowned, and this contrast, this partitioning of time into genres, articulated a sense of duration, of endured if not always endurable history.

I suffered now. I felt isolated to the point of craziness, but with a faint recourse to melodrama, to a potential audience and an attendant end to loneliness, for if I imagined *complete* despair I pictured it as an emptying of the theater, a feeling that the stalls and boxes would never be peopled again but would vacantly surround the stage on which the sole actor writhes and sobs, then sleeps, then wakes to speak in a voice he need no longer project. I hadn't reached that point. I was conscious of the emblem of proud and tragic loneliness I was embroidering stitch by stitch before the eyes of the other boys. Every time I crossed the wintry quadrangle alone or sat alone in my room during free period (but with a door open to expose my solitude) I knew I was drawing another silk thread through the cloth.

By day I gave myself over to a covert yearning for men. I'd linger in the locker room and study the brawny back of a senior, a body builder, a German with blond hair greased into symmetrical waves, with a faint dusting of brown hair on his shoulders and (he's turning around, he drops his towel) with an almost pinkish red puff of seemingly rootless pubic hair somehow floating in a cloud of smoke above his penis, as though the big gun had just been fired. In the shower room I'd linger as long as possible and watch the water turn wintry chalk into summer marble. Imprisoned under all our layers of long underwear, thick socks, shirts, vests, jackets, coats and hoods were these tropical bodies; the steam and hot water brought color back into the pallor, found the nacreous hollow in a hip, detected the subtly raised triceps, rinsed a sharp clavicle in a softening flood, swirled dull brown hair into a smooth black cap and pulled evening gloves of light over raw hands and skinny, blue-veined forearms.

Just as each shell held to the ears roars with a different ocean timbre, each of these bodies spoke to me with a different music, though all sounded to me unlike my own and only with the greatest effort could I remember I was longing after my own sex. Indeed, each of these beings seemed to possess his very own sex: the Italian with the hairy butt, thick legs and jaw darkened by a four if not yet five o'clock shadow; or take the blond darling of the football team with the permanent blush in his full cheeks, the distrustful smile of someone hard of hearing and the smooth, fleshy body and incipient beer belly resplendent with quivering health, feminine on a Rubens scale were it not for the way he moved—pigeon-toed athlete's walk and lordly rocking tilt from side to side, something stiff in the back and shoulders and floppy in the hands and arms, loose ribbons around the rigid maypole.

I've heard that some boys' boarding schools are continuous orgies, that jealous rivals explode in fistfights over the favors of stunning first-form fags, that arrogant head prefects move favorites into their suites and exile castoffs without even a nod toward adult authority—but Eton was not like that at all. Half the students were day boys who had cars, families and girlfriends and came back every Monday with stories of wild heterosexual weekends. Each boarding student had his own room and the halls were periodically patrolled after lights-out. On Saturday night the students from our sister school were bused over for movies or dancing and under the gaze of chaperones romances sprang up between boys and girls even if they were seldom consummated. Who will ever know if any of those Eton boys ever longed for one another as they lay sleepless in their separate cells, each strumming the guitar of sex and humming who knows what tune or if they felt desire as I did during wrestling practice for the wiry, crew-cut boy with the sand in his eyes and the bluish false teeth that had replaced those lost in a bloody match last year, a boy who seemed to be everywhere at once and who, in spite of the sleepiness of his expression, crackled like a field of static electricity above me, a shower of sparks in gym shorts as he darted all over, found the exact point of leverage and effortlessly pulled me down. The Russians practice a kind of photography, called Kirlian, that reveals the subject's aura, the varying patterns of radiant heat projected by his limbs as a kind of oriflamme, if that means the golden banner a knight wraps himself in. For me every male body inhabited just such a rippling flag, just such a field of force invisible to all eyes but mine—but to mine resplendent and dangerous, a smooth sheath though upon close inspection engraved with fine lines of tension. How else can I explain the way I'd swallow hard and begin to lose my sense of balance whenever one of these enigma machines came toward me?

At that time I had a book on Rodin. Every afternoon I'd sit on my cot and look at a black-and-white photograph of an early sculpture, *The Age of Bronze,* a nude study of a Belgian soldier so realistic that the artist had been accused of casting it from life. I didn't masturbate over that picture, nor did I imagine coupling with the statue or the soldier. No, I loved him and I told him so, again and again, in whispers that never sounded right because I could never figure out who I was—his son? wife? brother? enemy? husband? friend? And there was the other problem of the century that separated me from the long-dead model and of the continent from the distant replica. I told myself that if I ever found him I'd know how to love him, but I had mistaken yearning for talent and I'd neglected to sort out the most essential thing, my own identity. Perhaps that's why I'd become so enamored of a statue, for with it the only amorous activity could be the circle of my steps around that still form. No encounter, no vying for position, no chance of perfect understanding or total confusion. That is, everything suspenseful and mutable about the society of lovers had been eliminated in favor of an embrace as simple and unvarying (as eternal) as it had necessarily to be cold. Or perhaps I worried that if I had a real, living lover I'd wound him, subject him to all the rage I'd been saving up.

Yes, I spent my days thinking about male bodies, each of which was as varied, as sequential as a long Chinese scroll through which the minuscule pilgrim travels in his straw hat, followed by a servant and a horse, now standing back from the steaming falls, now meditating cross-legged under a grass roof held up by bamboo poles as he surveys the valley filling up with mist or as he throws his head back in wild spiritual hilarity in response to the grandeur of the mountain or here, down here, where he's picking at his rice in the company of monks in the long, narrow hall opened up to the sweet, gasped *Oh!* of the full moon and the long exhaled *Ah-h-h* of its reflection in the pond. If I could have lain in a bed beside any of these boys I jostled past every day, whose feet I had to sit on while they did sit-ups or whom I sat beside, shoulder to shoulder, during chapel, I would have explored him just as the Chinese pilgrim traversed that majestic, intimidating terrain to whose rhythm he hoped to adjust himself and from which he expected to take a wisdom not quite tenable.

At night I'd pull the covers up to my chin in the cold and listen to the momentary gust of laughter outside as a master and his wife bade farewell to another couple after a late dinner ("Thanks, Rachel." "So long, Hal"). Car doors slammed. A cold motor struggled to turn over. Success. Lights on. Motor in gear. Final farewells. Then a handkerchief of brightness was drawn across my ceiling, next the magician pulled a beige out of the white, a gray out of the beige, finally black from gray. On that ultimate cloth I tossed the dice: I began to meditate.

I threw back the blankets, took off my pajama top and, shivering but determined to master mere flesh, sat cross-legged on my cot. I knew nothing of bona fide Oriental procedures, but I made up my own from scraps of information I'd gathered here and there, overheard table talk at the banquet of bliss. Not limber enough to hook my feet over my thighs, I contented myself with a drooping lotus and pressed my hands together in my lap, thumb tip to thumb tip, second joints of my fingers united (the "people" inside the "church" of a more Christian childhood game). I proceeded to regulate my breathing through my nose, careful siphoning off of aerial fuel, and while I concentrated on its flow my eyes turned upward and inward to the roots of my eyebrows until my eyes ached and I feared that they'd stick there, that I'd stay cross-eyed for life. Nor could I help wondering how I'd look to an observer, drugged lids over white crescents.

Much as I focused on my breathing my thoughts would nevertheless rub against homework or hyperspace off into a new dimension and start drifting down to pinkish red pubic hair, or they'd curl like a morning glory around the simple picket of a noise in the hall (whose footsteps?). As long as I gave myself commands to breathe I could almost exclude distractions, as though I were pressing a door against an invader, but then the ghost of an idea would float right through the door, I'd become distracted, soon the door was swinging wide open on its hinges, a hog was sniffing the floor for food, all was quietly, bucolically lost and whatever was vegetative in me had engulfed whatever had been vertebrate—which in any case had begun to ache and arc in response to the tropisms of the flesh.

But one night I soared. My brain, which ordinarily had too much resonance in it so that every thought boomed and echoed muzzily without definition, tonight had acquired an acoustical sharpness; I could actually *hear* my thoughts as they rose and fell. And it seemed I hovered energetically over myself, ready to play my mind as a nervous but competent pianist might do, fingers flexing hungrily above the keys. But the real difference was one of attitude: I'd decided to take the very futility I so often felt, the vacant hum, the sense of subsisting outside whatever was vibrant and to equate precisely this secular emptiness with the sacred void, to make of my shame a jewel, to call my poverty wealth. If most of the time I saw myself as my sister's despicable little brother, the nerd who smelled bad and walked and talked funny, tonight I stumbled on the happy idea of, yes, redefining this same insufficiency as a proof of salvation: the famous emptiness of the Buddha. Of course I admitted that nirvana was rest and what I knew was torment, that Gautama wanted nothing and I everything, that I was crawling with desire—but couldn't this very excruciation reverse itself and suddenly become peace?

Once I accepted my extravagant mendicancy I stumbled upon the sober, intelligent little boy I had once been. This was the kid with the sweet smile and an interest in all sorts of things, the boy with brushed hair and cloudless eyes, the child so whole he could forget himself: the birthday boy. Tonight as I sat cross-legged on my cot I could see shining out from within me that boy who'd been entranced by the marionette show: his smaller, sweeter body burned through this neglected exile I'd become. Or was I simply at fifteen learning to love myself at four as now so many years later I like the fifteen-year-old (even desire him), self-approval never accompanying but always trailing experience, retrospection three parts sentimental and one part erotic?

Perhaps this composite self, older cherishing younger, provided me with some companionship. At least tonight my attention wasn't out wandering the corridors. A warmth welled up out of the solar plexus, which, true to its name, I pictured as plaited sunlight, sensitive bands reaching out into the most remote points of my body, even the cold tip of my nose and freezing toes. Like a heated square of pavement in an otherwise snowy sidewalk, the child burned through the adolescent and, luminous within the child, glowed this shifting cat's cradle of sensation, whether spiritual or physical I'm unable to say.

I began to rise. I drew back for an instant, startled, but then I gave in: I was determined to be adequate to the miraculous. I rose and rose, not pneumatically as a swami might but imaginatively, that is, really. I was being enisled, the lotus rising out of the mud, and now I was being drawn, molten and blossoming, up through the void until we (for I was no longer alone)—until *we* entered a ring of the eager faces of infants called away from their games to this curved window from which they peered with mild pleasure, meaty hands pressed to the glass, moist lips open, eyes filmy with wonder. Their whispering was being dialed in, now amplified, and I was losing my whiteness and taking on a gold color, warm as a new tan.

Shortly before Easter I managed to become friendly with my gym teacher, Mr. Pouchet. He was French Canadian and a recent Olympics competitor in track who'd come to our school as a coach and math teacher for the lower formers. He was very good with those kids. He lived in their dorm. They could be seen hanging onto him wherever he went, which he seemed to like in his shy, melancholy way though he pretended to find them tiresome ("What a pain," he'd mutter as yet another giggler leaped onto his back). At twelve and thirteen the boys alternated between being babies and being brutes, sometimes clinging sulkily to his waist, sometimes socking him and screaming. He couldn't keep them out of his room. They were always finding an excuse to sidle in and to look once again at his sports photographs and medals. I avoided talking to him about his medals, for his success had been neither major nor minor—in fact his was exactly the sort of ambiguous success calculated to invite regret.

To the degree that he was not concerned with his past he was interested in me, since I could talk to him about everything except sports. I don't mean to suggest we had a great, flourishing friendship (that kind of friendship came later, with another teacher and his wife). But Mr. Pouchet and I did go to church together. At Eton we were expected to attend services every Sunday, ordinarily those conducted by our own Anglican chaplain, an overgrown boy of startling good looks, great prowess as a skier and no imagination who lived on a strangely easygoing, joshing basis with Our Lord. The matey tone of Eton forbade preening of any sort; the chaplain, true to form, acted as though Christ had been putting on airs and needed to be brought down a peg. When forced to relay some real stunner (And then, on the third day, He arose from the dead), the chaplain would widen his eyes with mocking astonishment (Oh, come now), and after he had finished speaking, he'd snicker skeptically (God only knows how he pulled off *that* stunt). Mr. Pouchet was too discreet to complain about the chaplain but I'm confident Pouchet, a good Catholic boy, found chapel every weekday morning insupportable enough without having to submit to the longer Sunday sermon as well. He and I happily slipped away to services elsewhere, semi-anthropological field trips in his old car to a Greek Orthodox church one week, Roman Catholic the next, Baptist the third, a spiritual smorgasbord I found to be a natural continuation of my earlier sect-hopping.

Mr. Pouchet had very full lips the color of raspberry ice when it's still in the carton, before it's licked lighter, and slightly protuberant eyes as liquid as a spaniel's. His skin was very thin and olive and his mustache, though shaved close every morning, appeared as a black band by noon, nor did it grow close to his lip but well above, the sort of narrow, absolutely horizontal dash a child might charcoal in on Halloween. His chest was hard and covered with swirling, soft, lustrous black hair from his stomach up to his shoulders; his nipples were small and almost purple. His belly, ridged with muscle, stood out as a distinct zone, tucked in betwen the arc of his rib cage and cupped by his pelvic bones—the shape of a turtle's shell. Those famous legs were surprisingly lean. They were not the massive machinery I would have anticipated. As a naïve materialist, at least when it came to men, I missed the carnality of limbs that could perform so astonishingly. Where did the strength come from? When he was at rest, where did the speed go?

During our field trips I'd sit beside him in a hardwood pew or stand close to him under a dusty chandelier as men's voices chanted behind the iconostasis and I felt as though I were already Mr. Pouchet's lover and why not, for he was as much a superfluous man as I was an excluded boy.

Every morning at six he was out on the track running through the mist, stopwatch in hand, puffs of vapor issuing from his mouth, but surely he was running down. I had no idea how old he was (twenty-something), but doubtless he was declining physically. Here he comes, blood drained from his dark cheeks, lips purple and open to reveal wet, white teeth, legs lean and slightly bowed, the calves compact, not bulging, his whole body so *intelligent* that despite its hairiness nothing about it suggests an animal. He's the cautious, isolated man who sleeps alone, rises before dawn, runs, irons his chinos, pares his beautiful nails that haven't a single ridge or moon in them but that seem built up out of layer after layer of clear lacquer, who never seems to have a headache or hangover, who's a well-maintained machine but idling, idling, who approaches each new experience (the iconostasis doors break open and the black nave floods over with candlelight: Christ is risen) in a spirit of mildly detached curiosity, and yet nothing has touched him. He is vulnerable and he's untouched. He is a man to whom something is about to happen.

In the meantime he sits under the buzzing fluorescent lamp over his desk in his dorm room and grades algebra quizzes. Between the first and second hour in the study hall in the evening the boys have ten free minutes. A bell rings, they explode out of their rooms, toilets flush, four guys are pounding a fifth where the stairs turn and Mr. Pouchet winds the gold wristwatch he received for high school graduation not so many years ago, stands and looks out his window across the courtyard at the opposite windows filled with yellow light and the coming and going of the upper formers. Mr. Pouchet is waiting. His mind is open, patient, expectant. Perhaps he's the Buddhist, perhaps the Buddha, and if he doesn't focus on this state of grace, then that oblivion is proof he's blessed.

If I imagine Mr. Pouchet masturbating I see him turning the light on and blinking as he hunts for some tissue, which he puts on the night table beside his cot. An annoying but necessary task. He's wearing a clean white T-shirt and blue cotton pajama bottoms. He's an entirely serious person, a lonely adult. Off with the light. He folds the blankets down till their doubled weight rests on his knees. He pulls the sheet halfway up his chest, so that whatever happens under it will seem less sordid— or so he tells himself. (The truth is, the sheet declares the autonomy of desire, just as a tan line, by isolating the genitals, emphasizes them.) His dark hand pulls open the pajama flap and grabs his penis, which in a moment is as hard as hickory, but his thoughts are scattered, the flesh is strong but the spirit is weak. He assembles the features of various girls he's known or seen in magazines or movies into a face he kisses, then violates— wrong, cancel—kisses again.

And then he sees mental pictures of that time Julie and he

were lying on the rug and talking about their futures. They were going to different colleges, they'd be apart for a year, suddenly his hand is rubbing those panties over a mound that just barely hints through the thick spandex that there might be an opening below—and then he's wriggled under the armor into something flossy, ringleted and then hot and wet and labyrinthine and straining up to meet his fingers even as her throat moans no and she gasps, "Too sweet, you're so . . ." And she buried her face in his sleeve, bit a fold in his shirt. She pulled away and sat him on a chair across the room from her and mimed fluffing her skirt and straightening her hair and said, "There, now," but she didn't turn on the lights, he noticed, and in a moment he had scooted back over and was sitting on the floor below her chair and he was kissing her knee very tenderly, respectfully, but his hand was straying almost in spite of itself back up between her smooth warm legs, as lean as a boy's, as warm as new bread, while his other hand clawed at his own trousers and he whispered, hoarse and dry-mouthed, "Julie, just let me, just this much, something to remember—"

I came. I had seen. He could conquer me. If I was Julie or Helen or whoever else, just so long as I was in his mind somehow. Or no, perhaps I didn't want to be a character in Mr. Pouchet's head, just a virus that had entered the very gland of his consciousness from which I could study, even experience, his longing for a woman. I didn't want him to like men, just me, not even me as a man but me as discarnate ardor, pure willingness in his naïve, manly, exquisitely untested arms.

Using the same ill-fated parchment on which I'd written Helen, I indicted a love poem to Mr. Pouchet. I didn't sign it and I was careful to disguise my handwriting, to imitate laboriously the long, lean eccentricities of an italic script I traced out of a copybook. His compliance in going to church with me every Sunday and his reluctance to talk to me about his private life (if he had one) had enabled me to fancy he was quite prepared to love me—his compliance and reticence were the soft wax I impressed with the intaglio of my daydreams. In the afternoon, when I knew he'd be with the track team, I flew by his room and pushed the poem under his locked door.

Now it was done.

Would he read it and search me out after supper, invite me to drive with him into town where we'd sit in a dirty hamburger joint and feed nickels into the miniature jukebox at our table? Would he frown and pretend to be studying the song titles on the movable cards revolving under the smudged glass while he muttered his love for me, almost as though he were angry at me or embarrassed?

Or would he really be angry? Would he grab my arm as I came out of the dining hall and sadistically dig his nails into my biceps as he steered me down brick walkways glittery with ice and gritty with cast sand until we reached the deserted gymnasium, where he would unlock door after door, pushing me ahead of him onto a varnished, echoing, suddenly floodlit basketball court and would order me to do hundreds of push-ups and jumping jacks in expiation, hours and hours of exercise as punishment and cure?

But he never lifted his long-lashed eyes at dinner except to wisecrack with one of his kids and to hand out the pudding. I kept looking at him from my table. He was illegible. Had he, come to think of it, been able to read my fancy writing? Was he so dim he didn't recognize, in spite of my flimsy precautions, that I was the author of this great love poem? Did he—oh, many questions, one fear: he would hate me.

I never found out. He didn't mention the poem to me. He didn't invite me to go churching with him the next Sunday, nor did I seek him out. We both attended our fatuous chaplain's service. "Dearly beloved," the chaplain said, his eyebrows bouncing roguishly, "let us pray," and then, since he had no style for seriousness, he became horribly boring. He bowed his head and spoke in a monotone so dull it repelled attention. A rich person's smell of wet wool and perfume pressed down on us. The dismal leaking of the hushed organ trickled out around us. Sunlight came and went behind a rose window coarsely stenciled in lead, harshly colored with aniline shades, an industrial rose. After that, whenever I'd pass Mr. Pouchet in the hall, he'd smile and say hi, softening his rejection as much as possible: faintest watermark that had to be held to the light to be seen at all.

I decided I had to go to a psychiatrist. In the back of my mind I had kept hoping I'd somehow outgrow this interest in men, an interest I had nonetheless continued to indulge. But now I was becoming frightened. I was being pushed out of the tribe. I had a dream in which I was a waiter in an elegant restaurant where I served happy, elegant couples. That was upstairs. Downstairs the filthy kitchen was staffed by bald, grizzled men, convicts, really, mute, bestial with grief. They wore blood-stained aprons and gleamed with sweat. I was one of them and, although I could rise to circulate among the happy diners, I always had to descend back down to the hopeless workers, each suspicious of the others. And then the police van arrived and the help, all of us, were dragged out into the night street ablaze with revolving red lights. We were hauled off to prison, where we'd remain forever. As I was being herded into the van I could feel on my back the eyes of the diners looking down from the windows upstairs. Now they knew I wasn't one of them but one of the convicts.

I woke with tears in my eyes so salty they burned the canthus. Everything I touched or did spoke to me of sadness. Each article of clothing—shirt, tie, jacket—felt cut out of different bolts of sadness, each a peculiar weave and shape and hang of sadness, as though sadness came in lots of styles. My shoes posed above their reflections on the glossy floor, and they looked to me like imperfect molds cast from the original, perfect sadness; I mean they were big, solid things, crude actually, and yet the frayed end of a lace, the rim around the opening that bulged here and there, the unevenly worn heels—they all spoke of use, my use, they were sensitive records of dailiness, nothing sadder.

The father of a classmate was a local psychiatrist and he arranged for me to see a famous analyst John Thomas O'Reilly. O'Reilly's office was next door to his home, the two buildings unassuming suburban clapboard houses separated by a concrete drive. Once I was inside the office, however, I found the decor to be luxurious and exotic, not at all what I had expected. The waiting room was carpeted in delicate tatami mats bruised by horrid Western shoes. A large birdcage, woven out of bent reeds to resemble a Baroque Brazilian church, confined a dozen bright choristers all cheeping at once. Long scrolls, rubbings from Han Dynasty tombs, pictured featureless warriors standing in tall, narrow chariots under stiff fans and drawn along by surprisingly small ponies twisting nervously in their traces—a whole traffic jam of military chariots describing interlocking curves, fan beside palmetto fan, one horse's neck dipping behind and below another's raised hoof. The artist had been at least as interested in the abstract pattern as in the subject and as a consequence had turned a dusty pandemonium into immaculate machinery. I studied these details because I had so long to wait (I'd arrived early and the doctor was running about an hour behind schedule).

At last he emerged with a red-nosed woman in a green dress who was humble, even cringing. She slipped into a full-length black coat made of the wool of unborn lambs; once she'd extinguished the color of her dress she regained her composure and accomplished an unsniveling exit.

Dr. O'Reilly smiled at me, teeth spaced and white, lips full and raw, *gnawed* raw, it seemed, under full mustaches, his hair white and to his shoulders—a startling length in those days. His costume also gave one pause: a piece of rope to hold up baggy, stained trousers, bare feet in hemp sandals, a great tent of a minutely and intermittently pleated lime-green Havana shirt containing his corpulence, and in the stubby fingers of his right hand a dirty hanky he kept pressing to his red, raw face, for though we were still in midwinter, sweat lent an incongruous dazzle to his face.

"Come in, come in," he said, stepping aside to usher me into the inner office, a soundproofed cube with one wall all glass looking out on a garden and a small replica of the Kamakura Buddha, gilt everywhere save for a lap full of new snow. "See that log and that hatchet?" the doctor said, pointing to a palisaded enclosure just to the right of the garden. "My patients dub the log Mom or Dad as the case may be, usually Mom, and then have a grand ol' time hacking away at her." His small blue eyes, veined in red, rotated dryly in their sockets to take in my reaction to the idea of murder—except his act of "observation" was so stagy it preempted the need for another response. There was nothing about this actor that couldn't be read from the top balcony.

I declined the analytic couch's invitation to the voyage and chose an earthbound chair that faced the desk. Not that I wasn't eager to test the couch's splendors, which I instinctively (and I hazard astutely) equated with those of sexuality. It was just that I felt somewhat abashed by the couch's very explicitness, as though it were someone's beautiful mother who wouldn't cross her legs, who had even decided to flaunt her most intimate charms. That was just how musky and startling I found the couch, which so shamelessly resembled itself in a thousand cartoons, although now I understood the cartoons had done nothing so much as to sensitize me to its heroic and decidedly unfunny actuality.

My first sight of the analytic couch constituted the primal scene, for only its existence jarred me into recognizing that the world is governed by a minority, the sexually active, and that they hold sway over a huge majority of the nonsexual, those people too young or too old or too poor or homely or sick or crazy or powerless to be able to afford sexual partners (or the luxury of systematic, sustained and shared introspection, so sexual in its own way). All advertisements and films and songs are addressed to sexuals, to their rash whims and finicky tastes, but these communications cleverly ignore nonsexuals, those pale, penniless, underdeveloped bodies, blue nipples flung like two test drops of ink from a new pen across the blotting paper of a chest, or high, hairless buttocks, unmolded by hands into something lovely, something enticing, left pure and formless like butcher's lard. The patient who always preceded me was the lady in the Persian-lamb coat; she left behind the peculiar perfumed smell of the paper tissues she wept into, a weak solution of those chemical towels handed out after lobster in family restaurants, and the heavier, more aggressive and I suppose offensive smell of her stubbed-out cigarettes (eight or nine in the sterling silver cupped hand that served as the ashtray). These smells and the ghosts of smoke circulating through the sunlight, colloidal souvenirs, seemed to be the echoes of a just-completed drama by Racine in which lambent passions had glowed within the glass chimney of formal measures, in which all the action must occur offstage and is merely reported here and the only permissible emotions are the great ones—incestuous longings, guilt, and the impulse to murder—whereas the dimmer, more usual feelings of sloth, boredom, spleen, irritability are airily dismissed. For psychoanalysis feeds on intensity, as though life were all flame and no ash.

Dr. O'Reilly was not a good listener. He was always scooping up handfuls of orange diet pills and swallowing them with a jigger of scotch. As a great man and the author of several books, he had theories to propound and little need to attend to the particularities of any given life—especially since he knew in advance that life would soon enough yield merely another illustration of his theories. To save time, O'Reilly unfolded his ideas at the outset and then rehearsed them during each subsequent session since, as he explained, although these notions could easily enough penetrate the conscious mind, they soaked less readily into the hairy taproot of the unconscious. When he wasn't presenting his theories, O'Reilly was confiding in me the complexities of his personal life. He'd left his wife for Nancy, a patient, but the moment his divorce had gone through, his wife had discovered she was dying of cancer. O'Reilly complied with her last wish and remarried her. The patient promptly went mad and was now confined in an institution in Kansas. O'Reilly, to console himself, was throwing himself into his work. He was taking on more and more patients. He saw the last patient at midnight and the first at six in the morning.

Sometimes I would have both the last hour and the first and I would get permission from the school to spend the night on the analytic couch. I'd set the alarm for five-thirty. I'd arise and hurry over to O'Reilly's apartment next door. It was decorated like a ship's cabin, complete with bunk beds, coiled ropes on the walls, portholes for windows, a captain's desk and red and green lights to indicate port and starboard. To awaken O'Reilly I'd put on his favorite record, "Nothing Like a Dame," a song he considered "healthy." I'd then make a cup of coffee for him and with it hand him his jar of Dexedrines. By six-thirty at the latest he was alert, dressed and ready to return to his office. I associate those morning hours with the smell of his lime cologne.

Just as years before, when I was seven, I had presented myself to a minister and had sought for his understanding, in the same way now I was turning to a psychoanalyst for help. I wanted to overcome this thing I was becoming and was in danger soon of being, the homosexual, as though that designation were the mold in which the water was freezing, the first crystals already forming a fragile membrane. The confusion and fear and pain that beset me—initiated by my experience with the hustler, intensified by Mr. Pouchet's gentle silence and made eerie by my fascination with "The Age of Bronze"—had translated me into a code no one could read, I least of all, a code perhaps designed to defeat even the best cryptographer. Dr. O'Reilly was far too Mosaic to read anything other than the tablets he himself was carrying on which he'd engraved his theory. I subscribed to his theory, I placed myself entirely in his care, because learning his ideas was less frustrating and less perilous than teasing out my own.

I had no one and he liked me or at least he said he did. Of course, he needed someone to talk to about his problems, and I was a good listener.

I see now that what I wanted was to be loved by men and to love them back but not to be a homosexual. For I was possessed with a yearning for the company of men, for their look, touch and smell, and nothing transfixed me more than the sight of a man shaving and dressing, sumptuous rites. It was men, not women, who struck me as foreign and desirable and I disguised myself as a child or a man or whatever was necessary in order to enter their hushed, hieratic company, my disguise so perfect I never stopped to question my identity. Nor did I want to study the face beneath my mask, lest it turn out to have the pursed lips, dead pallor and shaped eyebrows by which one can always recognize the Homosexual. What I required was a sleight of hand, an alibi or a convincing act of bad faith to persuade myself I was not that vampire. Perhaps—yes, this must be it—perhaps my homosexuality was a *symptom* of some other deeper but less irrevocable disorder. That's what Dr. O'Reilly thought. After I'd confessed all, he pressed his hankie to his glistening forehead, gnawed his raw lips and said with a dramatic air of boredom, "But none of that matters at all. In here, you'll find"—the traveling blue eyes stopped meandering across the ceiling and fixed me—"that we'll ignore your acting out and concentrate on your *real* conflicts."

How thrilling to discover one had depths, how consoling to find them less polluted than the shallows, how encouraging to identify the enemy not as a fissure in the will but as a dead fetus in the specimen jar of the unconscious. My attention was being paternally led away from the excruciating present to the happy, healthy future that would be enabled by an analysis of the sick past, as though the priest had nothing to do but study sorry old books and make bright forecasts, the present not worthy of notice.

Since Dr. O'Reilly was a very famous analyst, his fees were high; since he considered me to be acutely ill, he decided I had to see him three times a week; the result was a staggering monthly bill. My mother agreed to pay half the cost, but my father refused my request. He couldn't find any good reason for me to be in therapy, nor was he at all convinced that therapy worked. "It's just a bunch of crap," he said over the phone. "I thought sending you to Eton was supposed to straighten you out."

I assured him it had in that it had removed me from my dependency on my mother. Paraphrasing Dr. O'Reilly, I added, "But you see, Daddy, I've *internalized* my mother and when I fall in love I merely project her introjected image—"

"Love?" I could hear the wires singing between us as they dipped and rose in rhythmic arcs over the cindered sidings of railroad tracks or plunged underground and threaded their way through the entrails of American cities. Instantly I recognized that in such a big, hardworking country and in the vocabulary of such a sober man the word *love* took on a coy, neurasthenic ring. Women lived for love and talked about it and made their decisions by its guttering, scented light; men (at least a real man like my dad) took the love that came their way gratefully but suffered its absence in silence. Certainly no real man ever discussed love or made a single move to woo it.

"Let me put my thoughts on paper," I said, for by now I'd learned he preferred personal transactions to resemble business invoices.

That night during study period, as I sat in my cold room at my desk, my pen flew over page after page as I drew in a portrait of myself as an adolescent desperate for medical attention. Once again I wrote on my special parchment, once again I was petitioning someone. But this time I had more confidence, for I felt I was within my rights. I knew Dr. O'Reilly was my one chance to escape the cage and treadmill of neurosis, to head out, ears up and whiskers twitching, into the enchanting unknown.

The dorm master tiptoed past my open door. He was on the lookout for boys breaking rules. Across the hall from me at his own desk a square-jawed German lad—who wrestled for the team, excelled at trig and played records of music he called "easy listening"—was working a slide rule and jotting down figures in his minuscule hand. His glasses blazed when he cocked his head at a certain angle, as though the numerical intelligence projected light rather than drank it in. On the wall above his head was an Eton pennant, placed with mathematical precision at the correct, casual angle, Gustav's concession to frivolity. The master tiptoed back past my door. In fact, he was cutting up, taking giant, slow-motion steps, his hands raised high as a marionettist's, his mouth turned down as though he himself were a truant who feared making a floorboard squeak—good for a chuckle.

In my letter to my father I used the word *homosexuality*, thereby breaking a taboo and forcing two responses from him: silence and the money I wanted. Much later my stepmother told me I'd caused my father weeks of sleepless despair and that at first he had chosen to believe I wasn't really a homosexual at all, merely a poseur hoping to appear "interesting." Dad never asked me later if I'd been cured. He was no doubt afraid to know the answer. Certainly he and I never discussed my problem. Indeed, horror of the subject led to a blackout on all talk about my private life. My father didn't like other men; he had no close male friends and he behaved toward the men in his own family according to the dictates of duty rather than the impulses of his heart. He so often ascribed cunning to other men, a covert plotting, that he approached them as enemies to whom he must extend an ambiguous hand, one that when not offering a cold greeting could contract into a fist. I was one of the men he didn't like.

Or should I say he simply didn't like my nature—the fact that I was drawn to art rather than to business, to people rather than to things, to men rather than to women, to my mother rather than to him, books rather than sports, sentiments not responsibilities, love not money?

And yet he always ended by lavishing his money on me, more than he spent on my sister, whom he really did adore in his obstinate, silent, astringent way.

Difficult as my father might be and obsessed with him as I might have been, Dr. O'Reilly had decided my dad was merely a son of a bitch but not the true villain, not like Mom. It was she who had broken past the immunological barriers of my frail psyche and infected every last inch of my soul. It was she who'd ensnared me in silk fetters, she who'd shorn my strength and blinded me to the gross imposition of her will. Indeed, she'd so thoroughly invaded me that scarcely anything of my own remained to me. Dr. O'Reilly's mission was to purge the invader and to fatten up my ego. Although he'd never met her he spoke of her with real venom. His blue eyes blazed with scorn. When I said I feared what would happen to her if I rejected her, he said, "That old cow? She'll outlive us all," as though he and I were a pair of young boys and she all the tenacious wickedness of the adult world.

During World War II O'Reilly had served as an army doctor in Polynesia, where he had studied the child-rearing methods of the natives. There no infant was ever punished, he said, and none ever cried. An infant's deepest insecurity, he went on, was derived from its physical smallness and helplessness. The Polynesians, especially those on the happy isle to which fortune had blown the good doctor, countered this insecurity by carrying their babies on their backs in a sling pitched so high that Baby's eyes peered out over Mama's head. This literally superior position insured the infant against all future anxiety and guaranteed him a life-long serenity. Eager to spread these advantages to America, O'Reilly insisted his patients emulate the Polynesian mode of transporting a baby. I saw those patients, men and women alike, all over town, sheepishly stepping over snowdrifts or gliding down supermaket aisles, their infants, petrified with fear, squawling and clutching locks of parental hair.

But this practice figured as only one of the many ways in which O'Reilly reformed our lives. Unlike those tight-ass Freudians, he said, who never suggested anything, who judged silently and interpreted rarely, he quite cheerfully broadcast his wisdom by spilling handfuls into fertile minds he himself had furrowed.

He believed that since I'd missed out on a loving childhood I had to feel my way backward in time, to regress in order to be raised all over again by him. "An adult," he said, "has no right to expect unqualified love, but a child does. That's what I'm offering you: love with no strings tied." He invariably made that mistake—"tied" not "attached." Sometime during each session he would repeat this extraordinary assertion of his love, and each time I felt embarrassed, for I couldn't help noticing how poorly he remembered the names of my parents and best friends and the major facts of my life. Perhaps foolishly, I thought of knowledge as a necessary if not sufficient condition for love. When I told him of my doubts about him he chastised me for being overly cerebral. "But you see," he said, "that's your unconscious pushing me aside because on some level you realize how much I love you. You're afraid of intimacy. Real love would force you to discard the mother imago you've introjected."

Spring approached and the gold Buddha grew more resplendent as rain washed away winter smuts. Although we were hundreds of miles inland, on some days the air smelled of salt and I half expected to see a gull perching on the statue's topknot like Maitreya, the bodhisattva of the future. Everything quickened, even my heartbeat. The sense of smell, so long banished from out of doors save for a whiff of exhaust or the scent of desultory smoke unspooling from a chimney, now returned and released memories long buried in the pockets of earth's apron. I'd cross the piazza at school and smell something earthy or rusty or a dog's stale turd, much washed and often salted, leeched of everything except its palest quintessence. Or last autumn would rise like a revenant from a scattered pile of burned leaves long covered with snow, and behind that ghost stood one even taller, more deeply shrouded in sadness—the memory of the hollow behind the house where I'd lived and played as a child. But if all these odors awakened memories, the salt smell, suggesting nothing of my past, promised a future, a journey, and I could hear sails luffing and snapping as they were cranked up the mast until they shivered under the weight of the cold wind.

Two developments were unfolding within me, or rather two quite different stories about a single life were getting told. In one, Dr. O'Reilly's version, I was wrestling with my unconscious, an immense, dark brother who seeped around me when I was awake, flowed over me when I slept, who sometimes invaded my body, caused my pen or tongue to slip, who erased a name from the blackboard of memory—a force with a baby's features, greedy orifices, a madman's cunning and an animal's endurance, a Caliban as quicksilver as Ariel. This doppelgänger was determined to confine me to what I'd already experienced and to deny me adventure, as though life were a cynical editor of gothic romances who demanded that every novel conform to a formula, who might accept slight variations in detail so long as the plot remained the same. O'Reilly's job was to outwit this brilliant tyrant.

While I observed the rounds in this psychoanalytic struggle, a quite different, less lurid, more scattered sort of story was taking place within me, one that lacked narrative drive or even direction. It sprang up without warning like mushrooms after rain; it came and went, circled around itself, died away and then was crawling like moss over the rock face of my will. Like a whole rootless plantation of algae, it washed in tides of longing and self-loathing. For the real movements of a life are gradual, then sudden; they resist becoming anecdotes, they pulse like quasars from long-dead stars to reach the vivid planet of the present, they drift like fog over the ship until the spread sails are merely panels of gray in grayer air and surround becomes object, as in those perceptual tests where figure and ground reverse, the kissing couple in profile turn into the outlines of the mortuary urn that holds their own ashes. Time wears down resolve—then suddenly violence, something irrevocable flashes out of nowhere, there are thrashing fins and roiled, blood-streaked water, death floats up on its side, eyes bulging.

If I had the skill I'd write about the way that place—the cold corridors of the school, its symmetrical parterres of snow, the replicas of the *Discobulos* and *Dying Gaul*—how that place became the espalier which my moods crept up. I'd find a way to connect moods to weather, to rhyme books I was reading with bouts of illness I endured, to link pop tunes of the moment with persistent fantasies I concocted (I was Rimbaud; Verlaine loved me so much he fired on me; I endured, lonely, smoking cigarettes on an African beach), I'd place Buddhism over Hesse, divide a laugh I borrowed from a popular senior with an incurable rash on my left ankle I scratched day after day—all figures in an algebraic equation in which X would stand for *Stimmung* and Y for truth.

What I was doing in those spring months was once again steeling my social nerve. I was becoming popular—not in a big way, of course, but as a bit player. I started smoking cigarettes in order to join the Butt Club, a coterie of fascinating disreputables who'd obtained parental permission to meet for fifteen minutes after lunch and dinner and for half an hour before bedtime to smoke. Serious athletes, admired prefects, good school citizens—they all looked down on us. We were not square, we were bums, hoods, bad characters. One small windowless room in the basement had been set aside for our regrettable hobby. Someone pinned up the famous nude calendar pose of Marilyn Monroe on the cinder-block wall, but even her maraschino charms looked bilious under the low-wattage green bulb screwed into the ceiling for "atmosphere."

I had never been bad before. Of course I'd been intolerably wicked or maybe just sick in sleeping with other boys and men, but those transgressions were secret and solitary. Now at last I, who'd always been considered obedient, even docile, was rubbing shoulders with guys who were about to flunk out, who got drunk and totaled cars, who knocked up girls, who got into fistfights with their dads, who stole motorcycles and went off on joy rides, who had created such chaos at home they'd been banished to Eton. These boys accepted anyone at all so long as he was a smoker and a failure. Here came the hell-raisers who sneaked off campus after lights-out, who downed a quart of vodka a day and nodded off in class, who faked medical excuses to get out of gym, who went weeks without showering ("Give us a break"), who jerked off in the back of class to the amazement of their neighbors ("Yuck"), who farted and popped their zits in assembly ("Ee—yuh"), who bought term papers from brains or beat the brains up, who in one case seduced a master's wife ("Neat"), in another a fat Latvian washup girl with greasy braids on the kitchen staff ("Barf").

My favorite smoker was Chuck, a gangly, pimply, popular guy with the gift of gab and the ambition to be a writer like Hemingway. Chuck was rumored to have the biggest dick on campus, but I never got to check it out. He was from a rich family and after listening to his stories of life at home I pieced together a glamorous feature film of two-seater planes, a sheep ranch in Montana, a fishing camp in Canada, a private island off Georgia—though Chuck didn't give a damn about possessions, all he wanted to do was stuff two fat black whores into his rattletrap Chevy and head south with them and a case of beer and of painful but not quite incapacitating clap and holler curse words at Arkansas cops and pass out from tequila, fatigue and sunburn at a two-bit rodeo in some dusty Texas town before he revived long enough to slip over the border into Tijuana, where he'd find those magic mushrooms or whatever the hell they were and that fabled gal in a straw basket hung on ropes from the ceiling, just her cunt exposed as she's lowered onto your stiff prong as you lie back and let the big-eyed nine-year-old girl assistant slowly, solemnly spin the basket and fan the flies off your face.

Chuck forged an invitation from his mother to me, something I could show the school authorities, and he drove me for the weekend to his family's deserted beach house. His parents were off in Florida. Everything here was gray and thawing, the sky and the lake anagrams for each other, iceberg of cloud above a cumulus of ice. We played a record of Big Bill Broonzy over and over again as we lounged about and looked out the plate-glass windows at a surrealists' world in which whatever had been hard seemed to be going soft. We drank beer after beer (Chuck pried the caps off with his teeth), we fell asleep in our clothes on adjoining couches, we were continuously hung over, we set out giant steaks to thaw, we awoke at dawn or dusk, who knew which in that long weekend of freedom, melting ice and nausea.

Although I certainly wasn't a straight-A student I'd at least always been conscientious in school. In one sense my doggedness was a way of hedging my bets, so that no matter how despairing I might be I was implicitly counting on my eventual happiness. Even as I made much of present miseries I was cautiously planning my bourgeois future.

There was nothing cautious about Chuck. He had his own trust fund from a grandmother who owned a cosmetics firm. He had a loud, maniacal laugh, he was big physically and knew it and half-scared people with his craziness, his drunk sprees,

the way he'd twitch or shoot his cuffs or without warning
scythe the air between you with a closed fist and shriek like a
samurai. He scared the masters because he didn't want or need
their approval and because he'd set himself up as an arbiter of
absurdity. If a teacher said something banal or foolish or
pompous in class, Chuck would quake with silent laughter until he was weeping and had slid halfway out of his seat onto the
floor, a helpless sprawl of laughter. He appeared to be in actual
pain and every eye was on him.

No number of demerits or revoked privileges or low grades
intimidated him. He had no particular ambition to go on to
college, nor did he doubt his own intelligence which, in the
Amercian fashion of that day, had been Tested; he'd been Cer-
tified as falling well within the Genius Range and declared that
most appealing of creatures, the Underachiever, a status he jeal-
ously preserved except in English class, an honors section conducted by a half-blind white-haired amphibian who paddled at
the air with one wounded web, who pronounced *poetry* as "pu-
trid" minus the final *d* and who was so absentminded he'd
once heard the bell for class and stepped off a high library ladder into thin air. This eccentric teacher was also a Genius; every
summer he played Falstaff in an outdoor theater and he'd once
written a textbook on semantics. For Dr. Schlumberger, Chuck
knocked himself out composing a novel about an oil driller in
Oklahoma much given to epic drunks and fornications—a
novel in which terse dialogue and tersely narrated violence alternated with nature descriptions of a shocking delicacy, silver-
point tracery against a wash of Chinese white. I read and praised
Chuck's book, and that made him like me. And the book made
me like him, for though he continued to slouch about and swear
and weep with laughter and refused to say an intelligent word,
nevertheless I'd had that written glimpse into his temperament,
and just as oils can be made fragrant by saturating them in the
perfume of flowers, in the same way in my imagination Chuck's
character had been transformed by this literary enfleurage.

Chuck decided we should visit a whorehouse. He picked up
four day students from their houses and we lurched and wheezed

in Chuck's Chevy down through the black section of the city. It was midnight and though this was the weekend the streets were deserted; only here and there a few neon lights outlined the windows of a tavern. The bordello was a dingy wooden house behind a larger one. To get to it we had to squeeze down a narrow strip of sidewalk past a sturdy metal fence behind which a neighbor's German shepherd kept barking and running back and forth.

After we rang the bell for several minutes and Chuck pounded the door and sang a love song in warbling falsetto, which elevated the dog into new ecstasies of rage, the door at last was cracked open and a tall Negro man looked out. He had a tight black silk kerchief on his head and a few short white curly whiskers growing out of a shiny mole beside his mouth.

Inside, two young black women and one woman who was white and middle-aged were sitting in slips in front of a television set. One of the black women had on pink-rimmed glasses and was knitting. The room beyond them, a waiting room lined with crude wooden folding chairs, was deserted and harshly lit. Three pictures leaned forward off the dirty walls, one a reproduction of a painting of Jesus praying in Gethsemane while his disciples dozed unmindful of the approaching Roman guards. The other pictures were of cloth behind glass, each embroidered with a motto: "Peace on Earth" and "Bless This House"— puns, I guess, but who could be certain. The house smelled of cooking fat and pork.

"Now, you boys sit in here," the white woman said, indicating the waiting room with a precise push of her hand, as though her hand were a croupier's rake, "and choose your women." We filed in under the harsh light. Chuck's nose looked huge and cratered, his teeth as big as a dog's. I felt my penis and scrotum contract, inchworm above a buckeye, but I was counting on the whore's discretion—the guys need never know of my failure.

"Girls, get your lazy black asses in here so these men can look you over."

One of the women, who'd fallen asleep in front of the television, had to be prodded awake. As she waddled past us on tiny, high-heeled slippers, the soles engulfed by her fleshy feet, she rubbed her eyes, protruded her lower lip and made a fretting sound. So massive and quivering were her breasts and hips under the slip that the garment seemed to be the body of a vaudeville horse which at least two people were inhabiting. At the same time her physical grandeur did nothing to diminish the impression she gave of being a little girl, an impression heightened by the sass with which she planted a fist in her hip and asked nastily, "Seen enough?" We nodded. She said defiantly, "*Good*. I goan back to mah TV shows."

The other black woman, the one who'd been knitting, kept her glasses on and the embryonic maroon sweater in her hand as she sleepwalked past, counting stitches, never looking up. Hers was also an ample, indoor body of seraglio proportions but her face seemed older, thinner—in fact, she was a dead ringer for our white dietitian at school, if a *ringer* is a racehorse entered under a false name and posing as another, less successful one. (Horse, dog, inchworm—nature takes her revenge on stories from which she's been excluded by smuggling herself into them under the guise of imagery.)

"Well?" the white woman said.

"Is that it?" Chuck asked.

She smiled a not especially pleasant smile and said, "There's always me," with an edge to the *always* to suggest how long she'd been in harness, how weary of the road she'd become.

"I'll take you," Chuck said. His voice didn't crack, he didn't soften the blow of his words with a giggle, nor did he drop his eyes. He knew exactly what he wanted.

"Yeah, me too," each of us said in turn on a descending scale of confidence ending with my whisper.

"Then come on," she said, walking away from us and unzipping her dress in a single gesture. She paused at her bedroom door and glanced back. The dress had somehow evaporated into just a wisp of teal-blue smoke in her hand as she tossed it aside. There she stood, door open and behind her a shaded floor lamp dangling fringe; her naked body looked pale as a night moth and as powdery. Her pubic hair had been shaved into a black rectangle. Her legs were ropy. She went in and disappeared from sight. The sound of running water could be heard and a cat's paw of steam stretched out into the bedroom to bat at a ball of cold air. A cricket chanted in the radiator. (Teal, moth, cat, cricket—the chorus of animals chirps and twitters, ready for its entrance into the enfeebled, cicatrized world.)

Chuck put his hands on his knees like a retired farmer and levered himself up out of the chair. "I don't know about you boys, but ol' Chuck's not taking no sloppy seconds."

I'd never heard before the expression *sloppy seconds*. Cursed as I was with an overly literal imagination—so that such stock phrases as *motherfucker, pussywhipped* and *shitfaced* took on horribly vivid pictorial detail for me—I couldn't help seeing now a bruised and drooling indentation. For the first time my inchworm twitched, in response not to this damaged cloaca but to the idea of the five penises beside me, each a masquerader behind a domino of buttoned or zipped cloth, all mysterious and of an unknown girth, slant, heft, scent and hardness. I hotly envied the white whore what so obviously left her cold; I would have been content just to watch from her closet.

Chuck returned to us surprisingly quickly but with a smile on his face and a huge transverse rod (that seemed worthy of its campus-wide reputation) in his trousers pointing up to the right of his belt buckle—one o'clock until it ticked down to two. As the second boy went in, Chuck wandered out into the other room, asked for a beer and got it and sat down to watch TV. He called me in to see something. I found myself sitting on the overstuffed arm of a chair covered with a fabric that felt like unshaved beard and suddenly there was a dimpled black hand on my knee belonging to the huge little girl who'd been dozing but was now contentedly half awake and sipping a rum and Coke. "Want some?"

"No," I said.

She breathed out a faint snort. "Don' know why all you fellas go for that ofay bitch."

"Ofay?"

"Yeah, she a ofay cunt."

"*Ofay* means 'white,'" Chuck muttered between mouthfuls of potato chips, his eyes drinking in a shoot-out on the screen. He cocked his thumb up out of his fist, sighted his way down his forefinger and fired at the television; his body was jolted to one side and he buried his head in his armpit for a second, played dead, sniffed, said, "Yuck, time for my monthly shower."

"Hey, honey," the woman beside me was saying, "I got me a crazy little crib downstairs. Why don' you and me party? Wanna party? That ofay cunt take ten bucks. I give it to you for eight. Eight for straight, ten for round-the-world."

"What's that?"

She hissed a goose giggle into her pink palm. When she lowered her hand she was still grinning. "Don' you know nothin'? You kids sho 'nuff *green*. Round-the-world means I start at yo' mouth and kiss you all round, top to bottom, round the world, with a long wait on your south *pole*!" Another hiss behind her hand.

I felt sorry for her. I thought she might really need my ten dollars. After all, this was Saturday night, and yet she didn't have any customers. Somehow I equated her fatness, her blackness, her unpopularity with my own outcast status. She'd show me sympathy, which would magically awaken my virility. In her adoring eyes I'd become a slender-hipped young prince under a gold crown of hair, skin as smooth as petals under a light green tunic. I'd protect her. I'd earn money and buy her freedom. We'd be outcasts together as a mixed couple, she a Negro whore and I her little protector. But no matter, for if this fantasy kept me a pariah by exchanging homosexuality for miscegenation, it also gave me a sacrifice to make and a companion to cherish. I would educate and protect her. I would nurse her back to decency after her years of debauchery.

We went downstairs into a cellar room curtained off from the furnace by a flannel blanket suspended from a clothesline. Her night table was a wooden crate. Her mattress had no sheets on it and was resting on the floor. She pulled her slip over her head and said, "Get your clothes off. I don' have all night."

She didn't even watch me as I undressed. As I pulled my underpants off I worried she'd laugh when she saw my fear-shriveled penis, but her indifference to me was complete. I creaked awkwardly as I lowered myself onto the bed beside her. Her fingers started blindly grubbing for my penis, which she found and yanked. Then she sighed, heaved herself up onto an elbow, finally lowered herself and plopped my penis in her mouth. Nothing happened. I could scarcely feel anything.

"I don' have all night," she said again as she unthreaded a hair from between her teeth and looked at it suspiciously.

"Sorry," I said. It dawned on me that neither of us was enjoying this and that she was as eager as I for it to be over. "For some reason I'm not in the mood tonight," I said. "Let's just talk a minute and then go upstairs. And if any of the fellows should ask—"

"Yeah, yeah," she said, "Ah'll say you was great, a real stud. And in the future, my man, drink gin. Gin make you hard. It do. It make a man hard."

The following summer I spent with my father at his cottage—the summer of my exciting, frustrating idyll with Kevin. When I returned to school the next September I was switched to a new room in a new dormitory next door to the housemaster's suite. Mr. and Mrs. Scott seemed an odd pair, he a grinning, skinny, forgetful little Latin teacher behind glasses cloudy with thumbprints, the fly of his gray, unpressed Brooks Brothers trousers sometimes open, usually half open, his hair worn in a salt-and-pepper crew cut, his shoulders fallen, perhaps broken under a perpetual burden of sin and duty and uxoriousness, which must be either one or the other. He was at his sweetest with Tim, his four-year-old son, a lovely wide-awake kid who alternated between bouts of boyish roughhousing and almost seraphic spells of listening. Yes, listening to adult conversation, to the radio, to the muted shoutings of the dorm during free time, to practically anything, even silence, which for him came across as a plenum, supersonic scrape and lift and settling, the sound of the feathered jets of the spheres.

Whenever Tim clung to his father's leg or sat on his lap and asked questions, Mr. Scott seemed most in focus. An admiration of his handsome, intelligent, good-natured little boy brightened and fattened the wavering flame in Mr. Scott's eyes and sweetened the vinegar of his smile, for usually Mr. Scott smiled as if in queasy anticipation of a practical joke about to be played on him. Indeed, the students *had* offered him "a new bike" at an end-of-semester ceremony last year, but when he came bounding up the aisle with a glad grin they greeted him not with some sleek English racer to replace his battered old Schwinn but with a Bike athletic supporter (sour smile, "Very funny, you guys, a big yuck for your side").

His students counted on his being dazed. In Latin class, when he called attendance, someone different responded to each name each time, nor did Mr. Scott appear to notice when the same person answered to three different names in a row. Kids were always taping on his back the message "Kick me." When he had to make an announcement in general assembly, he'd be unable to read his own writing. Soon he would have shoved his glasses up onto his forehead and he would be holding the paper an inch away from his eyes.

He himself was the product of prep schools and his natural position in this rough, raw society would have been as one of those skinny little kids who don't hit puberty until sixteen and who learn to take a lot of teasing until then and know how to dish out a few practical jokes in return (dead frog under the pillow). He was one of those kids who serve as manager of the football team and become the mascot, the sort of boy who's dying to be included by the team but hides on the day the yearbook photo is being taken: lovable, starved for affection, elusive. Yet here he was having to play disciplinarian. Whenever someone made a commotion during chapel, Mr. Scott's eyes flared for a second with sympathetic mirth, which he immediately doused in favor of the stern visage of the leader, boy giving way to man. As a man he was a fake, and this very fraudulence was what dazed him, sank his self-esteem, introduced confusion into his voice.

I was asked to baby-sit for the Scotts, and since little Tim and I got along I was invited back more and more often. Tim liked a bedtime story I made up about the ghost train that floated outside his window and that only he could see and hear as it went "Whoo-o-o . . . ," its whistle a high, sad, soft wail lost on the winter wind. The whole point of each episode was the repetition of that sound, which I'd hoard until the end; then his eyes would grow wide. The sound seemed to correspond to that heavenly ruckus he alone could hear, that burn-off of angelic fuels at the center of the universe.

Something about that child seemed so wise and cool but tender, and for a moment the idea of rebirth did seem convincing to me, for how else could one explain the wisdom of many lives, cleaned by the refiner's fire, and placed large and bright and constant within this merest excuse for a body? I felt Tim understood all my own fears and hopes, understood everyone and everything. When I'd brush his hair and see the blue artery ticking in his temple or wash his face and observe the awakened capillaries in his cheeks rush full of bright red blood, or help him out of his shirt and into his pajama tops, as I glanced in that interval of nudity at the inhaled diaphragm pressing up and into the minute ribs, this live and breathing glove pulled over the cupped, inflexible hands of bone guarding his heart— oh, at such moments I sensed that only the thinnest tissue separated me from spirit itself and that the roar Tim was listening to was not far away but here, inside, here.

Tim was the agent who humanized Mrs. Scott for me. If he loved her, if he could let her tickle him, if he could cling to her knee as she read to him, then she must not be a monster, all appearances to the contrary. When I dropped by their apartment in the afternoon she always had the curtains drawn and was always sunk into a stupor on an old, feeble couch broken in the shanks and bleeding from the arms. Mrs. Scott squatted heavily on this piece of furniture, her chin on her palm, as though she were Death meditating on its latest convert. Sometimes I'd want just to fly through, to kiss Tim or to leave my Latin assignment with her husband, but she couldn't be ignored. She drank in all the oxygen around her and reversed the magnetism of all metals; one was drawn to her even by the fillings in one's teeth. Her hair was black and dirty and cut into a pageboy only because hair must be worn in some style; undoubtedly she would have preferred it thick with twigs and matted with mud. She always wore a formless madras blouse flown like a flag announcing defeat over the battlements of her corpulent body. Her teeth overlapped. Her eyeteeth were unusually long and pointed and wet.

Mrs. Scott was a poet. Her husband also wrote verse. It was understood between them that his lines were very learned but a bit dry and completely the work of the conscious mind, hence inferior. He was of the school of T. S. Eliot—classic, ironic, religious. Her poems, which appeared seldom but then cataclysmically after a night white with lightning, had been purloined from the danker, more sulfurous regions of the unconscious. She spoke with the lentor of alligators through skeins of Spanish moss white and frangible with death; epochs of prehistory bubbled voluptuously and broke with gluey smackings in the lower regions of her sinister art. On the day after one of her nights of vision I'd find her panting with fatigue on the couch, her eyes ringed in black, her smile slightly goofy with sanctity, a reminder that *silly* once meant "blessed."

I stood in front of the cobra throne, her couch, and said, "I understand from Mr. Scott that you've written a wonderful poem."

"*Wonderful?*" she asked, aghast, chuckling silently, her many teeth various beiges, yellows and browns, even the odd blue. "Did he say *wonderful?*" By now her body was heaving under the madras blouse with horrific scorn.

"Well, I don't mean to get him into trouble," I said nervously. "That's probably not the word he used; I just gathered that he's crazy about your new poem."

The terrible silent chuckle continued behind clouds of smoke. The Cumaean Sybil swayed hysterically over the tripod.

"Do you think I might hear it sometime?" I asked, my question unexpectedly sounding rude and trivial to my own ears.

"Don't make me read it today," she begged. "Not today." It seemed her energies, mortal after all, had already been taxed to the limit by creation.

"Of course," I hastened to assure her.

"Help me up," she said.

I rushed to assist her. I took her hand and pulled. When she was at last standing beside me, breathing audibly, she let her eyes travel up and down my body in a surprisingly frank way. Then she scuttled off to the kitchen. I followed. She brewed us instant coffee. Sitting with a master's wife discussing poetry or gossiping about the other teachers and kids struck me as "sophisticated," that game in which grown-ups pretended I was one of them, that my opinion counted, indeed that I was autonomous enough to have an opinion. Nothing I did or said among the other boys came to me naturally. As a result, in every encounter, even the most glancing, I had to be a performer, for at all times I was aware I was impersonating a human being. "Sophisticated" conversation with Mrs. Scott was itself inauthentic, of course, delightfully so, since by its very nature it prized artifice—a release from the vague, always changing but ever-stringent demands of teenage sincerity. I wanted to be sincere but I didn't know how. I could find no method for it except when alone. Sophistication suspended this anxiety, since to be sophisticated is to adorn oneself rather than to strip oneself bare.

Mr. and Mrs. Scott got to like me, perhaps to need me, and they arranged for me to stay up with them after lights-out and after little Tim had gone to bed. Outside their apartment the long corridors resonated with silence. We inhabited a cube of warmth and light and babble. Mrs. Scott ("Call me Rachel") would descend from her mystic platform and could even become quite chummy. The heat in the whole dormitory would go off at midnight and we'd move to the kitchen and sit around the lit oven, its door ajar. We drank cup after cup of coffee.

Soon Mr. Scott ("DeQuincey") and his wife were confiding bits and pieces of their story to me. He came from a rich Boston family, father remote tycoon, mother perfectionist socialite, three older sisters, all wielding hockey sticks. Little DeQuincey hadn't been able to keep up, nor did he feel at home in this boisterous female world. Various prep schools followed in a descending, depressing order of academic credibility. The unsavory names at the end of the list were interchangeable with those of mental hospitals or juvenile detention homes. Next, some real hospitals made their shadowy flight over his life ("Quince, don't go into all that"). A bit of college, some analyst-hopping, more college, a degree in Latin, another breakdown. By this point he'd somehow strayed to Miami, Florida, where two saving events took place: he met Rachel and he converted to what he liked to call "the Church of England."

Night after night the story of their lives came together, as though in puzzle pieces, a clump of sky confining the still-empty silhouette of a tree, another piece shaped like a running dog but turning out to be a child's elbow against four pickets in a fence. One passage, complete in itself but not yet oriented to the rest, would float wonderfully to its correct position on the board.

Rachel had been brought up by her father, a Miami real estate investor of a cruelty that surpassed description, though incest, starvation and frequent beatings were hinted at. His evil nature I confused with his daughter's poetic genius. Whereas DeQuincey sniggered, stuttered and shrugged his way through his gruesome account, never more than a wisecrack away from pain, Rachel refused to tell her story, but when she relented she proceeded with great gravity. Each of them, in fact, competed for my sympathy. One night I told the Scotts of my struggles against homosexuality and of my present effort to be cured through psychoanalysis. Although I maintained a flippant tone about sex, the Scotts both stood as I spoke, then came over to my kitchen chair, drew me to my feet and embraced me, tears in their eyes. "You poor boy," Mr. Scott said again and again, searching my face for the stigmata of mental illness. "You poor, poor boy. But surely you haven't *acted* on these impulses, have you?"

It took a moment for me to realize they hoped I had only thought about sex with men but never actually engaged in it. I assured them I was very experienced, though I wasn't. I exaggerated the depth of my depravity. Although I was content to accept their sympathy, I didn't want them to pity me for crimes

I had merely contemplated. My admission put them off a bit, as though the fact of sex were a coarse redundancy and the idea of it quite sinful enough.

My confession spurred them on to more daring feats of self-disclosure. I learned that DeQuincey had also been homosexual briefly, a period just before his marriage and conversion, a period adumbrated as a time of faltering, of humiliation, exhaustion and confusion, of bouts of madness alternating with briefer and briefer zones of lucidity, as an accelerating train leaving the station might roll faster and faster under dim lamps before plunging into the blackout of night. Now he was no longer homosexual, not in any way, nor did he ever experience even the slightest twitch of forbidden desire. This complete change he attributed to Christ and Rachel.

The November night went on and on endlessly, exactly like that ghost train in my story, dim rolling stock gliding slowly over the clicking place where the tracks switched, the constant bass hum of that somnolent progress passing over that one tenor break, the riveted and rusting bulkheads emblazoned with the mud-spattered logos of distant places, everything stately as destiny. I could hear the night's freight cars clicking past, and the sky shook out its hair, silver clouds backlit by the moon.

In this measured silence Rachel told me about her own conversion from Judaism to the Church of England, an enlightenment she attributed to her chance reading of C. S. Lewis's *Screwtape Letters* and the simultaneous revelation that Jesus had quite literally died for her sins. She spoke with peculiar emphasis about the nails in Christ's wrists and hands and she even drew a little sketch on the telephone message pad of how she thought the nails had looked (she'd been doing some research into Aramaic pig iron).

When I nodded respectfully but with a visible mote of scorn in my eye, she quite accurately read my thoughts. "Oh, I see, you think I'm some no 'count Baptist, huh, some raving redneck?" She spoke with an unaccustomed crudeness.

"Well, I respect your religion," I spluttered, "but I'm a bit of an agnostic personally and I—"

"You're full of shit," she told me. She was looking right into my eyes. She was breathing emphatically, as though breath were psychic italic marks. She'd pushed her pageboy back from her face and shoved the sleeve of her madras blouse up to expose a pale bicep. She was halfway up out of her chair and leaning toward me. "Shit," she said, her eyes darting for a second up to some invisible cue card before fixing me again. I felt she was torn between shyness and holy fury. "Jesus died for you," she said, "and that's something the greatest poets, Eliot and Dante and Donne, that's something they knew—and they weren't Florida crackers."

"Bravo," DeQuincey whispered in awe. He turned to me with an isn't-this-gal-great? grin—"She's done it again, she's really done it this time"—and he shook his head in admiring disbelief at the sheer wacky brilliance of his wife's spiritual daredevilry.

Exhausted by her performance, she shrank back into her chair, then rose and toddled off to the dark bedroom beyond. The moment DeQuincey and I were alone he stiffened, which I attributed to the embarrassment he must be feeling about his confession to me of his homosexual past. Not that he was attracted to me, nor I to him, but the possibility of attraction existed now and our sexual self-consciousness ricocheted like sunlight in the Hall of Mirrors.

That autumn with the Scotts I remember as a tender haze of tiredness, as the sight of their bright windows projecting a lattice of cross-barred shadows on flower beds filled with chrysanthemums, then dead leaves, then snow. The talk was continuous, it lasted for months, with interruptions only for our lives, which we grabbed at in short, obligatory snatches. Even during the day I'd pop in for ten minutes before lunch or on my way to class. I'd find Rachel foundered on her couch, a bilingual volume of Rilke cast aside, the air around her streaky with angelic transits.

More and more I was spending my long afternoons with Rachel rather than with my old friend Howie. Over the summer

Howie had grown taller and his skin had cleared up. A broad pair of shoulders had been clapped like football padding onto his previously sloped body. Last year he'd worn his fussy, dandified clothes from Paris even when he was alone in his room, and I had often found him rooting about in sachet-scented drawers full of paisley foulards, mauve pocket squares, silk shirts, horrible black garters and knee-length ribbed stockings. Now everything was different. Now he was getting himself up in button jeans, cowboy boots and bright checked shirts, a style that flattered his newly acquired height and slimness. He still wore his crooked horn-rimmed glasses (which looked preposterous the one time he donned his ten-gallon hat in my presence), he was still shy and still refused to undress in front of me or even to walk about in his underwear, but this shyness, so to speak, had now gained confidence and he no longer needed to disguise his shyness as belligerence.

Along with his cowboy clothes he had taken up a gentle Western manner. No longer did he inveigh against Jews in high finance, he no longer denounced our idiot teachers, parents, classmates, the entirely barbaric hemisphere we were unfortunate enough to have been born on. The Juliette Greco record had been banished in favor of one by the black folk singer Odetta. Howie himself had taken up the guitar and he favored the old songs of the IWW period. His change in height had led to a change of wardrobe that had in turn inspired a change in his politics. No longer did he pore over hagiographies of the Führer; now he was reading Emma Goldman's *Living My Life.* And this change was as temperamental as ideological, for suddenly he seemed sensitive to the labor of the many gardeners and cooks and janitors at Eton who were always in the background of everyone's snapshots and who maintained the miles and miles of grounds. We'd stroll past a frosted-over greenhouse on a cold November afternoon and through the cloudy glass we'd see the Scottish gardeners hovering and stretching and reaching as they bedded down bulbs for the winter or repotted plants or misted giant tropical ferns, and Howie would start grumbling about the unfairness of things: "Why should they have to work so hard to make things beautiful for us?" I felt like pointing out that a gardener's life was pleasantly varied by the seasons and offered chances for self-expression and in any event was a skilled craft, but Howie's sympathy for what he called "the poor" came as such a welcome relief to last year's fascism that I scarcely wanted to discourage it. Any sign of suffering moved Howie, even to the point of tears.

He was also treating me with kindness and for the first time was willing to listen to me when I talked about my shrink or my homosexuality or my infatuation with the Scotts, although he was dubious about most of my enthusiasms. He thought psychoanalysis was a terrible waste of money and breath. As for homosexuality, he didn't know what to think about it. Last year he had told me with a saurian little smile that the Führer had liquidated Ernst Röhm for his "inversion." But now all of Howie's views were becoming mammalian. I saw that the anger and hauteur of the past, which I'd accepted without interpreting, had been merely a counterpart to his isolation and the terrible shame he'd felt about the way he looked. If he couldn't participate in the festivities of friendship and romance, then he'd burn the tents and poison the wells.

This intransigence had now given way to a new optimism and tenderness and a gracious, civilized uncertainty. "I don't know what to say about homosexuality," he said to me as we kicked our way down a long hillside of autumn leaves that crackled like the bright, cast-off shells of boiled crustaceans. "But at least you have *some* sort of sexuality. And you've actually had some sex. Which is neat, if you think about it. Not many kids can claim as much." We were heading toward a Japanese stone lantern half mossed over beside a bridge wreathed in mists rising from the stream that fed into the man-made pond, empty now but in warm weather the home of corpulent, whiskered white fish freckled with pale brown spots. "Now, as to these High Church Scotts of yours, they seem like fanatics to me. Of course, they're fascinating, I can see why you like them." He compared them to characters in Proust, but the names meant nothing to me. I envied him his Olympian sureness in placing people according to the typology of classic fiction. I, too, would read Proust someday, but only after I'd mastered Pound, Moore, Eliot, Gerard Manley Hopkins, Donne, Dante and all the other poets the Scotts discussed every night.

The talk with the Scotts was not exclusively literary. When we were alone, Rachel would confide in me how much she despised DeQuincey, how unworthy of her he was and how she longed to escape him and to remove little Tim from his debilitating influence. "DeQuincey's just a creep, weak, ineffectual. You can see it for yourself. I hate him." She lowered her head and her eyelids fluttered disquietingly as she spoke; she was ashamed of both her husband and her spleen.

It dawned on me (or rather sunset on me, for this recognition felt old, familiar, auburn) that Rachel loved me or would have had she met me at some more favorable moment in her life or mine, or had I been even a few years older. All these objections, and her proud fear of exposing her love to someone who might not welcome it, made her break off, sigh, fidget with her hair, strum the *Duino Elegies* and squint into already feeble sunlight further filtered by drawn curtains. That distant, scarcely audible whistle must belong to a coach on the playing fields half a mile away. Her chair creaked. Tim materialized, rubbing sleep and fever out of his eyes. He'd been kept home today with the flu. Without hesitation he climbed up onto my lap and butted his head dully, stubbornly against my chest, frustrated because he was sick. I sipped the hot coffee and smiled inwardly at the thought of this wife and this son I'd acquired, these phantom dependents. Sometimes I caught DeQuincey sneaking an unpleasant glance at me, but I knew he would never exile me or even antagonize me, for he needed me to placate his implacable wife. Once, only once, on a Saturday night we three drank two bottles of wine and we let the talk drift to sex. "Yeah," DeQuincey said, "Rachel's got her fantasies. She'd like—"

"Shut up," Rachel said without any particular emphasis. An

incongruous smile flickered over her features. "Just shut up." The smile suggested she was anticipating his next move, as a sitter lights up the moment before he is finally shown his portrait.

"Yeah, Rachel wants two pricks, one in each hand."

I drew back inwardly at the terrible words and the smile that was leaking out of DeQuincey's face like candlelight from a carved pumpkin. He had just given a haywire emphasis to the words *two pricks* that made me no longer think of him as a lovable, befuddled, overgrown preppy but rather as a man who had really had real mental breakdowns, whose imagination had festered. I looked for a reflection of my disgust in Rachel's face, but she was grinning and staring at her accomplice, perhaps her impresario. There was an air about them of driven but thoroughly professional gamblers. He had just placed a roll of chips on a number. She more than matched him and pushed forward with both her small hands, slowly but firmly, all her remaining wealth. "Okay," she said softly. Her terrible silent chuckle had begun. She spread her legs under the full skirt, planted her elbows on her knees and looked up at us. Her gaze was steady and provocative, although from time to time she had to steal a glance at the cue card to break the tension.

"Oho!" DeQuincey shouted. Then he said in a stage whisper to me, "She thinks we'll be the first to chicken out." (I liked that *we*.) "But she's got us pegged all wrong." He raced about the room turning off lights and saying over and over again, "Ooh-la-la," as though sexual adventure must be French.

In the past, whenever the Scotts had come close to a decisive action, they'd annihilated it through paralyzing discussion. That's what kept them together, I imagine, their Sisyphean talk. He'd annoy her, she'd lapse into ponderous, savage silence, he'd cajole her out of it, she'd tongue-lash him, he'd whimper, then cringingly strike back, she'd retreat, he'd pursue—and all these feints and thrusts they simultaneously analyzed from so many angles and with such a strange blend of vanity, self-hatred, Christian moralizing and cross-cultural reference that finally nothing took place. Rachel didn't walk out on DeQuincey. DeQuincey didn't burn his poems, his "life work," as he threatened to. She didn't send Tim off to her monster father in Miami ("At least he's a real man, and absolute evil is preferable, far preferable to your *mauvais foi*"). He didn't run away to become an Augustinian. She didn't turn on the gas to asphyxiate them all. None of this happened. They outsat each other, the air turned blue with tobacco smoke, irony and exhaustion. Dawn made its killjoy appearance, like a parent returning home to halt the children's party, by now a seedy, nearly comatose event.

But tonight talk wasn't sapping resolve. In fact tonight the Scotts seemed in collusion, as though they'd decided in advance to seduce me. Given my failure with the black prostitute, I feared I wouldn't be able to get it up for any woman, much less a teacher's wife. But I didn't want to be the one to back down.

When we all three finally got into bed, DeQuincey kept the wisecracks coming. He was the eternal kid who's forgotten to change his underwear, who keeps his socks on and can hardly wait to dive in ("Oh boy, oh boy"). Rachel, however, lost her bravado. She wasn't frightened or ashamed but she was shy, even a little romantic. She lay between us. DeQuincey took no interest in me; perhaps Christ really had driven out all his homosexual devils. As it ended up, he mounted her while I stroked her face. When we were all dressed again, the Scotts seemed exhilarated—too much so, to my mind, considering how little had happened. Only gradually did I come to understand that whereas the Scotts certainly did have a serious Anglican admiration of sin, they had an equally strong horror of seeming to themselves bourgeois. Their desire to be bohemian outweighed their resolve to be good. Our "orgy," as they called it, reassured them that their morality must be of a higher sort, no mere suburban primness.

Sex now seemed a strange thing to me, a social rite that registered, even brought about shifts in the balance of power, but something that was more discussed than performed, a simple emission of fluid that somehow generated religious, social and economic consequences.

What I daydreamed of was a lover who would be older than I, richer and more influential, but also companionable. He would prize me for my sexuality, which was at once my essence and also an attribute I was totally unfamiliar with, like the orphan's true name, a magical identity he knows nothing of until the very moment of revelation. The name ennobles the orphan, just as one's sexual nature confers a previously undivined but achingly anticipated *human* nature upon love's candidate. I knew I was worthless and at the same time I was convinced somebody would find me worthy, would worship me for this sexual allure so foreign to my understanding yet so central to my being.

Although I lived surrounded by people and regularly visited a psychoanalyst, it never entered my mind to discuss with anyone my fantasies, those in which the Belgian soldier or a silver-haired stranger in a dove-gray suit seated in his Silver Cloud took me away and married me. For other boys, who can legally marry their fantasies, marriage itself must seem less magical. It is, after all, a ceremony they will eventually go through. But for me, who'd never even read about the sort of union I longed for, marriage became more and more impossible, a transubstantiation as eerie and irreversible as death. Perhaps by framing this ideal and funereal homosexual marriage in a prospect of poisonous flowers, I was making it more and more remote, thereby putting off the day when I'd have to decide whether I myself was a homosexual or not. Of course I wanted to love a man and to be heterosexual; the longer I could delay sorting out this antinomy, the better.

I didn't go home for Thanksgiving but spent the long weekend with the Scotts. They took the opportunity to introduce me to Father Burke, their "confessor," and spiritual guardian. Rachel had told me that he regularly wrote her long letters full of counsel and prayer, although he lived only some fifty or sixty miles away and she and DeQuincey saw him often. Father Burke also wrote Quince long letters, which Quince would never show to Rachel. Father Burke had taken over the poorest, oldest, most backward parish in the state: a mortification, I suppose. In his unheated, shabby little church he officiated at several services a day. He was famous, at least to the Scotts, for his short, lucid sermons—"Worthy of Boussuet," DeQuincey assured me, "little miracles of theology and common sense."

In his letters to Rachel, Father Burke argued in page after page of his effortlessly flowing script against her longing to leave DeQuincey. Once she even showed me an excerpt from Burke's latest: "Nor, my daughter, can you leave your husband any more than Our Lord can abandon the sinner or God the prodigal. In a very special, very private sense DeQuincey is your Cross and your marriage is your Calvary. Don't imagine for a moment, my child, that I am insensitive to your plight. I know what sort of man DeQuincey is, and I know how little he is suited to you in the way the world thinks. What, then, could have been God's plan in linking you to such a man with an eternal vow except to purify you through pain? Rather than despising and fleeing our sufferings, we should treasure them and thank the Lord for them, since we are each given the exact sort of suffering we require to break our will and to increase our spirit, as though the will were the seed's hull and the spirit its germinating embryo."

Something in me thrilled to this talk. Certainly such a religion raised our flat, squirming little lives into the high static relief of allegory. The Church had set aside its legal and political ambitions in order to ensure its continued colonization of dailiness. This invasion advanced into every last corner of consciousness by virtue of a flair for drama. Reality isn't dramatic but the mind is; the Church accommodates itself accordingly to mental physiology rather than to the anatomy of the real.

For the Scotts the medieval ring to Father Burke's style made it all the more seductive. Far from impressing them as a drawback, the far-fetched nature of his language and his insistence on its literal truth had for them all the appeal of the antique. They belonged to that generation of humanists who found the advances of science alarming and who imagined the atelier and the chapel must defend themselves against the laboratory. To me this view of things seemed quaint; I was content to accept every truth science might establish, though at the same time I recognized that what most interested me science couldn't address: subjectivity.

The Scotts weren't willing to reduce the claims of the spirit. They wanted to vaunt the "higher" truth of religion and art over the somehow mechanical or merely factual truth of science. Father Burke, clearly intelligent, erudite and dedicated, thrilled them when he insisted on the literal miracle of the Virgin Birth and the actual existence of hell, although in his version hell got improved, its status as fiery real estate changed to a cold, unreal state in which the degree of damnation is measured by the soul's distance from God. "Hell is God's absence," he told me.

For Thanksgiving Mrs. Scott had on an unprecedentedly girlish blue dress and a mauve ribbon bobby-pinned to her still-wet hair. She kept blinking mildly and smiling meekly as she brought in dish after dish to the heavy oak dining room table. DeQuincey stood to carve. He performed the ritual with solemnity. When we toasted one another with red wine, DeQuincey said to Father Burke, "I welcome you to the hospitality of our table; you are our honored guest," and the priest smiled and inclined his head. I kept feeling that everyone but me was following a secret book of etiquette and that the deliberateness of the courtesy was as medieval as Burke's theology.

The dinner conversation was philosophical. Aristotle was dismissed in favor of Plato, a preference I again ascribed to the very improbability of Plato's thought. It seemed that the more bizarre a belief, the more poetic it must be, and hence the more noble it was to embrace it. I couldn't help sensing that the Scotts were, underneath everything, as American as I, just as skeptical of ideas, and that like me they were convinced by the sincerity of an impulse rather than the rigor of a system. Very well. By a snobbish reverse, the preposterous claims of Platonism and a Platonic Christianity were what most excited them, as though anything that so taxed one's credulity must be—well, not true, but aristocratic, superior. When they'd talk about Original Sin or the Creation or the Devil they'd become agitated, their cheeks would flush and their eyes would sparkle, as though they were hypnotizing themselves into espousing this obvious nonsense. And the more vague and absurd the things they discussed (angels, the resurrection of the body), the more they used such words as *precisely, undoubtedly, clearly* and *naturally,* and each time they uttered such a word their eyes would dilate with glee—lying made them gleeful, just as children shriek with pleasure as they egg each other on to think up more and more gruesome details in a ghost story.

After dinner I found myself alone with Father Burke. Tim was taking his nap and the Scotts had rather stagily gone out for a walk. The priest was by no means the dour figure I had pictured him to be. He was small, clubby, wore a gold seal ring, swilled his brandy in a snifter and inhaled its fumes with his eyes closed and eyebrows raised as though he were hearing a tenor float a high note. When he spoke he did so with a faint Tidewater accent. Like other upper-class Southerners he had an interest in history and acted as though he were on an intimate footing with the famous dead. The Roman Republic had been discussed over the pumpkin pie and Father Burke had winked at me and said, "You know that Julius Caesar was a terribly *attractive* man. He made conquests wherever he went, and not just among the ladies." I dared to hope he meant Caesar had loved men as well, although possibly ladies were being contrasted to sluts. Assuming Burke had meant men, was his wink a way of showing me the Scotts had told him about my homosexual problem and that he was too worldly to be appalled by it?

I'd never known this particular shade of Christianity before. I'd met know-nothing Fundamentalists, or at least heard them rave over the radio. Higher up the social ladder came the suburban Presbyterians and Unitarians and Congregationalists who joined a vanilla-pudding sort of earnestness to a complete lack of charity. Fortunately, they had no urge to proselytize, since they maintained their faith as a closed club, a Rotary lodge for well-heeled businessmen. Then I had had my brush with Marilyn's Catholicism, but it was all rapture and votive candles and tears, something I filed in my imagination next to Puccini arias and the names of expensive perfumes (*Poème d'Extase*). The Scotts, however, were serious people. They cared about the poor. They liked their pleasures. They were well read. And they were spiritually on the make; they wanted me to convert. Father Burke himself was both cerebral and sensuous, unshockable. He had small dark eyes that he would let deliberately cloud over only so that they could suddenly clarify. As I spoke he'd tap his fingertips together and wear a wan smile that said, "I've heard this all a hundred times before. Please continue." At the moment I was spelling out for him my objection to God, an argument I'd worked out previously but that the wine was muddling: "But if God is all-knowing He must have foreseen from the beginning how people would suffer, and if He foresaw it, then we didn't really ever have a choice, and if He was all good, then why did He let us suffer, wait a minute, wait a minute . . ."

Father Burke had stopped tapping his fingers. His smile had faded and his eyes had gone cloudy. He'd let his face become old and weary, as though to say I had done this to him. Suddenly his eyes were homing in on me, a flicker of his tongue stung his lips back into life and he said, "But shouldn't we set aside this *philosophy*"—generous dollop of irony to suggest that if he was interested in my soul he was bored by my mind, for my soul might be eternal but my mind was all too obviously adolescent—"and move on to something a little more urgent." He pressed his fingertips to his brow and hid behind his hands. "Haven't you something you want to tell me about?" he asked out of this manual tent, his voice hollow.

But he was trying to intimidate the wrong person. I was, after all, a Buddhist. I'd never believed, or only in fleeting reverie, in a warm, concerned, touchy Christian God, who seemed all too obviously a conflation of what people wanted and feared. As a character, Burke intrigued me more than his deity. I appreciated the sense of drama he wanted to inject into my existence and I was flattered he thought I, or at least some essential if rather abstract principle within me, was worth saving.

But I also felt surging within me a fierce need to be independent. Of course I responded to the appeal of divine hydraulics, this system of souls damned or crowned or destroyed or held in suspense, these pulleys and platforms sinking and lifting on the great stage, and I recognized that my view of things seemed by contrast impoverished, lacking in degree and incident. But the charming intricacy of a myth is not sufficient to compel belief. I found no good reason to assume that the ultimate nature of reality happens to resemble the backstage of an opera house.

On a more emotional level I had an aversion to anything authoritarian. I might long for the capacious, sheltering embrace of a father but I detested paternalism. I was quite hostile to it, in fact. "Well, yes," I said, "I am seeing a psychiatrist because I have conflicts over certain homosexual tendencies I'm feeling."

At these words Father Burke's face lurched up out of his hands. Not the nervous little confession he had expected. He recovered his poise and decided to laugh boisterously, the laugh of Catholic centuries. "*Conflicts?*" he whooped, in tears of laughter by now. Then, sobering for a second, the priest added in a low, casual voice, "But you see, my son, homosexuality isn't just a *conflict* that needs to be *resolved*"—his voice picked up these words as though they were nasty bits of refuse—"homosexuality is also a sin."

I think he had no notion how little an effect the word *sin* had on me. He might just as well have said, "Homosexuality is bad *juju.*"

"But I feel very drawn to other men," I said. Although something defiant in me forced these words out, I felt myself becoming a freak the moment I spoke. My hair went bleach-blond, my wrist went limp, my rep tie became a lace jabot: I was the simpering queen at the grand piano playing concert versions of last year's pop tunes for his mother and her bridge club. There was no way to defend what I was. All I could fight for was my right to choose my exile, my destruction.

"Just because you feel something is no reason to act on it," the priest said. "Americans hold up their feelings as though they were . . . dispensations." He drained off the brandy. "For instance, I've taken a vow of chastity and I abide by it."

"What do you do for relief?"

He smiled at my impertinence. "Do I masturbate, is that what you're asking? I don't. Occasionally there's a nocturnal emission." He touched his lips with his fingertips. I wondered if the women of his parish who volunteered their services as house-keepers to the priest treasured those stiffened linen relics of sanctity.

The pastoral chat was not turning out. Father Burke was miffed. He was most irritated with the Scotts, who'd misrepresented to him my readiness to leap up into the lap of Mother Church. The priest consulted his pocket watch, then worked a toothpick behind a screening hand, a nicety that seemed to me nearly as repulsive as nocturnal emissions.

My stubbornness caused the Scotts to cool considerably. When I dropped in on Rachel the Monday after Thanksgiving, she scarcely looked up from her *Imitation of Christ*. At last she sighed impatiently, set it aside and said, "I don't think you should spend quite so much time here. It's not healthy for you. You should run and play with the other boys. Besides, I'm doing a lot of reading in *The Golden Bough* for my next poem and I can't just chew the fat with you for hours and hours and hours." Tears sprang to my eyes and I hurried away.

Recently a new part-time teacher had been added to the staff, a Mr. Beattie, who had been hired to instruct three afternoons a week those students interested in jazz. Beattie himself was a jazz drummer and had even toured with a band; he still held regular jam sessions somewhere downtown on weekends. Chuck told me Beattie was a "character," his highest accolade. Chuck was so sure of himself he was always seeking out "characters" in order to introduce dissonance into his otherwise tonic experience.

Chuck was famous for his escapades. He'd regale me for hours with the details. His current girl was the pert grand-daughter of an almost comically conservative senator, one of those mastodons my father voted for. At the moment Janie had her own house, an unusual possession for a girl of seventeen. Her mother, who was supposed to live with her, was off sailing the Aegean with an Argentine. Her playboy father, about to divorce his third wife and already separated from her, lived on a neighboring estate by himself. He'd lost his license after repeated arrests for drunk driving, and his daughter had to chauffeur him everywhere. They looked like brother and sister.

A maid cooked and cleaned for Janie, but the maid didn't live in. Someone else maintained the indoor pool.

At night Janie was alone and she was free to invite anyone she liked to stay over. That would usually be Chuck on weekends. Even on some weeknights Chuck would escape the dorm after lights-out. Janie would be waiting for him at the gate in her battered old MG, lights off. She'd return him to school before dawn. In the interval he'd persuade her to perform some new sexual stunt. They'd experiment with exotic lubricants (papaya juice, chocolate syrup, cold bacon grease). He'd insert a balloon in her and then inflate it. Eventually she would return the favor as they both drifted on an air mattress across the heated swimming pool on a subzero December night. Snow blew up in banks against the thick glass doors and spun in minor swirls under the porch lights. Farther up the hill stood pines laden with snow like ermined dons gathering for the procession.

Chuck grew more boisterous, reckless, impatient after every adventure. No outrage was enough for him. Only a war would have been equal to his hunger for danger. He and several members of the Butt Club became friends with Beattie. Just before supper every other afternoon they'd sit around with him down in the music building and smoke cigarettes in one of the record-listening booths. They'd spin jazz records. Sometimes Beattie would play along on his own drums. The noise of their talk, laughter and drumming was confined to the soundproof room. Whoever might report they were smoking off limits and at an impermissible time of day could be spotted at a safe distance through the glass window set into the wall separating the booth from the glee club's big practice room.

Beattie wore black suede shoes and had his hair cut in a flattop, longer in back than in front. It sloped down toward you like a ski jump. If he bent his head, his scalp showed white. His handshake was limp, but a second after he'd removed this cold, boneless fillet from your hand he was slicing the air with a powerful snap of his fingers in response to some mental or recorded riff he was hearing. He'd squint and bite his lower lip and his head would bob up and down in an accelerating rhythm. Soon he'd be whispering, "And-a one, and-a two . . ." He had, it seemed, only one suit, a shiny gray sharkskin, the baggy pants radically pegged, the jacket's lapels narrow and usually turned up as against a draft. On off-hours he wore no tie but just a black shirt buttoned tightly at the neck to give him a throttled look. His neck and face and hands were pale and big; he seemed like a prisoner in a cheap suit he's been given on dismissal. He projected a strong, almost rancid sexuality, but it was hard to place. It was too canny and too asymmetrical to seem robustly masculine in the old sense. He had a way of grabbing his crotch and holding it, sometimes even shaking it for a second while he was talking. I suppose he'd picked this up from the Negroes he'd met in the jazz world.

This gesture seemed designed to lend an extra weight to his words. Or perhaps it was a proof to the listener that he was being honest, all there, a body behind his words.

His ears were a shade pinker than his pale face. His eyebrows were very solid and dark and looked as though the draftsman had pochéd them in quickly. His upper lip was so thin as to form just a line, but his lower lip was full. On some days he laughed hysterically at simple statements; he'd double up and keep repeating an ordinary word someone had chanced to use as if he hoped to wring some new meaning out of it. When he held his crotch, his baggy pants would ride up to reveal how powerful his thighs were. He wore socks of bright pinks and purples and they were only ankle-high. His responses were sometimes weirdly delayed. Someone would ask him a question and he'd study his face a moment, two moments, before saying a soft, feathery yes or an even less audible no.

I sat around with the Butt Club boys and Mr. Beattie on two or three different afternoons, but I didn't like him. He reminded me of that hustler I'd met two summers ago. He had the same air of being a con man. Something shifty.

One day Chuck told me Beattie was about to receive a shipment of marijuana. Did I want to buy in or at least try a joint or two?

"What is it, exactly?" I asked. "Isn't it like heroin?"

Chuck laughed. "No. Great stuff, Beattie tells me. Makes you happy. Good for sex. Good for listening to music. Come on down next Wednesday to the music room and we'll blow some weed." He snapped his fingers with a hard snap. But this was precisely the invitation to a lifelong addiction I'd always heard about, a fate so dire no one actually had ever had to warn me against it. Not that I'd met an addict, but I had seen movies in which a handsome musician—exactly!—sweated in a hotel room and vomited and pleaded with his girlfriend to put him back on the needle or weed or whatever, but she refused him for his own sake, despite his hallucinations and writhings on the floor. Why had Mr. Beattie come to Eton? Perhaps he was so addicted to marijuana he could no longer afford to maintain his habit unless—that's it—unless he also became a dealer to bored teens.

In those days all drugs except alcohol, tobacco and diet pills and sedatives were unknown to conventional Americans. I wasn't sure what I should do. I wanted to do the right thing. Chuck and the other guys in the Butt Club seemed hopeless to me. They would succumb to any temptation, I knew, but not if the temptation was removed. They valued nothing. One of them had lost an eye in a fight, but all he could say was, "So what? I've still got one left."

During my next session with Dr. O'Reilly I asked him for advice. He didn't want to discuss my problems. He was telling me about his daughter's latest escapade. While he had been addressing a parents' group, she had gone into the best restaurant in town, been careful to identify herself as his daughter and then tried to set the place on fire.

When I brought O'Reilly back to the subject, he snapped, "I can't tell you what to do, you know that."

"Then give me some information. Is marijuana dangerous?"

"Can be." He was picking his nose in an elaborate way, examining his handkerchief for portents.

"How?"

"It can cause a psychotic break." He had just received a shipment of Polynesian carvings, statues with real human hair and giant phalluses; three of these totems stood behind his chair, lending force to his opinions.

"What's a psychotic—"

"Craziness."

"And does marijuana always lead to heroin?"

"It can, if only because you start living in the drug world and you think you might as well try everything."

"What does it do, marijuana, to ordinary people?"

"Makes them paranoid."

I thought I knew how my father must feel all the time: lonely and responsible. No one looked to my father for amusement. He was dull. He wasn't fashionable. He was deliberate, but he didn't shirk his responsibilities. He could always be counted on to do the right thing.

I went to the headmaster's secretary to make an appointment. "I must see him now."

"What is it exactly?" she asked. "Do you want to argue over a grade? It's too late for that—"

"No, no," I said disdainfully. "It has nothing to do with me personally. It concerns the reputation of the school and it can't wait a moment."

She nodded and went into the headmaster's paneled, carpeted office for a moment. When she emerged she told me to come back at four.

I was agitated. I knew I was doing the right thing and yet I feared what Chuck would say when Mr. Beattie was fired. Would Chuck drop me, persecute me, organize a cabal against me, tell everyone I was a hateful little prig?

I knew I wouldn't be able to face Mr. Beattie. I'd never spoken out against anyone before. Would his wife and children go hungry? Would he ever find another job? Never before had I wielded so much power over an adult man; the power excited and scared me. Paradoxically, I who didn't much like Eton, I who concealed sexual longings most Etonians would have condemned far sooner than dope peddling, I who had rejected the school's religion and slept with a master and his wife, I who had once bought a hustler ten years older than I and last summer had slept with a boy three years younger, I who'd serviced Ralph, the special camper—paradoxically, I was the one whom circumstance had chosen to defend this institution I despised. I was to be the guardian of public morality.

Anxiety swept through me. Like most of the other students I refused to wear an overcoat even on the coldest days. Now I was trembling as I hugged myself and hurried down the brick walkway toward the music building. My teeth were chattering by the time I ducked in the door.

There was Mr. Beattie picking out chords on the piano. No one else was around. "Hi," he said. He stood and gave me his limp hand, a courtesy that puzzled me. No other master routinely shook hands with students. I felt shame rise to my face. I looked at the clock: it was three-fifteen.

He asked me if I played the piano and I said just a bit. He surrendered the instrument to me. I played a recital piece from long ago, something simple by Brahms my father used to like.

"Hey, Mr. Beattie," I said, "Chuck tells me some famous jazz guy's coming to visit you this weekend."

"Bugs Tice," he said. He was standing in the incurve of the grand piano's embrace, one hand pressing down on the polished black lid. "He's staying in the parents' suite here at school. You'll have to hear us jam—he's the greatest on the horn."

Somehow I was picking up the sound of sex. I was always on the alert for it, I studied boys as they came out of one another's dorm rooms, I lounged on other guys' beds during free time, always in expectation of a held glance, a missed beat, but I never heard a single hint. Now I was hearing something—tentative to be sure, but something real.

"These jazz guys?" I said as I struck the final chord.

"Yes?"

"Some of them are oddballs, right? No offense, Mr. Beattie. I mean, the jazz world's pretty progressive, right?"

"Yeah. We say hip."

"Is this Bugs hip?"

"How do you mean, exactly?"

I smiled. The clock hands refused to move.

"No, how do you mean?" Beattie repeated. He was also smiling.

"Well, I was just wondering why you were putting him up in the parents' suite instead of at your own house with your wife and kids."

Mr. Beattie's eyes widened rhetorically; he wanted me to see them widening. "Boy," he said, shaking his head, "you're wild." He covered the next beat by miming playing a saxophone. His fingers ran up and down imaginary keys and his cheeks swelled. He closed his eyes and rocked back on his heels.

"Seriously," I said, breathless and exhilarated but only in my capacity as spectator; as a performer I was beautifully calm. "Chuck says that marijuana—"

"Sh-h-h!" Mr. Beattie hissed. "Don't go talking that shit. That's real bogus, man."

"Sorry," I said, "Mr. Beattie."

"So what did you want to know?" His smile had migrated back and now he was wailing one more long note on his imaginary sax.

"I just wanted to know if it's good for sex."

"Is it—? Well, yeah." He laughed. "Yeah. I had you pegged all wrong. I thought you were the Little Lord Fauntleroy type, but you're hip. I like the way you just truck right in." He mimed driving a truck. He took a swerve, then pressed down on the brake, glided to a halt, switched off the key, pulled it out, twirled it once and pocketed it. "Just as neat and simple as you please." Very deliberate, now: "Yeah, kid, it's great for sex. Next question."

I played a C-major scale. "Are you going to make me do all the work in this conversation?"

"Possibly." He grabbed his crotch, then looked down at his white hand, the white of cooked ham, gave it an extra shake and, as though satisfied with his test, smiled. "You're a good kid," he said, releasing himself.

I could hear the football team shouting as the guys entered the athletics building next door; that must be the thunder of their cleats on the stone floor just inside the double doors. "Say you and Bugs are listening to music or something and you're all alone in the parents' suite and nobody's around, because it is real isolated after all, and say you smoke some—"

"We get high. So go on."

"You both get high and . . ." I closed the lid over the keys and rested my hands on the curved, reflecting wood. "Suppose he was the kind of guy who wanted to fool around. Who wanted to party." I used the word the black whore had used.

"I'm with you. You're amazing. Here we are in goddamn suburbia and I've got some fuckin' teenage hipster on my hands. Go on."

"Well, suppose he gets high and wants to blow you, nothing more, you don't have to do a thing, just dig the music, would you let him?"

Mr. Beattie was brushing his right hand back and forth over his crew cut. He seemed to be concentrating on this job, getting the feel of those soft quills against his palm. He wasn't looking at me. "That's a pretty funny question. Why do you ask? Is your question *academic* or what?"

"I'm asking," I said, "because I'd like to party with you."

He nodded quickly. "Got it. Groovy." He looked at the clock. "I could make it real good for us both. Come back at five-fifteen, five-thirty and it'll be dark and the fuckin' animals next door"—head jerk to indicate the athletics building—"will have cleared out by then. We'll be all alone down here and I'll put on some nice classical music and we'll blow some weed, I've got nice stuff, and we'll see, just see what happens. Okay?"

I who was always conscious of the formlessness of real life now saw it imitate art, though the meaning of this action, which was surely turning out to be tragic, escaped me. I had my appointment with the headmaster at four. At five-thirty, after I'd betrayed Mr. Beattie, I'd return to have sex with him. The next day he'd be fired. He'd learn of my denunciation and he wouldn't be able to say anything against me. He wouldn't be able to discredit me by saying I was a practicing homosexual since we would have practiced homosexuality together. He'd be powerless. I would have gotten what I wanted, gotten away with it and gotten rid of him: the trapdoor beside the bed. At last I could seduce and betray an adult. This heterosexual hipster would be my momentary Verlaine.

I smiled at him, nodded encouragingly, even grabbed my own crotch in friendly imitation of his trademark gesture. Once I was outside I looked up at the gray and white clouds boiling and flowing over the tower beside the chapel, a brick reminiscence of the silo it had replaced (the whole estate had once been a farm). I hurried under a stone arch carved with the motto "A Life Without Beauty Is Only Half Lived." A shiny black head of a woman was poised in a niche above the arch. Though the sculptor had undoubtedly hoped she would appear ageless, in fact her hairdo was all too patently a style of the 1920s, giveaway finger waves.

But everything I observed was at the edge of consciousness, for I thought of myself as a sturdy cutter slicing through waves of cold air, as a tough, almost square vessel set on a straight course. Usually I'd sense I was permeable, insubstantial, at most a bank of moving air, a cold front, and only in conversation did I condense into a downpour of being. But now I was dense and potent. There were no eddies of empty time to swirl me off course, no horse latitudes of nothingness to becalm me.

The headmaster found my information too upsetting to accept readily and I observed his dithering with scorn. I was summoning him to battle, but he kept fussing over how he should wear his uniform. "Well, of course Mr. Beattie is not a full or even regular member of the Eton faculty," he said, as though that made any difference one way or another. He was performing all the tiresome operations of cleaning, fueling and lighting a pipe. "I suppose we'll have to report him to the federal—would it be the Treasury Department? Is the Bureau of Narcotics a subdivision of the Treasury?"

"I don't know," I said, by now just a boy again.

After the headmaster had covered every subsidiary issue, as though he were constitutionally drawn to the incidental, I brought him back to what was essential at least to me. "You must promise you won't talk to Mr. Beattie until after I've gone home for Christmas vacation," I said solemnly. "And then you must make sure he's out of here by the time I get back. I don't want to have to see him. That might be dangerous for me." I thought the headmaster owed me at the very least this protection in return for my having saved the school.

"Nonsense," he said, peeved, "I can't promise a thing." He looked longingly at the closed door as though he hoped someone would open it and end this eternal interview. "And are you quite sure you haven't become an addict yourself?" he asked. "Shall I have the narcotics people bring you some of their interesting literature on addiction? I'm sure they have some splendid brochures, they should, our tax dollars, you know . . ." And he went on mumbling to himself until I was able to slip out.

No one was worthy of me.

I had twenty minutes to kill before my rendezvous with Beattie, an interval I resented, so habituated had I already become to the tight scheduling of the great man, the man of the world.

THE HEADMASTER, as it turned out, botched everything. He did bring in the narcs, who did give me a brochure about heroin; I was basalt with indignation. Mr. Beattie was fired, but he was allowed to hang around until well into the next semester. Since Beattie couldn't say we'd had sex, at a faculty meeting he accused me and DeQuincey of being lovers. Good old Quince stood by me, though he was badly shaken; the accusation had been just accurate enough to scare him. At last Beattie left us; I didn't see him again until three years later, when I was in college and he was playing drums in a two-bit band at a fraternity dance. His eyes locked with mine. I felt I should tell him how much I repented what I'd done to him. I'd used and discarded him—just as my dad had mistreated Alice, the Addressograph operator.

Oh, there are lots of stories I could tell. Dr. O'Reilly, who of course turned out to be a speed freak, had a breakdown one day and had to be hauled off to a clinic for several years. My friend Howie, true to his prediction, died before he was twenty. I saw him when he was very ill in the hospital. He was yellow and bloated from nephritis. I had to hold a mirror for him while he trimmed his own hair: "Don't want to leave my last haircut to these hacks," he said gallantly, a trace of the old Nazi dandy having reemerged in extremity. At the funeral Howie's father turned out to be a young middle-level executive for a big corporation. The funeral was held at the McCabe Funeral Home (I pronounced it "macabre"). I was a pallbearer. There was a Hammond organ toothlessly mouthing hymns as though the music were bread soaked in milk. Our handsome, oafish chaplain gave the sermon. He'd never spoken for two seconds to Howie, who in any event had been a militant atheist. Oh, and the chaplain was found soon afterward in another master's wife's bed and he was not only dismissed from Eton but also defrocked. His brother found him a job leading ski tours of eager coeds to Switzerland, where he was last heard yodeling on his way to his death as he missed a turn and sailed off into a crevasse.

The college I went to was near Eton and I often visited the Scotts. One day I discovered Rachel laughing and sobbing. Finally overcome by curiosity, she'd broken open the casket where DeQuincey kept his pastoral letters from Father Burke. They were all love letters, hysterical avowals of pornographic desire, some of it clearly referring to actual nights of passion they'd spent together. "To think Burke kept urging me to stay with Quince," she said. "I was their cover." She kept sifting through the letters, and her horrible silent chuckle resumed. Tim, older now and in first grade, looked in, but when he saw his mother talking to herself he frowned and clattered up the stairs to his room.

AS I LEFT the headmaster's office that day I noticed the wind was now sharp with snow needles. Evening was coming on rapidly. It had been implicit in the dim day all along, just as the snow had been. In the gray light the snow could be felt but not seen; suddenly lamps along the walkway snapped on and their halos were grained by a million, million lights. The return to the music building wasn't lustful or fearful but ceremonial. I felt as though I were a dancer not up to his role but inspired by the expectation everywhere in the darkness around me. Or I felt like someone in history, a queen on her way to the scaffold determined to suppress her usual quips, to give the spectators the high deeds they wanted to see.

Mr. Beattie was stoned. His smile was unfocused and perpetual. He started telling me a long story I couldn't follow, something about something someone had once said to him somewhere, but then he noticed we'd drifted into the listening booth. He didn't turn on the light. The darkness was illumined by light reflected up through the windows off the snowdrifts outside. He put on a record. He sat in an armchair, lit another marijuana cigarette and blew smoke at the ceiling. When he offered me a drag I smiled with what I hoped passed for affection and shook my head. A moment later I was kneeling on the floor beside him. I opened his fly and pulled out his large and already erect penis. "Here," he said, "let me make it better for you," and he undid his belt and dropped his trousers to his knees. I'd been right; his thighs were very powerful. He took my right hand and guided it to his testicles in the loose, floppy bag. I gathered I was supposed to roll them around.

I can swear that not even one volt of desire passed through me. I did my job; I simulated excitement. But I was scandalized when Mr. Beattie asked me to lick the bright red head, to roll my tongue around the head of his penis. I'd forgotten that this act was not as purely symbolic for him as it was for me. I remembered that he considered all this to be pleasure, as Herod thought Salome's dance was fun until he heard what she wanted as a reward.

At last it was over. Mr. Beattie told me to go on up to the dining hall for supper. He'd follow me in a few moments. He didn't think we should be seen together, just in case.

Sometimes I think I seduced and betrayed Mr. Beattie because neither one action nor the other alone but the complete cycle allowed me to have sex with a man and then to disown him and it; this sequence was the ideal formulation of my impossible desire to love a man but not to be a homosexual. Sometimes I think I liked bringing pleasure to a heterosexual man (for after all I'd dreamed of being my father's lover) at the same time I was able to punish him for not loving me. My German teacher and Mr. Pouchet had not loved me. Tommy had not loved me. My dad had not loved me.

Beattie was a friend of sorts, or at least an accomplice, but he was also a stand-in for all other adults, those swaggering, lazy, cruel masters of ours (how refreshing it was that at Eton the teachers were actually *called* masters). I who had so little power—whose triumphs had all been the minor victories of children and women, that is, merely verbal victories of irony and attitude—I had at last drunk deep from the adult fountain of sex. I wiped my mouth with the back of an adult hand, smiled and walked up to the dining hall humming a little tune.